The Urbana Free Library

To renew: call 217-367-4057
or go to *"urbanafreelibrary.org"*
and select "Renew/Request Items"

5-12

	DATE DUE	
JUN 18 2012		
JUN 25 2012		
SEP 08 2012		
SEP 29 2012		

FAIR
COIN

an imprint of **Prometheus Books**
Amherst, NY

Published 2012 by Pyr®, an imprint of Prometheus Books

Cover illustration © Sam Weber
Jacket design by Jacqueline Nasso Cooke

Inquiries should be addressed to
Pyr
59 John Glenn Drive
Amherst, New York 14228–2119
VOICE: 716–691–0133
FAX: 716–691–0137
WWW.PYRSF.COM

16 15 14 13 12   5 4 3 2

Library of Congress Cataloging-in-Publication Data

Myers, E. C. (Eugene C.), 1978–
    Fair coin / by E.C. Myers.
        p. cm.
    Summary: When evil versions of himself and best friend Nate appear one day, teenaged Ephraim embarks on a dangerous odyssey through parallel worlds to make things right.
    ISBN 978–1–61614–609–2 (pbk.)
    ISBN 978–1–61614–610–8 (ebook)
    [1. Fantasy.] I. Title.

PZ7.M98253Fai 2012
    [Fic]—dc23

                                                          2011045841

Printed in the United States of America

For Mom, the best of all possible mothers

ACKNOWLEDGMENTS

A lot of people helped change this book from a wish into reality. Many thanks to Carrie Wright for encouraging me to write it and for being its first reader and editor, even if she did insist I lose most of the puns.

Thanks to the brave members of the Clarion West Class of 2005 and my writing group, Altered Fluid, who read early manuscript drafts and offered encouraging but honest critiques and advice. I am especially grateful to Kris Dikeman (for the infamous plot graph, of course), Amy Sarah Eastment, Alaya Dawn Johnson, Rajan Khanna, Mercurio D. Rivera, Karen Roberts, and Katie Sparrow.

I'm fortunate to have family and friends who understand why I ignore them for weeks and months at a time, yet are always there when I'm suddenly looking for company. Maia Bernstein has been my biggest cheerleader since I first began writing, and so many others have supported me and my work along the way, including Torie Atkinson, Sean Boggs, Lucy Chen, Dan Crucy, Liz Gorinsky, Jackie Hidalgo, Megan Honig, Scott Kletzkin, Dayle McClintock, Rachel Perkins, Ben Turner, Carrie Wright, and Di Zhang.

I truly appreciate my super agent, Eddie Schneider, and everyone at the JABberwocky Literary Agency, as well as Katherine Mason, for pulling my manuscript from the slush. And of course, my utmost gratitude goes to my editor, Lou Anders, who took on this weird book with enthusiasm and turned it into something really special, and to the entire Pyr team, who worked hard to make me look good.

I couldn't hope for better people to share this with.

CHAPTER 1

Ephraim found his mother slumped over the kitchen table, her right hand curled around a half-empty bottle of vodka. A cigarette smoldered in the ashtray beside her; it had burned into a gray cylinder up to its lipstick-smeared filter. He ground the butt in the tray forcefully and waved wisps of smoke away from his face.

"I suppose this is *my* fault," he said to her still form. She'd drunk herself into a stupor, but she'd probably blame him for not rushing home from school to wake her for her late shift at the supermarket. He picked up the vodka bottle. Even if he woke her now, she wouldn't be in any condition for work. Besides, she was already an hour late.

"Mr. Slovsky's gonna dock your pay again," he muttered. Ephraim slipped the vodka out of her hand and took it to the sink. He filled a quarter of the bottle with tap water and swirled it around, diluting the alcohol. It stretched out the liquor supply; they already couldn't afford her two-bottle-a-week habit. Of course, it would be better for both of them if she didn't drink their money away at all. He screwed the cap on tight and thumped it onto the table where he'd found it. She didn't even stir.

"Mom?" Normally she'd be coming to by now, slurring incoherent curses while reaching for another drink. But there was no motion at all. Everything seemed to still around him, the sound of the humming refrigerator and the ceiling fan dropping away. Something was very wrong.

He touched her on the shoulder and leaned over her face to check her breathing.

"Mom."

There was something clutched in his mother's left hand. An

amber pill bottle. A few purple capsules littered the scratched formica around it. Ephraim's chest tightened as he realized that he'd never seen her take any kind of prescription medication.

"Mom!"

Ephraim shook her shoulders gently, then more roughly when she didn't respond. More of the candy-colored pills flew from the bottle and skittered across the table to the floor. The soft capsules popped under his sneakers as he stepped around her and took the bottle from her limp hand. The long chemical name on the pharmacy label meant nothing to him.

Ephraim eased his mother to a sitting position. Her head lolled forward. "Mom." He patted her cheek gently. "Wake up. Wake up!" He felt her breath against the back of his hand—that was something, at least. "Please, wake up."

"Mmmm . . ." she murmured. Her head twitched.

"Mom!"

Her eyes fluttered open, and she stared at him glassily. "Ephraim, where are you?"

"Right here, Mom. Look at me."

She blinked a couple of times, trying to focus on his face. "Honey?"

"Yes, it's me."

She was really out of it.

"What happened to you?"

She shook her head and tried to push him away. He held her shoulders tighter, worried that she would hurt herself. "No!" she said. "No!"

"What's wrong?"

She scrambled out of her chair and struggled when he tried to grab her arms. The chair fell between them and he bumped his hip painfully against the side of the kitchen table. She was stronger than she looked.

"You're dead!" She jerked away, more awake now. "Ephraim's gone!"

"Calm down, Mom. I'm right here."

"Ephraim's dead." She sobbed.

"You just imagined it. Mom, look at me. Look at me! I'm fine."

She stumbled toward the stove and grabbed onto the side, then leaned over and retched. Clear liquid splashed onto the faded linoleum, along with some of the pills she had taken.

"Jeez!" he said.

She wobbled, and he rushed over to catch her if she fell.

She collapsed to her knees, head bowed. She coughed a couple of times and stared down at her own mess. Finally she looked up, and this time he knew she recognized him. She was crying; eyeliner was smeared under her eyes like bruises. "Ephraim? But . . . I saw your body." A thin trail of saliva dangled from her chin.

"Do I look dead to you?" he snapped.

"A bus, it hit you, and— " She rubbed her face. "But you're here. You're alive? Are you really my Ephraim?"

"Why'd you do this, Mom?"

"You were so young." She closed her eyes. "My poor baby . . ."

"Mom, stay with me. You have to stay awake," Ephraim said.

"Stay . . ." she echoed.

"Mom!"

Her lips moved, murmuring something too low for him to hear. As he leaned closer to listen, she slumped back against the oven door and stopped moving.

Ephraim snatched the phone and dialed 911. While the line rang he lowered his mother gently down on the floor, using her purse as a pillow. His hands shook and hot tears blurred his vision.

A calm voice spoke from the phone. "911, what is your emergency?"

"My mother took some pills," he said.

CHAPTER 2

If one more doctor or nurse came by to tell him he'd saved his mother's life, or tell him how lucky it was that he found her when he did, Ephraim thought *he* would be sick.

It was still sinking in, what his mother had done. What she had tried to do.

During the ambulance ride to Summerside General, she had drifted in and out of consciousness. Each time she awoke, she'd stared at him as though she couldn't believe he was there. She'd thought he was dead, she said.

He looked up and saw a nurse at the open door with curly brown hair and a kind smile. She seemed familiar, though he'd never met her before. The badge on her chest identified her as Julia Morales.

"Ephraim Scott?" She pronounced his name "Eff-ra-heem" with a rolling R, the way his dad did, instead of "Eff-rum," the way everyone else said it. He liked the exotic sound of her Spanish accent.

"Yes. How's my mother?" he said.

"She's still in Intensive Care, but resting comfortably. Thank God you found her when you did."

Ephraim winced.

Her expression softened, and she sat down next to him, placing her hand on his arm. "Your mother will be okay now. Dr. Dixon doesn't think there'll be any permanent damage, but we have to hold her overnight." She frowned. "Possibly longer."

"Longer?"

"We can't send her home until we evaluate her. To make sure she won't try this again."

"It was an accident," he said. "She mixed up her medications. She had a little too much to drink, that's all."

"Sweetie—"

"She's never done this before. She didn't mean to!" The loudness of his voice in the small room shocked him into silence.

"Okay," the nurse said. "How are you doing?"

"How am *I*?"

"With all of this. It's a lot for someone your age. If you want to talk—"

"I'm just worried about her."

She sighed. "You go to Summerside High?"

He nodded.

"Maybe you know my girls. Mary and Shelley Morales?"

That's why he'd recognized her—she was Mary and Shelley's mother. The resemblance was clear now: her hair frizzed like theirs, she had the same thin nose and thick eyebrows. The same curvy figure.

"I'm in their English class." He didn't mention that they wouldn't know him. The identical twins were far too popular to pay any attention to Ephraim, especially with all the other guys fawning over them—including his best friend, Nathan Mackenzie, who they outright ignored.

He almost asked Mrs. Morales what was up with naming them Mary and Shelley; it was an indication of how well-liked they were that no one had made fun of them when the class read *Frankenstein* last semester.

"So . . . what happens now?" he said. "With my mother?"

"A psychologist is going to talk to her. Try to understand what was going on when she—" She left the sentence hanging, her eyes darting heavenward. He noticed a silver cross dangling from a slim chain around her neck. "Child Protective Services will want to talk to her too. And you," she said.

Ephraim clenched his jaw. "But she's fine normally, she really is." Aside from the alcoholism and depression.

"It's hospital policy."

Ephraim took a deep breath.

"She kept saying that I was . . . dead. Like she really believed it," he said.

Her hand jerked up then to the side in a quick motion, a bit like the blessing the priest gave at church, a cross drawn in the air.

"Someone made a terrible mistake," Mrs. Morales said.

"What do you mean?"

"We did have an accident victim earlier this afternoon. A boy, about your age and height, same hair color. His face was badly scraped, but honestly . . . I could see why someone might think he was you." She studied him carefully.

He tried to maintain a neutral expression, though his feelings were jumbled in a mixture of shock and anger. This was important, though—his mother wasn't crazy. She'd been fooled just like everyone else.

"He was hit by a bus?" Ephraim asked.

Mrs. Morales nodded, her lips pressed together. "Just outside the library. He was killed instantly, they said, a small blessing."

"So if you couldn't even identify him, how did my mother find out? Why didn't someone check with the school first? I was there all afternoon." Ephraim had stayed late, hoping for a chance to talk to Jena Kim, the hottest geek girl in his class, while his mother nearly killed herself.

"We had reason to think he was you. Your library card was in his wallet."

Ephraim's hand went to the bulge of his wallet in the right-hand pocket of his jeans. He'd used his card only the day before, and he remembered sliding it back into its usual place. Hadn't he?

"It was enough to make the identification, but we called in your mother to confirm it. I guess that poor kid must have picked it up some-where. We all thought you were dead until you walked in here tonight." She pursed her lips. "On paper, you still are. I'd better fix that."

"Can I have my card back?"

"We gave all your—*his*—things to your mother when she came in." She shook her head. "I'm sorry your mother had to suffer through that. If one of my girls. . . . Such a tragedy. Now we still have to find his family." She stood up.

Ephraim leaned forward as she moved to the door. "Is the . . . uh, the body still here?"

She gave him a puzzled look. "You wouldn't want to see it." She paused in the doorway. "I'm off shift in an hour. Do you have anywhere to go? Anyone you can call?"

Ephraim didn't want to return to his apartment. He would have to wipe up his mother's vomit, crawl around and pick up every one of those purple pills from the kitchen floor.

"Not really. Can't I just stay here?" he asked.

"You've done enough for her tonight, no? We have a spare room. My oldest son is working at his university this summer."

Ephraim almost smiled at the thought of telling Nathan he'd slept at Mary and Shelley's house. But he wanted to be close to his mother in case she woke up. She might need reassurance that he was still all right. He should have been there for her today, and he wasn't going to risk leaving her alone while she still needed him.

"No thanks," he said. "I want to stay here."

"Then I'll ask the other nurses to let you know if anything changes. At least you won't miss anything important at school tomorrow."

Ephraim didn't need the reminder. He'd been dreading the last day of school more than anything—until he'd discovered his mother at the kitchen table.

Mrs. Morales left to finish her rounds, and Ephraim sat still in the waiting room until his stomach gurgled loudly. He had missed dinner, of course. He didn't have much of an appetite but felt he should eat something. The hospital cafeteria was closed now, but he'd seen a vending machine down the hall. Unfortunately he didn't have any money for it.

Ephraim picked up his mother's purse. He'd grabbed it when the paramedics came, in case they needed her ID or credit cards or something at the hospital. He looked for change, rifling through balled-up Kleenexes smeared with mascara, tubes of lipstick, and an empty two-ounce plastic bottle of rum. He threw the bottle across the room; it clattered hollowly behind a row of seats.

Shoved down to the bottom of the purse was a clear plastic bag with "Summerside General" printed on it. He fingered the wrapped contents and felt a prickle along the back of his neck. The bag contained a wallet, a key ring, a black digital watch, and a single quarter.

Ephraim dumped the bag out on the orange plastic seat beside him. He counted the keys on the ring. There were exactly five, matching the ones in his pocket: one for the lobby door, two for the apartment, one for the AV Club storage space at school, and a little circular key for a bicycle lock.

The watch was a cheap Casio like the one around his left wrist, but the plastic face was cracked. Faded pixels danced across the shattered LCD screen when he pressed his thumb against it.

He hesitated before prying open the Velcro of the gray canvas wallet. It felt comfortable in his hands, well-worn and familiar, just like his own. If he'd closed his eyes, he would have thought it was his. He flipped through a few pieces of paper that looked like foreign bills or Monopoly money in assorted colors, faded receipts, and business cards from comic book shops he'd never heard of. It also contained a membership card to a new video game store; a ticket stub from the multiplex cinema for something called *Neuromancer*; an expired coupon for a free ice cream; three fortune cookie fortunes; and, in the zipped inner pocket, a sealed condom.

Ephraim's library card was tucked into the plastic sleeve, exactly where he would have put it himself. He tugged out his own wallet—similar but made of black canvas—from his jeans and looked inside. The card wasn't there. He hurriedly checked through all the sleeves and compartments, but his library card was definitely missing. He'd lost it after all.

Ephraim let out a breath. His palms were cold with sweat. He had really worked himself up, had halfway expected to find another library card. But it was all just an amazing, terrible coincidence.

Just one item left in the bag. The quarter gave him a static shock when he pulled it out. It was one of those commemorative US quarters: the back of it said "Puerto Rico 1998" at the top, with the mint date of 2008 at the bottom. The picture showed a little frog in front of an island with a palm tree.

He had a jar of those state and territory quarters back in his room, but he'd never come across one for Puerto Rico. They'd been released in limited quantities, making them rarer than the rest of the series. But the territory coins had all been minted in 2009, which meant this one could be a prototype that somehow had made it into circulation. Guiltily, he slipped it into his back pocket, reasoning that it was better off with someone who knew its value so it didn't end up in a parking meter or vending machine. He imagined if the hospital managed to contact the other boy's family, he could return it to them and explain why he'd held onto it.

Ephraim retrieved his library card, too, and dropped the rest of the things back into the plastic bag. He stuffed the bag back into his mom's purse and slipped it under his arm as he walked down the hall.

His mother only had a few dollars tucked into the plastic wrapping of a carton of cigarettes, so he picked out a bag of chips, Twinkies, and a can of soda. On his way back to the waiting room, he spotted someone rounding the corner ahead of him. It looked like Nathan.

"Nathan? Nathan, wait up!" Ephraim ran to the corner, but his friend wasn't anywhere in sight. A nurse at the station looked up at Ephraim and frowned. "Sorry. Thought I saw someone I know," he said.

It couldn't have been Nathan anyway. Ephraim hadn't told him he was going to the hospital.

Maybe the stress was finally getting to him. Ephraim turned

around and noticed a door near the corner. He wandered over and read the small sign mounted above it: Morgue. That was where they had the body that supposedly looked like Ephraim. He actually reached for the handle before he stopped himself. He wasn't really going in there, was he? He glanced back at the nurse's station. She wasn't paying attention to him anymore.

It was probably locked anyway. But when he nudged it slightly, it opened. It would just take a second to slip through.

No, he wasn't going to sneak into a hospital morgue. As morbidly curious as he was, he couldn't see himself doing something like that. He pulled the door shut and went back to the waiting room. He dropped his mother's purse on the seat beside him with the chips and Twinkies.

Ephraim popped open the soda can, and it fizzed all over his right leg before he could move it to arm's length over the floor. He'd shaken it too much when he ran down the hall.

"Perfect," he muttered. The dark wet patch on his jeans quickly grew cold and sticky against his skin in the air-conditioned room. At least that would keep him up for a while. He had a long night ahead of him.

CHAPTER 3

They moved Ephraim's mother out of the ICU in the morning to a room on the third floor, uncomfortably close to the Psychiatric Ward in the next wing.

She looked awful, like someone who'd had her stomach pumped the night before. Like someone who had almost died. The curtains were drawn against the morning sunlight, and the fluorescent bulb above her bed didn't improve her features. Her skin was sallow and her lips were dry and cracked. She didn't look like his mother at all. His eyes burned as if he was going to cry, but he was all out of tears.

"Hey, Mom." Ephraim saw fear on his mother's face when he approached her bedside, but it faded, replaced with a wan smile. He leaned over and hugged her, surprised at how frail she felt. A plastic tube ran from the back of her hand to an IV drip next to a monitor.

"Is that my purse? It looks good on you," she said.

He tugged the strap from his shoulder and placed the bag on the table tray over her bed.

"Oh, thank God," she said. She pawed through it. "I'm dying for a cigarette."

"Don't say that," Ephraim said. She looked at him sharply. "You can't smoke here anyway."

He dragged a chair closer and sat, suddenly exhausted. He hadn't gotten any sleep at all.

He wanted to take her hand. He wanted to talk to her, but she wouldn't look at him. He talked anyway.

"Mom. What happened last night?"

She shook her head. "I thought . . . well, never mind what I thought. I was wrong." She pulled the plastic bag out of her purse and cradled it in her lap.

19

"Those aren't mine," he said. "Mistaken identity." He took the bag from her gently and laid it on a side table. "I didn't die. Obviously."

She laughed. "Of course not."

"But even if I had . . . God, Mom. How could you do that to yourself?" He squeezed the bed railing. "Suicide, Mom? Really?"

"I'm sorry, Ephraim. I don't know what I was thinking." Her eyes filled with tears. "You're all I have, honey."

"It's my fault," he said. "I should have been home sooner. I was late leaving school. I had no idea you were going through all that." He tried to swallow the lump in his throat.

"School?" His mother looked around the room, squinting. "What time is it?" He wouldn't have been surprised if she'd asked him what *day* it was.

Ephraim checked his watch. "Just after seven. In the morning." He glanced at the broken watch in the plastic bag.

"Then why aren't you at school, young man?"

"Are you kidding? It's the last day. And you're in the hospital."

"You've never missed a day of school and I don't want you to start now. You shouldn't be here, Ephraim. I don't want you to see me like this." She wiped away her tears and smiled weakly.

What about all the times he'd found her drunk on the couch in front of the television? All the times he'd plucked a burning cigarette from her hand so that she wouldn't set their apartment on fire?

She got out a tube of lipstick and a small mirror. She examined her reflection then pulled out more makeup.

"I'm staying with you," he said.

"Go. You can't do anything more for me right now."

He wished people would stop saying that. Wasn't he doing something just being there?

"You can come back this afternoon," she said. "I'm not going anywhere."

"If you're sure . . ." He stood and took her hand. "I told them it was a mistake, Mom. You mixed up your medications, you were confused and drunk. You didn't mean to do anything."

"I'll see you later," she said firmly.

He bent over her, and she pecked him on the cheek.

"Have a good day," she said.

The last day of school was just one long assembly where they handed out awards and gave drawn-out speeches. Ephraim had never had much school spirit. As soon as it was obvious there wouldn't be news about a local teen dying in an accident, he tuned out the rest of the announcements. He kept falling asleep, and Nathan would jab him in the ribs to wake him up.

When Ephraim wasn't drifting off, his mind wandered. He pictured his mother unconscious in the kitchen. He wondered who had been killed by that bus; he could understand if the administration didn't want to make a statement before the student was identified, but it was strange that none of his classmates were gossiping about it either. *Someone* must have known the victim, even if he went to another school.

Most of all, he thought about Jena.

Ephraim was probably the only student at Summerside High who was sorry summer vacation was starting, for one reason: Jena Kim. He would miss seeing her every day, watching her at lunch, arranging "coincidental" run-ins at her locker between classes. It would be a challenge finding excuses to visit the library while she was working there without seeming too much like a stalker.

She was actually looking at him. Had she noticed him staring at her? Her short black hair was clipped back over her ears, and she wore her geek-chic red horn-rimmed glasses today. Though she tended toward plain T-shirts and jeans, she had an endless assortment of trendy frames, to the point where Ephraim wondered if she actually needed corrective lenses or just liked the fashion statement. Jena wore her intelligence proudly, while other girls were just trying to fit in.

This blatant individualism would usually draw the wrong kind of attention in high school, but she had such an easygoing personality that it only made her more appealing. Jena always had guys chasing after her, both because of her exotic half-Asian cuteness and for the homework answers she sometimes shared, or possibly because she presented herself as a challenge—she hadn't returned anyone's interest yet, including Ephraim's. Rumors sometimes flew around that Jena only liked girls, but Ephraim was not discouraged. He ignored them, just like the jokes that linked Ephraim and Nathan as a couple because they were together all the time. If there'd been any truth to that, it wasn't something he'd be ashamed of, so the comments weren't all that hurtful. Denying rumors gave them more power.

Jena was smiling now. He flicked his eyes away from her, then back. Still smiling. At him.

Nathan elbowed him hard. "Dude."

Everyone was looking at Ephraim, smiling. No, they weren't smiling—they were laughing.

"Ephraim Scott!"

He finally heard the principal call his name.

"Crap," Ephraim said, too loudly. He jumped up from his seat, and the laughter increased. His face hot, he edged his way to the aisle and moved to the front of the auditorium. The steps up to the stage seemed like a mountain, and the walk to the podium took an eternity. At least he didn't trip.

"Congratulations, Mr. Scott," Principal Crawford said. He handed Ephraim a paper certificate that looked like it had been laser printed on fake parchment.

"Uh, thanks." He shook Crawford's hand. The man's hand was thin and sandpapery, but he had a firm grip. Ephraim turned back to the stairs.

"The other way, son," Crawford whispered.

"Huh?" Ephraim turned.

Crawford jerked his head over his shoulder, toward the stairs on the other end of the stage.

"Oh. Sorry. Thanks."

He slunk past the podium while Crawford called another name. Ephraim missed the last step on his way down and lurched without quite falling. A flash went off in the audience, and he lost his sense of direction for a moment. He passed Jena's seat on his way back to his own and smiled at her. She didn't notice.

When Ephraim plopped back down in his seat, Nathan held up his digital camera. "Not smooth. But I got a great shot." He swiveled the LCD panel on the back out to show Ephraim stumbling forward at the bottom of the steps with a comical expression.

"Thanks," Ephraim said.

"Congratulations on your award," Nathan said.

Ephraim read the certificate in his hands: Perfect Attendance. He couldn't believe it—he had outnerded the nerds. Of course, he hadn't gone to school every day because he enjoyed it. He was happy to have any excuse to leave his apartment. He also liked to see Jena. He hadn't even skipped on the unofficial cut day, thinking that she of all people would be in school. She wasn't. She'd gone to Six Flags in Jersey like everyone else.

Jena got a host of awards during the rest of the morning assembly: National Honor Society, Science Scholar, Math Scholar. They probably should have given her a seat up on the stage to save time. Whenever she walked up, she was greeted with thunderous applause, cheers from the Chess Club and newspaper staff, and wolf whistles from the football team.

Ephraim tracked her graceful movements while she walked up to receive an award for most valuable member of the Quiz Bowl. He didn't even know the school had a Quiz Bowl.

"Why don't you just ask her out?" Nathan asked.

"She turns everyone down."

Nathan's camera flashed, and he showed Ephraim a zoomed-in

shot of Jena walking down the stairs, which more than made up for the embarrassing picture of Ephraim tripping.

"She's probably worried that dating will interfere with her studies. I don't get it. She's cute and all, but it's just not cool to obsess over a geek." Nathan frowned. "Even if she lets you copy her notes."

Ephraim had copied her notes more than once when he didn't actually need them, just for an excuse to talk to her. Jena had nice handwriting. It had lots of neat loops and circles dotting the i's, one of the only distinctly "girly" things about her.

"Like you know what's cool. Besides, *we're* geeks," Ephraim said.

"Yeah, but we're not *smart* geeks. That's a whole other thing. I mean, she's in Chess Club. Do you really want to date a girl who's smarter than you?"

"Yes."

"If she's too smart, she'll know better than to go out with you." Nathan shook his head. "Now, her friends, on the other hand . . ."

Jena slid back into her seat between Mary and Shelley Morales. They admired Jena's latest award, passing the plaque between them. He wondered if their mother had told them about seeing him at the hospital. He wondered if Jena knew.

"You okay?" Nathan said. "You've been out of it all morning. If I didn't know you, I'd suspect you were stoned."

Maybe summer vacation wouldn't be so bad. Chances were, no one would find out that his mother had attempted suicide, and even if they did, by September no one would care anymore.

"I'm okay," Ephraim said. "Just looking forward to getting out of here."

After the assembly, Ephraim and Nathan ran into Jena and the twins outside the physics classroom. The halls were emptying quickly.

"Hi, Ephraim," Jena said. The twins simply nodded. Few people could tell the willowy girls apart, so they were jointly called "Mary Shelley" most of the time, which didn't seem to faze them. They practically encouraged it, usually wearing matching outfits the way they had in junior high, though it was more sexy than cutesy now.

"Hey," Ephraim said. He swallowed, his mouth suddenly dry. "Congratulations on all your awards, Jena. I think you collected them all."

"All but one." She pointed at the rolled-up paper in his hand. "How much you want for it?"

Ephraim grinned.

The twin on Jena's right spoke. "Sorry to hear about your mother, Ephraim."

"Thanks," he said, worrying over how much they had been told. Wasn't there some kind of doctor-patient confidentiality?

The one on Jena's left nodded. "Our mother's dropping us at the train station on her way to work. I'm sure you could ride with her to the hospital if you're going back there for visiting hours."

"Um, yeah. That would be great." Ephraim still hadn't told Nathan about his mother. His friend was uncharacteristically silent, as if the conversation didn't register. He looked dazed, and his hands were locked tightly around his camera. Ephraim knew what was affecting him: the identical brunettes had the best figures in school, and they weren't shy about flaunting them.

"Where are you guys going?" Ephraim asked.

"Dinner and dancing in the city," Jena said. "To celebrate."

"A girls' night out," Mary and Shelley said quickly.

"Will your mother be all right?" Jena asked.

"She's fine now." Ephraim was embarrassed, even as he was pleased at her show of concern. "No big deal."

"Oh! Before I forget," Jena said. "I have something for you."

"You do?" Ephraim's heart started pounding, and he felt something quiver in his gut.

She rummaged in her bag then held out a white plastic card.

His library card.

He closed his hand over it, the hard edges pressing against his palm and fingers. Blood rushed in his ears.

"Where did you get this?" he asked.

"You left it at the circulation desk the other day. What's wrong?"

"Nothing. Thanks . . . I didn't know I'd lost it." He pulled out his wallet and snuck a glance at the one he'd recovered at the hospital. They were identical. He tucked the two of them inside together, then snapped his wallet shut and squeezed it tightly.

"I figured you'd need it, since I see you at the library a lot," Jena said. "I'll be working there again this summer, so I guess I'll run into you."

He nodded. Was that an invitation? Did she actually want to see him there or was she just being polite?

"Coming, Ephraim?" said the twin on Jena's right.

"I need to empty out my locker," he said. "Meet you outside?"

"Don't be long." The twins spoke in chorus. How did they do that?

"I'll be right out," he said.

The three girls split around Ephraim and Nathan as they passed, and then smoothly merged back into a row as they walked down the hall. Nathan turned and stared after them as they left, then he joined Ephraim at his locker.

"What was that about Madeline?" Nathan said.

Ephraim didn't know when it had started, but Nathan called Ephraim's mother by her first name. She actually enjoyed it.

"She's in the hospital. Nothing serious." He couldn't bear to go into the details right now.

"Shit, no wonder you're such a mess. Sorry to hear it. I'll drive you over there. I'd like to see her, too."

"No no, that's okay. Mrs. Morales is taking me, and I think my mom doesn't want a lot of attention at the moment. Thanks, though."

"Hey, I bet this'll take your mind off your troubles!" Nathan said. He showed Ephraim a picture of the three girls on his camera. They were cut off just below the shoulders and above their thighs.

"Your framing's off," Ephraim said.

"No, it isn't." Nathan grinned and pointed out Mary and Shelley's impressive cleavage in their blue summer dresses. "It's a shame Jena doesn't have much up there, but she isn't bad. Especially when she isn't wearing those frumpy shirts she usually has on."

Ephraim had to agree. It was nice to see Jena in a skirt. The growth spurt she'd had the summer before their freshman year of high school had distracted Ephraim into almost failing Algebra, the one class they'd shared that first semester. A lot of guys paid more attention to her that year, until she began covering herself up. Now they all wondered what she was hiding.

"She's hot the way she is," Ephraim said. "How did you sneak that picture anyway?" Ephraim was unable to tear his eyes from it.

"I turned off the shutter sound. But wait, there's more."

Nathan clicked over to the next picture, a shot of Mary, Shelley, and Jena from behind.

"Pervert," Ephraim said. "You should be ashamed of yourself. Make sure you e-mail me a copy of that as soon as you get home."

"I could charge for these!" Nathan leaned his wiry body against a locker and gazed blissfully at the camera screen. His long blond hair fell over his eyes. "Listen, when you get in their car, try to sit between them—"

"I'm not going to cop a feel. Their mother will be in the car." Not to mention Jena. He wondered if he could sit close to her, though he supposed he'd be forced to ride shotgun.

"That's what makes it extra naughty. They probably won't say anything in front of her. Come on, look at those calves!" Nathan exclaimed. Ephraim rolled his eyes.

When he opened his locker, a piece of paper fluttered out. He bent to retrieve it from the floor.

"'Make a wish and flip the coin to make it come true,'" he read. It looked like Nathan's handwriting. "What the hell is that supposed to mean?" He tossed it to his friend.

Nathan read it. "Weird. I don't know."

"That isn't your handwriting?" Ephraim was sure of it.

"I did not leave a note in your locker. That's so elementary school." Nathan scrunched up his eyes as he looked at it again. "It does look like my handwriting. A little. But I don't know what it's supposed to mean. What coin? It doesn't make any sense."

He handed the note back to Ephraim.

Ephraim stared at it. Could it be referring to the quarter he'd found last night? He hadn't even mentioned that to Nathan yet. This was as unsettling as the duplicate library card and the idea of another kid who looked like him. But what did it mean? And who had written the note?

He pulled the quarter from his back pocket and reread the note one more time.

"You're actually going to try it?" Nathan snorted.

Ephraim shrugged. "No harm in it." He held the coin flat on his palm and cleared his throat.

"I wish . . ." He glanced at Nathan. "I wish my mom wasn't in the hospital."

Nothing happened, of course.

"Flip it," Nathan said. "Like the note said."

"Never mind. This is silly," Ephraim said. He moved to put it back in his pocket and felt a jolt in his palm, as if someone had stabbed it with a pin. He dropped the coin, and it rolled away on the uneven gray tiles.

"Ow," he muttered.

"What happened?"

"It . . . *shocked* me," Ephraim said, glancing around. The coin had landed under the locker across from him. He crouched and picked it up, shaking off clumps of dust. It had come up heads. The metal felt hot for a second, but it quickly cooled in his hand. His vision swam and he suddenly felt nauseous. He clutched his stomach.

"Ephraim?" Nathan said. "What are you doing on the floor?"

He had to get to the bathroom. "I—" He wasn't going to make it.

Ephraim turned and stuck his head into his locker.

"Dude!" Nathan said. He moved to the other side of the hall while Ephraim vomited.

Ephraim wiped his mouth with the back of his hand. "Sorry," he said. He held his breath and closed the door of his locker, deciding he didn't really need the papers and comic books that had accumulated at the bottom throughout the year. He walked to the water fountain at the end of the hall to rinse out his mouth. The water was warm and tasted metallic.

"Are you all right? The nurse might still be here," Nathan said.

"I feel fine now." It was as though nothing had happened. Ephraim stuffed the quarter and the note in his pocket and grabbed his backpack. He suddenly realized how lucky he was. If that had happened while he'd been talking to Jena . . .

"But you just barfed in your locker. I mean, at least tell the janitor." Nathan turned his camera so Ephraim could see the screen. It was a blurry shot of Ephraim with his head tucked into his locker. It was enough to make him feel queasy again. He pushed the camera away.

"I'm so glad I have you around to document my greatest moments," Ephraim said.

"The camera doesn't lie," Nathan said. "You really are that much of a tool. You sure you're okay?"

"Maybe I caught a bug at the hospital," Ephraim said. He'd been sitting there all night, after all. But who'd ever heard of a twenty-four-second stomach flu?

"When were you in the hospital?" Nathan asked.

"I just told you, my mom went in last night."

"Oh no!" Nathan's eyes widened. "Is it serious? How's Madeline?"

"Did we not just have this conversation?" Nathan must have been more distracted by the twins than he'd thought. "She'll recover. I'm catching a ride with Mary and Shelley to the hospital now," Ephraim said slowly. "Remember?"

Nathan seemed even more surprised by that. "You're kidding.

I'd love to share a back seat with them. Man, I wish *my* mom were in the hospital."

"Careful what you wish for," Ephraim said.

Wait a minute. Wish?

He'd just made a wish that his mother wasn't in the hospital. Now Nathan didn't remember it . . .

"Hey, you should try to sit between them," Nathan said.

"Still not a good idea," Ephraim said.

Down the hallway, Michael Gupal came around the corner and grinned when he caught sight of them.

"Crap," Ephraim said.

Nathan looked at Michael calmly as he stomped toward them. "What? He's not going to try anything. It's the last day of school. That's like a truce."

"It's more like there's no one here to stop him," Ephraim said. It was Michael's end-of-year ritual, to track down his favorite victims and give them something to remember him by over the summer.

Michael stopped in front of them and crossed his arms, legs planted apart. He was as squat and thick as the twins were tall and thin, and almost as well-endowed with flabby man boobs. Ephraim had heard that he was taking steroids to bulk up for football.

"Where do you think you're going, Mackenzie?" Michael said. "We didn't have a chance to say good-bye yet."

"Time to go," Ephraim said, taking a step back. Nathan usually followed his lead in situations like this, but he seemed strangely unconcerned.

"Are you kidding? He doesn't scare me," Nathan said. "Have a nice summer, Michael!" He lifted the camera, and the flash went off. This only enraged Michael, like a bull with a flag waved in front of it.

"What's with you?" Ephraim asked Nathan.

Ephraim grimaced as Michael grabbed Nathan by the straps of his backpack and shoved him hard against a locker. The bag loaded with books took the brunt of the impact, but Nathan's head whipped back and rang against the flimsy metal. A number of locker doors around the school bore Nathan-sized dents; you could almost chart Nathan's growth over the years by them.

"Ow," Nathan said. "Sorry—I meant I hope you have a shitty summer."

Michael scowled and shook Nathan from left to right. "What's got you so happy, Mackenzie? Glad you won't be seeing me every day?"

Nathan's hair had fallen over his forehead. His eyes peeked through his bangs and he smiled.

"Sadly, I won't have the pleasure of summer classes with you. Have fun with that."

Ephraim winced. *Don't taunt him, Nathan.* His friend had always lacked an essential element of self-preservation. They'd met one day in the first grade when Ephraim had stuck up for him, but their friendship since then had only made Nathan even more reckless—he knew Ephraim would back him up. Still, this was taking things too far.

Michael growled and squeezed Nathan's backpack straps together.

"Study hard," Nathan wheezed. "Senior year wouldn't be the same without you. Third time's the charm, right?"

"Hey," Ephraim said to Michael. "Leave him alone." Some habits were hard to break. He wasn't afraid of Michael, but he knew he couldn't beat him, either. His protests were just for show. But Nathan would never forgive him if he didn't even try to defend him.

"You wanna be next? There's plenty to go around." Michael flashed him a feral grin.

"Actually, some people are waiting for me outside . . ." Ephraim said.

"I've got this, Ephraim," Nathan said.

"I can't leave you."

"I can't leave you," Michael mocked.

"Go on," Nathan said. "You don't want to miss that ride. Tell Madeline I said I hope she gets better soon."

"Okay. Are you sure? Call me later if . . . if you can still dial," Ephraim said.

"That's right, run!" Michael said.

Ephraim pushed the double doors open and stepped outside. Far from the fresh air of freedom, he sucked in the hot summer air and immediately began to sweat.

Ephraim scanned the parking lot, but there was no sign of Mrs. Morales's beat-up Volkswagen. Or the twins. Or Jena.

Or the school buses.

He checked his pockets, but aside from the quarter, he was broke; he'd already used the last of his mom's money to catch a bus to school from the hospital that morning. It was a long way back on foot.

There were a handful of cars in the lot, including Michael's black BMW sports car and Nathan's secondhand blue Chevy. Maybe he should wait for Nathan to drive him after all; his friend might need a trip to the hospital anyway after being tenderized by Michael's meat hands. Then again, Ephraim didn't want to miss visiting hours, so it would probably be faster to walk—unless he went inside to extricate Nathan from Michael sooner, in which case Ephraim risked an injury of his own. Better to go with the lesser of two evils.

Ephraim started walking.

CHAPTER 4

Ephraim's mother wasn't in her hospital room. Her belongings were gone, too, along with the plastic bag containing the wallet, keys, and broken watch from his unfortunate look-alike. He stood frozen in panic, staring at the carefully made bed. Had they moved her to the psych ward after talking to her?

Ephraim found Mrs. Morales at the nurses' station.

"Mrs. Morales! Sorry about before, I got sidetracked on my way out of school. Um. Do you know where my mother is?"

She looked up from her seat behind the counter. "Excuse me?"

"She was in room 302 this morning."

She glanced down at a clipboard. "There's no one assigned to that room. What's her name?"

Ephraim frowned. "Madeline Scott. Don't you remember me? Mary and Shelley just offered me a ride here after school."

"You know my daughters?" She sounded both surprised and disapproving.

"I'm Ephraim." He spoke slowly. "I was here last night in the ICU waiting room. You came to tell me how she was doing . . ."

"I was on shift last night, but I don't remember seeing you."

He raised his voice. "We had a whole conversation."

"Okay, calm down, sweetie. I'm sure I'd remember you and your mother."

"I would think so." Ephraim wondered if Mrs. Morales had a twin sister who also worked at the hospital. Didn't that kind of thing run in families? But her nametag said Julia Morales, definitely the same woman he'd spoken to before.

He took a deep breath. "Listen, could you just check? I know she's here. Maybe she was moved to . . . another room." She could be in a mental hospital by now if she had kept going on about him being dead.

Mrs. Morales slid a black keyboard toward her and typed, her fingers pecking the keys one by one delicately, with inch-long nails painted a bright green.

"I'm sorry, she was never here," she said. "Are you sure you have the right hospital? People make that mistake all the—"

"The computer must be wrong. An ambulance brought her in last night."

"There would be some record in the system," she said. "What was she admitted for?"

"She—" Ephraim pressed his fingers against the countertop. "Never mind. Sorry for the confusion."

"You're agitated. Why don't you have a seat and calm down? I'll find someone who can help you . . ."

Why would he be agitated? His mother was only missing. But he didn't want to draw the attention of Child Protective Services now, if they'd already forgotten all about him and his mother.

"I must have the wrong hospital, like you said. I made a mistake, that's all." Which reminded him . . . "Actually, maybe you can answer one more question. That boy who was killed in the bus accident yesterday. Did you ever find out who he was?"

Mrs. Morales's face hardened. "I don't know anything about an accident, either, and I wouldn't be able to share personal information with you even if I did. This is really inappropriate. I don't have time for games." She pushed the keyboard away from her, its plastic screeching against the metal desktop. He felt like she was the one playing a prank on him.

"No, there was a body yesterday afternoon that matched my description. They found my library card in his wallet. There was a whole bag of his stuff, I left it in my mother's room—"

Mrs. Morales scowled and stood up. "Mr. Scott, you aren't making much sense. Is there someone you'd like me to call to pick you up?"

"Forget it." He walked away quickly.

He paused by the elevators and glanced back. Mrs. Morales had come around to the front of the station and was watching him. He couldn't blame her. He knew how his story sounded.

The only proof he had was the coin he'd found in the plastic hospital bag yesterday.

Make a wish and flip the coin to make it come true.

It just wasn't possible. Coins didn't grant wishes. But he had wished his mother out of the hospital, and now she wasn't there—in fact, it seemed she had never been there at all. If the wish had wiped out her visit entirely, that might explain Mrs. Morales's memory lapse, just like the one Nathan had at school right after Ephraim flipped the coin. But then why didn't she remember the dead boy? He'd had nothing to do with Ephraim's wish. Of course, that didn't even matter, because wishes didn't come true, not by magic anyway.

Ephraim took the elevator down to the lobby. When the doors opened, Michael Gupal was standing there.

He looked like crap.

Michael had a gash over his left eye, which was swollen half-closed. Blood dripped down his temple from a nasty cut, and his lower lip was split in the middle.

"What the hell happened to you?" Ephraim said. No one had ever taken down the school bully.

Michael squinted with his good eye. "Your friend Mackenzie is a psychopath."

"What?"

"He went completely nuts on me."

"*Nathan* did this?" Nathan wasn't capable of causing that much damage to someone, except from behind the wheel of his car.

Michael coughed. It didn't sound good. "Yeah. No one was more surprised than me."

"When I left school, *you* were beating *him* up." If Nathan had finally managed to fight back, Ephraim didn't have much sympathy for Michael. As unlikely as it seemed, maybe Nathan had even planned this, the way he'd been acting. But he'd have needed a crowbar to do this to Michael.

Michael shook his head then grunted with pain. "I only shook him up a little. And stuffed him in a locker."

Ouch. That had been Michael's signature technique in junior high. Nathan was one of the few people still thin enough to fit—and even so, he wasn't as small as he once was. That must have hurt.

"Then you deserve whatever he did to you," Ephraim said.

Michael's one eye widened. "I don't know how he got himself out of that locker, but he was waiting for me at my car."

"You're sure it was him?"

"I've been punching that face since the first grade; I'd know it anywhere."

"That's when he beat you up?"

"He was strong. And he knew how to fight. He was like a different guy. Vicious. He smashed my car's headlights in with a damn brick."

A brick. That would do it.

But that didn't sound like the Nathan Ephraim knew.

"And then the asshole took my picture," Michael said.

That sounded like Nathan. He would never let such a victory go undocumented.

Michael had said Nathan was different. The thought gave Ephraim a chill. What if there was a guy out there who looked just like his best friend, the way that body in the morgue looked like Ephraim? But he doubted anyone could look so much like Nathan that Michael would mistake the two of them, especially within a few minutes; there must be some other, simpler explanation. Nathan had just gotten tired of being pushed around. It was over ten years in coming.

Michael grabbed Ephraim's shoulder, but his usual iron grip was weak.

"Listen," Michael said. "Don't go spreading this around, or you'll be sorry."

"Sure, Michael. Your secret shame is safe with me." For the first time, Ephraim wanted a blog so he could shout the news from the Internet. Ephraim hoped Nathan had gotten some good pictures. That kind of evidence alone would be enough to blackmail Michael for a trouble-free senior year.

"Just watch it around that guy. He's not as pathetic as he looks," Michael said.

"I know."

Michael stared at Ephraim then turned and limped into the open elevator. Ephraim grinned. He had to ask Nathan how he'd pulled this off.

Once again, Ephraim was annoyed that he didn't have a cell phone. He might have been able to afford one if he worked at the supermarket more often, but even when he did, they always needed the money for household expenses—and it was weird working there with his mother, especially since he did a better job than her.

Ephraim stopped at the pay phone near the hospital entrance, but he couldn't bring himself to slide the only quarter he had into the change slot. Even though the coin couldn't be magic, there was definitely something odd about it.

He hung up the handset. Calling Nathan could wait until he got home, after he had checked on his mother.

Ephraim pushed open his front door, worrying about what he'd find in the apartment this time.

His mother was there, dozing on the couch in the living room, another bottle of vodka nearby. No pills, at least. He switched the television off.

"What time?" she murmured.

"Just after seven." He glared down at her.

She groaned. "Shit. I have to call Slovsky and tell him I'm on my way."

"Again?"

"Why are you home so late?" she said. She sat up and reached for a cigarette.

"I was at the hospital."

"The hospital? What were you doing there?" She tried to pat her wild hair into order without much success. He didn't know why she bothered. She looked up at him suddenly. "The hospital! Are you all right, sweetie?"

"Me? I'm fine. I didn't think they'd send you home so soon."

"What are you talking about?"

"You don't remember?" he said.

"Remember *what*? I think I'd remember being in the hospital." She lit her cigarette and peered at him through the smoke. "You haven't been getting into my liquor, have you? Or something funny with your friends?" She laughed.

"Something funny?" He spat the words out. "This isn't funny, Mom."

"What's gotten into you?" She blew some smoke from the side of her mouth, turning her head away from him. It drifted toward him anyway, and he swatted it away angrily. His eyes teared up, but it wasn't because of the smoke.

This wasn't just one of her memory blackouts. She didn't remember trying to commit suicide. It had to be the coin. It had erased the event entirely; only Ephraim was unable to forget what he'd seen.

"Where were you last night?" he asked.

"At the store. Where else?" She tapped her cigarette into the ashtray. "Since we're on the subject, where were you? You weren't home when I left. And you're late again today. You know I need you to come straight home from school, Ephraim."

He sighed. "Don't turn this around on me, Mom."

She chuckled. "Who's the parent here?"

"Sometimes I wonder." Ephraim picked up the bottle of vodka. He screwed the cap on tight. "This has to stop."

"I know. I'm cutting back."

"So you're going to work tonight?"

"I don't know if I'm up to it."

Ephraim sighed. "I'll call and tell Mr. Slovsky you aren't feeling well." Her boss knew it was just a code for drunk off her ass, but he wouldn't raise much of a fuss, probably. If it wasn't too busy at the store tonight.

"You're a good boy," she said. She lay back down on the couch. He kissed her on the cheek and took the cigarette from her. He stamped it out in the ashtray.

"I love you, Mom."

Even if you're hopeless.

Ephraim went into the kitchen. There was no sign of vomit or purple pills or anything from the night before. That was a break—he hadn't been looking forward to cleaning up that mess. Maybe it had all been a bad dream, or maybe he was losing his mind. Or that coin actually could make wishes come true. Whatever the explanation, he was glad she was home and alive. They'd been given a second chance. He pressed the speed-dial for the ShopRite where his mother worked.

"Let me guess," Mr. Slovsky said. "She isn't feeling well."

Mr. Slovsky obviously had caller ID, though this had become enough of a routine that he may have simply taken a lucky guess.

"Hi, Mr. Slovsky. Yeah, my mother . . . she's sick. I'm sorry, but she isn't going to make it in tonight."

"I am so surprised. Maybe I don't feel like coming to work sometimes, but every night, here I am."

She almost died last night, Ephraim wanted to scream. He squeezed the phone. "She'll make it up to you. I promise."

"You promise? It's her promise I want. You are always a solid worker," Mr. Slovsky said.

"Thank you, sir."

"No more of this, understand? She has to get her act together. I mean it this time." Mr. Slovsky lowered his voice. "I notice some missing alcohol. I hope I don't find out it was Madeline. Our stock boy, he's not as good as you. It could have been an accounting error. Once."

Ephraim sighed. "Thanks, Mr. Slovsky."

"It would be best for you to keep an eye on her. You want a summer job, you let me know. She works when you're around. Not for her boss, but her son? Well."

"I'll think about it, sir. Thank you."

Ephraim slammed the phone into its cradle. He couldn't believe his mother was actually stealing liquor now. If she lost her job, he doubted she'd be able to find another one. She probably wouldn't even look all that hard, when she couldn't be bothered to go to the one she already had. For all their complaining about her boss, Mr. Slovsky had been more than generous with her.

Ephraim didn't want to lose his summer covering her shift.

He searched for the bag with the duplicate wallet, watch, and keys in her purse, but it was gone, just as mysteriously as the body had disappeared from the hospital. At least Ephraim still had the coin.

He went to the desk in his room, shoved the keyboard and comics aside, and put the quarter down in front of him, heads up. It looked so normal. He reached into his coin jar and pulled out another one for comparison.

They both had George Washington on the front, but the pictures were reversed—one faced to the left, and the other faced right, with a slightly different portrait. They had the same inscription all around, though: "UNITED STATES OF AMERICA," "LIBERTY," "IN GOD WE TRUST." They both even had a tiny P, which meant they had been struck in the Philadelphia Mint.

He weighed the two coins in each hand. The magic coin seemed slightly heavier, and shinier. Maybe it had actual silver in it? Starting in 1965, quarters were made of copper and nickel; since this one was newer, they might have changed the composition again.

He turned each coin over. Neither of them bore the standard eagle on the reverse side, but they both included "E PLURIBUS UNUM," whatever that meant. The one on the left had an image of the Statue of Liberty under the words "New York 1788," indicating the year that New York ratified the Constitution and became a state. The inscription read "Gateway to Freedom," and 2001 was printed at the bottom: the year the coin was issued.

So if that information also applied to the magic quarter, Puerto Rico had become a state in 1998, which was obviously wrong. Its caption read "The Enchanted Island," and 2008 was marked as the year of issue—a year before the territory coins were struck. Ephraim tapped the coin with his index finger thoughtfully, then fired up his computer.

After a few minutes on Wikipedia, he learned that the frog in the picture on the coin was called a *coquí*, a kind of Puerto Rican mascot, and he'd confirmed what he already knew: Puerto Rico was definitely not a state. The last vote on its status had been in 1998, the same year printed on the coin, but it had resulted in the island remaining a Commonwealth of the United States. And the actual territory quarter for Puerto Rico had a completely different design and was issued in 2009. That certainly made this coin an anomaly. But magic? It was far more likely to be a novelty coin minted for a private collector.

Ephraim pulled out the note he'd found in his locker. *Make a wish . . .*

All right. He would make another wish, to prove the first hadn't been a coincidence or some delusion.

"I wish my Mom wasn't so messed up." No, he should be clearer. "I mean, I wish my mother wasn't a drunk and had a better job and acted a little more . . . like a mother."

And flip the coin to make it come true. How had the note writer even known that he'd found the quarter? Another mystery on top of all the others.

He flipped the coin. His toss was awkward, and he failed to catch it on its wobbly downward arc. It bounced off the edge of his desk, landing heads up on the carpet. He leaned over and scooped it up.

Was the coin a little warmer than before? He felt a head rush, a brief moment of dizziness like last time, vision blurring for just a second, but otherwise . . . nothing.

He'd probably just stood up too fast; nothing magic about that. He went out into the living room, but his mother was still asleep on the couch, just as he'd left her. If the coin had improved things, she would be at work right now.

He felt like an idiot. He had actually started to believe—had *wanted* to believe—that the coin could grant his wishes. He dropped both quarters into his collection jar and tightened the lid.

He went to throw the note out, but he couldn't find it.

It had been right there, but it was no longer on his desk. He rummaged through the trash in case it had fallen in, checked all over the floor, but it had completely vanished.

Now he was really getting worried about his own mental health.

CHAPTER 5

Ephraim woke the next day to the delicious aroma of cooking bacon.

The lamp beside his bed was still on, its bulb overpowered by morning sunlight that streamed through the window. When he sat up, a thick hardcover copy of *The Lord of the Rings* slipped from the bed and thumped against the carpet. He picked up the book and tried to smooth out its bent pages by folding them in the opposite direction, but that only made it worse. He closed the book and hoped that its considerable weight would flatten the creases.

When he'd seen Jena reading it, he figured he would try to impress her by reading it himself, make some connection with her, but she hadn't noticed him lugging it between classes for the last month. Now that school was over, he might as well return it to the library. Thanks to the movies and the Internet, he could probably fake it anyway, if he ever had the chance for a real conversation with her.

He dropped the book on his desk then pulled off his rumpled T-shirt. He sniffed the armpits and crumpled it into a ball—it was definitely past its prime after two days. He hated sleeping in his clothes. It always made him feel like he hadn't actually slept, that the day was just a continuation of the day before.

Oddly, his laundry basket was empty. He'd washed his clothes last week but had never gotten around to putting them away. When he checked his dresser, everything was neatly placed in the drawers, the way his mom used to fold them when she had bothered with housework.

He pulled on a fresh shirt, tried to smooth his hair, and headed toward the sound of clattering pans.

Breakfast was on the kitchen table. An actual breakfast. Crispy bacon was piled on a plate, with a paper napkin soaking up the grease. There was a platter of french toast, and a glass of orange juice waited for him at his place.

"Good morning, sleepyhead." His mom smiled at him from the stove. "I was about to wake you."

"Mom?" Ephraim stepped into the kitchen. The air was smoky, not from cigarettes but from whatever she was frying in the pan. "What are you doing?"

"I thought you should have a good start to summer vacation. Don't expect this every morning."

"But . . . you don't cook." *Not anymore.* He had become accustomed to cold cereals and flavored oatmeal from paper packets, or cold PopTarts from foil packages when he was running late. He couldn't even remember the last time he'd seen his mother out of bed before eight in the morning, let alone up and dressed and *cheerful*.

"Are you all right, hon?" she said.

When he passed the stove, his mother put a light hand on his shoulder to stop him. She pecked him on the cheek then tousled his already-tousled hair.

"You were up late again, weren't you?" she said. "I just put some coffee on."

There was a squat coffeemaker on the counter. It was shiny, all bright chrome and black plastic. "When did we get that?"

"Do you have a fever? Let me feel your head." She reached for his forehead, but he ducked away.

"I'm not sick!" Ephraim grabbed a mug and poured a half-cup of coffee from the coffeemaker. It smelled better than the instant Folgers coffee his mom favored. It tasted better too. He took it to the table and sat down. "How are you, Mom?"

"Nice try. I'm worried about *you*. You don't sound like yourself."

She was one to talk. She seemed like a different person, and she looked good, better than usual. Her auburn hair was brushed and tied back in a high ponytail that made her look a few years younger. Her face had a healthy color, and she seemed slimmer, too.

"What are you doing up so early?" he asked.

She slid scrambled eggs onto a plate and placed it in front of him. "A little thing called work. You'll learn all about it one day." As if he hadn't been picking up shifts for her and working summers since he'd started high school.

"You're on the morning shift today?" Slovsky sometimes had her work doubles to make up for missed hours.

"Now I'm really worried. Is something wrong, Eph?"

"Never mind." Was he still asleep? He wondered if he was dreaming all of this, but if he was, he didn't want to wake up yet. Not until after he'd had some of that bacon.

"How was your last day of school? Sorry we didn't have a chance to talk last night. I guess I fell asleep on the couch."

Because you were drunk again. He shrugged. "I got an award," he said.

"Really? For what? Let me see."

Ephraim went to his room and brought her the certificate. He sat back down and forked some eggs into his mouth.

"Perfect attendance." She chuckled.

"What?"

"I'm proud of you." She almost kept a straight face then laughed again. He snatched it away from her.

"As well you should be. I value my education."

"Sure it isn't just that girl you like? Jena Kim?"

Ephraim choked. "How did you know about her?"

"You've only been mooning over Jena since the second grade. What was that school play she was in?"

He'd never mentioned his crush to his mother, and she had never cared enough about his life to take an interest. Ephraim picked up a bacon strip and crunched it. It crumbled then melted in his mouth. Delicious.

"You're quiet all of a sudden. Penny for your thoughts," she said.

A penny . . . The coin. His wish! He slapped his fork down on the table and sat straight up.

"Now what's wrong?" A note of impatience slipped into her voice. She shook a cigarette out of a pack then picked up her lighter. "I'm trying, Eph. I really am."

He had used the coin to make two wishes, and they each seemed to come true. That was more than coincidence. More than a hallucination, unless he had completely lost hold of reality.

It was magic. He had a magic coin.

He smiled. "Everything's perfect, Mom. Thanks for the breakfast."

She lit the cigarette. She took a drag and blew the smoke away from the table. "You sure there isn't anything you'd like to tell me?" she said.

He swallowed. "I . . . love you, Mom."

"That's just your stomach talking." She stood and untied her apron, cigarette dangling from her mouth. She brushed off her sleeve and patted her hair to make sure it was all in place. "I better get going. I don't know how much of this you're actually going to eat, but it made me feel better to do something. I know I've been at work a lot lately and I want to make it up to you."

She slung her apron over the back of her chair. "Any plans for your first day of freedom?"

"I'm just going to hang out with Nathan," he said around a mouthful of toast. "At the library."

She smiled. "Give the girl some space, huh?"

Ephraim coughed.

"And clean up before you go. Just pop everything in the dishwasher."

Ephraim looked up. "We have a dishwasher too?"

His mother shook her head. "What's gotten into you? I hoped you were going to skip this whole phase, whatever it is."

As soon as his mother had gone, Ephraim raced back to his room. He took his coin collection and shook the jar out onto his unmade bed. He sifted through the jingling coins frantically. What if it had disappeared like everything else?

Ephraim's mother had changed so much since last night, but she had been that way once, when his father was around. Before things got bad. He couldn't believe he had her back.

There it was! He plucked the magic coin from the rest. The metal hummed gently against his skin as he turned it over and over.

He didn't know what his next wish would be, but he would have to plan it carefully. He didn't want to rush it—for all he knew, the third wish could be his last. They always came in threes, didn't they?

The summer was looking a lot more promising.

Ephraim locked his bicycle to the rack in front of the Summerside Public Library. He paused before the stone lions flanking the entrance. They were half-scale replicas of the lions at the main branch of the New York City Public Library—a bit ostentatious for a Westchester suburb like Summerside, but they had always impressed Ephraim. He'd named them Bert and Ernie when he was a little kid. Bert, the one on the left, was his favorite, even though they were mirror images of each other.

Ephraim patted Bert's left paw on his way up the stairs. He passed the book return box and pushed his way through the turnstile, headed for the circulation desk.

He used to come here every Saturday afternoon with his father. Ephraim had never really enjoyed reading much more than comics, but he liked spending time with his father so he'd always looked forward to those trips. He would gather an armful of books to take home, for his father to read with him at bedtime through the week.

Some things never changed, Ephraim thought. He was still using the library as an excuse to get closer to someone. He pulled *The Lord of the Rings* out of his backpack, lightening the load significantly, and approached the circulation desk.

Jena sat behind the counter, her face bent over an open book, of course. Her short hair curtained down on either side of her face. He was surprised to see her wearing a tank top; he was even more surprised that he could see straight down the front of it. He felt faint.

"Checking something out?" she said, eyes still glued to the page.

"Uh," Ephraim said. How did she know he'd been staring at her?

Jena looked up and pushed her bangs back. "Hi, Ephraim. Checking out?" she repeated.

"Oh. Returning, actually." He placed the book on the counter. She stood and pulled it toward her. She ran her fingers over the worn cover gently, then turned it over and aimed a scanner at the barcode on the back.

"Getting something else today? Or are just you here for the computers too?" she asked.

"Too?" Ephraim responded.

"Nathan's over there already. Better not let Mrs. Reynolds catch him trying to download porn again."

Jena slid the book onto the cart behind her desk, then returned to her reading as though Ephraim weren't still standing in front of her.

Well, what had he expected? She was at work, she probably didn't have time to chat with friends. And he wasn't really a friend. But she didn't look exactly busy, either—there weren't many other people in the library this early, on the first day of summer vacation.

"Hey," Nathan said when Ephraim rolled a chair over.

"You did a pretty good job on Michael yesterday," Ephraim said. "I meant to call to find out how you pulled it off." He'd been so distracted by the situation with his mother, and the coin, it had completely slipped his mind.

"Say what now?" Nathan glanced at Ephraim.

"I saw him at the hospital last night. After you schooled him."

"You've got it backwards. That asshole shoved me in a locker." Nathan rubbed his shoulders. "I bet he used to shove the circles into the square pegs in kindergarten too."

Ephraim laughed. "He did. But you finally got back at him. How'd you escape from the locker, anyway?" Ephraim usually had to rescue Nathan after the coast was clear.

Nathan frowned. "I was in that locker for over an hour. Ms.

Kelly finally heard my yelling. She had to find the janitor to get me out with the master key. I thought I was going to be trapped in there all summer." Nathan's face was bright red; he'd had a crush on the curvy Social Studies teacher since freshman year. Even though he classified for honors level, he'd chosen Ms. Kelly's survey class and opted for extra tutoring with her as often as possible—and he'd still nearly flunked the class.

"Well, someone beat him up in the parking lot. Why would he lie and say it was you?" That would have to be more embarrassing for him.

"I wish I could claim credit for it," Nathan said.

Ephraim had wished his mother wasn't in the hospital, and the coin made it so she'd never been there. Maybe his last wish had also changed the incident with Michael? He just didn't know why the coin would have affected the outcome of Nathan's fight, which seemed completely disconnected from his wish.

Ephraim put his hand in his pocket, but he hesitated short of drawing the coin out. Should he tell Nathan about the wishes? How could he explain something like that? Since Ephraim seemed to be the only one who remembered the way things were before the wish came true, there was no way to prove the coin was magic.

"What were you doing at the hospital?" Nathan asked.

There was no point to having this conversation again. "Forget it. I'm glad you made it out all right." Nathan looked a lot better than Michael had. "I suppose it could have been worse. He might have locked you in my locker with the vomit."

Nathan gave him a strange look.

"Oh no. Tell me he didn't," Ephraim said.

"What the hell are you talking about? Who left vomit in your locker?"

"You took a picture of it!"

Nathan wrinkled his nose. "I don't recall any vomit, and I'm perfectly okay with that."

Ephraim sighed. He didn't know why the coin would have wiped that event too, but he had no complaints if it removed the photo evidence of one of his least favorite moments.

"Speaking of pictures, what are you looking at?" Ephraim asked, ready to move on.

Nathan spun his seat to face the computer screen.

"Let me show you," Nathan said. He logged into his image hosting account, where he uploaded the dozens of pictures he took every day. Even though he had his own computer at home, his parents insisted on monitoring his online activity closely. His father was a corporate IT guy and compulsively ran gatekeeper programs on their household network. So Nathan did all his personal stuff from school and the library, which ironically had fewer restrictions.

Nathan clicked on a folder, and a set of thumbnail images popped up. He expanded one of them, and Ephraim saw a picture of Jena, Mary, and Shelley at school yesterday. They were standing around with their backs to the camera.

Ephraim snuck a glance at the circulation desk, but Jena wasn't there anymore, and the cart of book returns was gone. The librarian, Mrs. Reynolds, was hunched over the computer keyboard, typing away madly. All the kids knew she was writing a novel; they just didn't know what it was about. She never talked about it, which probably meant it was one of those Harlequin romances she read all the time.

Which made him think of Jena again. He was disappointed he hadn't made the most of his brief encounter with her. He'd been planning to find another book just to swing by her desk again, but she'd probably be shelving for the rest of the morning. He didn't want to be too obvious by looking for her.

"This is my masterpiece," Nathan said. "I call it 'three hot girls.'"

"That's inspired," Ephraim said. "What happened to the good stuff?"

"I made a slideshow," Nathan said. He clicked on the mouse again and the screen dissolved. A photo of Jena sitting in the assembly came up. Then a photo of Ephraim tripping down the stairs.

"Did you have to keep that one?"

"It is not for us to alter history. I merely observe and capture the moment for posterity."

"Whatever." More pictures of the assembly passed, then the photo Ephraim had just seen of the girls, then pictures of Nathan's cat.

"Hold on." Ephraim grabbed the mouse and stopped the slideshow. "Where's the picture of their . . ." Ephraim lowered his voice. "Tits?"

Nathan's jaw dropped. "Getting that kind of shot would be like finding the Holy Grail. Then photographing it."

"No fair holding out. You promised me copies."

"I'd share it with you if I could, buddy, but I don't have any pictures like that. Yet."

Ephraim clicked through the set of pictures, but several photos he clearly remembered were missing—most notably the ones Nathan had taken in the hall just before Ephraim made his first wish, while he was talking to Mary and Shelley about his mother.

"Until then, we'll have to be satisfied with these." Nathan clicked on another set of pictures. He shifted his seat to shield the screen from Mrs. Reynolds's view with his body. A picture flashed on the screen.

It wasn't a nude, but it might as well have been. At first all Ephraim noticed were breasts in a tight white tank top, wet through to show the dark circles of the woman's nipples. Then he checked out her face. It was Jena.

"What?" Ephraim said. He took a breath. "Where did you get this?"

Nathan smiled and clicked forward to another picture. It was Mary—or Shelley—in a bright blue bikini, splashing in surf on a beach. This time Ephraim recognized the picture.

"That's . . . you stuck her head on a model's body!"

"Magicians never reveal their secrets. But yeah, I've been practicing with Photoshop."

"This is a new low for you. You can't let them see these," Ephraim said. He peered closely at the next picture, with Jena's face grafted onto a lingerie model. "But you do have talent, my friend."

"What are you guys up to?" Jena said. She stood behind the computer terminals, looking over at them. Ephraim glanced from her to her image on the screen.

"Nothing!" Ephraim said.

"We aren't looking at porn," Nathan said.

Smooth, Nathan. "Of course not," Ephraim said.

"Okay," Jena said. She moved on, pushing a book cart ahead of her. Nathan pulled out his camera and fumbled with it. He turned it on and zoomed in on her back just as she moved out of view into an aisle.

"Too late," Nathan said.

Ephraim groaned.

"So when are you going to ask her out?" Nathan said.

"Why would I do something like that?"

"Because you like her."

Ephraim would be confident enough to ask Jena out if he knew she liked him, but the only way to find out for sure was to ask her.

Ephraim took out the coin and balanced it on his thumb with his forefinger around it.

"Why don't you ask out one of the twins? Whichever one you like this week," Ephraim said.

"I'm going to wait until you get close to Jena, so you can set me up with Shelley. Or Mary."

"Sounds like true love," Ephraim said, toying with the coin.

"Hey, I double the probability of scoring with one of them if I go after both, right?" Nathan grinned.

"You never were very good at math."

"Anyway, I suppose you do have all summer to work up the

nerve to talk to her. Though you'd think you'd be ready after ten years of pining," Nathan said.

"I haven't been 'pining.' And I'm not afraid to talk to her, I'm just not very good at it. I wish she liked me, that's all." The coin warmed up in his hand. "Oh crap. I didn't mean that."

"Then what did you mean?" Nathan said. He was paging through other photo collections online, finding more images of girls that verged on porn but didn't quite cross the line. He knew better than anyone how to get the most from a restricted network.

The coin became hotter, the way it had after Ephraim had made each of his other wishes. If the coin only granted three wishes, he'd just used up his last one. He didn't know how to cancel it, if he could. He had no choice but to flip it.

When he caught the coin, the air rippled before him, like heat waves on pavement. The huge breakfast he'd eaten roiled in his stomach, and he tasted acidy bacon, but he swallowed and the slight nausea passed quickly. The coin had landed on tails.

Nathan poked him in the arm. "What's with you? You spaced out."

Nothing seemed different yet. The same picture was even up on the screen. "I'm gonna head home, I think," Ephraim said. "Too much excitement for one morning."

"Okay, I'll come with."

"Um, I don't know if that's a good idea." Ephraim rarely asked anyone over to his apartment, Nathan included, because he never knew what state his mother would be in. It was safer to just hang out at Nathan's like usual, especially since he didn't know whether his last wish had changed anything else. "Let's just hang at your place," Ephraim said.

"Okay. My dad just brought home *Duke Nukem Eternal*. He'll be pissed if I beat it before he does." He smiled. "So I'm going to play it all day."

"You mean *DN Forever*?"

"No, this is the sequel. It just came out." Nathan gritted his teeth and murmured through pressed lips. "She's doing it again." He'd gone through a brief period studying ventriloquism in the fourth grade, but he'd never quite mastered the technique.

"What?"

Nathan pointed his left hand toward the circulation desk, hiding it behind the monitor. "She's staring at you."

"Mrs. Reynolds?" Ephraim asked.

"Blech. That would be gross. Not Mrs. Reynolds—Jena Kim."

Ephraim turned and saw Jena behind the desk instead of the older librarian. She was looking at him, but she quickly diverted her attention to her book.

"Don't turn around! What's her problem?" Nathan said. "Doesn't she get that you aren't into her?"

"Why would she have that impression?"

"Because you've been mooning over her best friend for years."

"Who?"

"What do you mean, 'who'? Mary." Nathan rolled his eyes.

"Mary Morales? You're the one who has a thing for the twins," Ephraim said.

"Hey, I'm holding out for her better half."

Ephraim kept an eye on Jena, but she didn't look up at him again. He sighed.

"Wait. Are you serious?" Nathan said. "Since when do you like Jena Kim? And why? Did you hit your head?"

Ephraim felt like he'd been dropped into the middle of a different conversation than the one he'd been in a moment ago. The coin had worked its magic again and rearranged his life, but this time not for the better. If Jena was aware of Ephraim's supposed interest in Mary, his situation had just gotten even more complicated.

Had anything been different about the coin this time around? It had come up tails . . . he tried to think back over his wishes. He was pretty sure the coin had shown heads after his first two flips.

Ephraim slipped it back into his pocket, wondering if he'd ever get used to it.

"I'm going to talk to Jena," Ephraim said. From the way Jena had been staring at him, maybe his wish had come true after all, regardless of its other effects. If so, there had never been a better time to find out how she felt about him.

"What about the plan?" Nathan asked.

"We can still do something after."

"Not that. The double date, man! We're supposed to date the twins. You with Mary, me with Shelley. We've been planning this since puberty."

"But I like Jena, Nathan. I always have."

"Oh, I get it. You're gonna go for both Mary and Jena. Play the friends against each other, do a switch. It's risky, but you'd be my hero if you pulled that off." Nathan shrugged. "Well, you're my hero anyway, but you know. That'd be something. You're an inspiration, Eph."

"Yeah. Don't get all weird on me. Weirder. I'll be right back."

He headed for Jena's desk, trying to think of something clever to say. When he reached her, she closed her book and smiled at him.

"Hey, Ephraim."

"Hey, Jena. Um. Wasn't Mrs. Reynolds just sitting here?"

That wasn't the best opening line ever, he had to admit. Jena blinked at him.

"She's been out all day. She sprained her ankle last night stepping down from a ladder."

"I could have sworn I just saw her . . ." Ephraim said. He knew he'd seen her at the desk, just before he made that accidental wish.

Could the coin have caused Mrs. Reynolds to injure herself, just so he would have this chance with Jena? That was a much worse outcome than Ephraim supposedly crushing on Mary instead of Jena.

"Is she all right?" he asked.

"She'll be back tomorrow," Jena said. She took a deep breath.

She seemed as nervous as he felt. "Can I ask you something, Ephraim?"

"Sure."

"I'm having a little party tonight. Nothing big, just a few people from school. To celebrate summer vacation and everything."

Ephraim nodded.

"So, I was wondering . . . if you'd like to come." She tapped a pen against the book in front of her.

Ephraim opened his mouth but no sound came out.

Jena laughed. "Just nod or shake your head."

"You're inviting me to your party? Tonight?"

"I know it's short notice." She looked past him, and he turned to see Nathan watching them. Nathan gave him a thumbs-up. Jena couldn't have missed that; Ephraim reminded himself to kill his friend later.

"I've been waiting to talk to you alone," she said. "It's a *small* gathering, you know?" She smiled, a little uncertainly.

"Yeah." Ephraim nodded again. He got it. She didn't want him to bring Nathan. "Um, what time?"

"Eight." She handed him a slip of lavender notebook paper with her address and phone number scribbled in sparkly blue ink. "That's my cell phone number," she said.

He forced his hand not to shake when he took it from her. "Um. Yeah . . . I'll be there. Thanks," Ephraim said. "I'll hold onto this." He waved the slip of paper around.

He'd been worried he had wasted what was potentially his last wish, but maybe the coin was giving him exactly what he wanted after all. If things worked out the way he hoped with Jena tonight, he wouldn't need a single wish more.

CHAPTER 6

Ephraim didn't do well at parties. Jena had greeted him enthusiastically at the door, but before long she'd been called off to fulfill her duties as hostess. Ephraim stood alone by the snack table in the dining room, watching everyone else mingling and having a good time.

He never hung out with his classmates outside of high school, aside from Nathan. He figured they were all just forced together by circumstance, so why bother? He didn't have much in common with most of them, and he probably wouldn't see many of them ever again after high school—especially if he got out of Summerside like he planned.

Some of the guests cast puzzled glances his way as they approached the food table, then veered off to avoid talking to him. Ephraim watched Michael Gupal talk to Jena on the other side of the living room. He seemed to have recovered from his injuries; Ephraim didn't even see any bruises or cuts on his face. Perhaps that had been wiped out by his latest wishes, too, which would explain why Nathan had no memory of beating up Michael. There went his dreams of blackmailing the bully and ending his reign of terror.

"Do I need to give you a code word?" A girl's voice came from his right.

One of the Morales twins stood next to him, one hand on the dining table.

"Er. What?" he asked.

"I figured you were in charge of the food. You haven't budged from this table since you got here." She glanced over at Jena, who was still deep in conversation with Michael near the massive entertainment center. "Or are you admiring the view?"

"I just kind of ended up here."

"Well, you're really good at it. Standing."

"Thanks."

"No, thank you. You're saving me from unnecessary calories."

Ephraim picked up a plastic cup. "Can I pour you a drink?"

"Now you're the bartender? I suppose that's a step up."

"The tips are better."

She looked over the selection of sodas. "Just a Coke, please."

Ephraim reached for the Diet Coke, and she put a hand on his. He froze.

"Do I look like I need Diet?" she asked.

She wore a yellow tank top that showed off exactly how little she needed a diet soda. She had a baby-blue knee-length skirt on and pink sandals. Her toenails were neon green.

"Not even a little bit. It's just . . . you were talking about calories . . ."

"Diet's fine." She smiled. He handed her the cup, and she sipped it delicately, peering around him. He turned but didn't see anyone there.

"What?" he asked.

"I was wondering where your sidekick was."

"My sidekick? Oh. Nathan, uh, couldn't make it." *Because he wasn't invited.* Ephraim felt guilty about ditching Nathan and lying about his plans for the evening, but since the presence of Mary and Shelley Morales at the party was a given, Nathan would have insisted on tagging along. The betrayal would hurt his friend either way, but better to beg for forgiveness than risk his chance to spend some time with Jena. Of course, the other major downside to keeping Nathan in the dark was he couldn't get a ride to Jena's house, which was clear on the other side of town. It had taken over an hour on a bus to get here, and he'd have to leave early if he wanted to get home the same way.

Ephraim swiveled his head to follow Jena as she disappeared into the kitchen with Michael. He took a half step in that direction.

"That's a shame," she said. He snapped his attention back to the

Morales twin, whichever one she was. She noticed him studying her nervously. "I'm Mary, by the way, if you were wondering."

He laughed. "Am I that obvious?"

"I recognized the look in your eyes. It's not just you. We've had the same classmates since junior high, and still no one can tell us apart. Just Jena, which is probably why she's our best friend."

"Or is it *because* she's your best friend?"

"You know? Maybe that's it." Mary smiled.

"So where's *your* sidekick?" Ephraim asked.

"Shelley's around here somewhere. We aren't attached at the hip, you know."

"No, then you'd be Siamese."

Mary laughed. "Score. That's the first twin joke I haven't heard a thousand times."

"What do I win?"

She raised an eyebrow. "What do you want?"

Jena sidled up to Ephraim's elbow. She glanced from him to Mary a couple of times.

"Are you two having a good time?" Jena asked, with a weird edge to her voice.

Michael hovered behind her with a platter of cookies cradled in his arms. He placed it on the table and eyed Ephraim before heading back to the kitchen.

"I am," Mary said. "But I don't think Ephraim is. Yet." Mary popped a potato chip into her mouth.

"Shelley's looking for you, Mary," Jena said pointedly.

Mary smiled. "I'd better find out what my dear sister wants. So much for not being Siamese." She raised her plastic cup toward Ephraim like a toast and wandered off.

"Are you really not having a good time?" Jena asked. She gave him a frowny pout.

"You know. I just got here," Ephraim said. The music got louder, so he raised his voice. "Are your parents around?"

"Are you kidding? My mother would be having a nervous break-down if she were here, and my father would be sitting in the corner making sure no guys talked to me without his permission. They're visiting my aunt in New York this weekend. As long as they can't hear us in Flushing, we'll be fine."

He was surprised that Jena would be throwing a party without her parents' permission; she always seemed to follow the rules at school. But that's why he was here, to get to know her better and find out what she was really like. She was obviously more than a bookworm.

"Hey, do you want a drink?" he asked.

"No thanks." Jena cleared her throat. "I'm glad you came tonight. I wasn't sure you would."

"I said I would. Thanks for the invite." He took a deep breath. "I was happy you asked me."

"Really?"

"Well, yeah. I . . . thought you didn't like me," Ephraim said.

"What?" Jena's voice squeaked. "I thought *you* didn't like *me*!"

"What gave you that idea?"

"All the times I asked you to hang out with me! You always have some excuse."

Ephraim would have fallen all over himself to accept if Jena had ever asked him out, like he had tonight. It would be nuts to turn her down.

"But you've been avoiding me all night," he pointed out. "You couldn't get away from me fast enough when I showed up."

Jena looked down at her feet. Her toenails were a dark blue. "I was nervous."

"Oh. Really?"

Ephraim and Jena stared at each other for a moment then laughed.

"You'd think I'd seen enough episodes of *Three's Company* to know better than to jump to conclusions," Jena said.

"Three's Company?"

"It's an old sitcom my dad likes. People were always misunderstanding each other on the show: overhearing conversations, drawing wild conclusions." She took his arm and led him over to a cabinet by the television. The shelves were crammed full of DVDs and videocassettes, many of them labeled by hand. "He's into vintage programs. He bootlegs a lot from the museum." Mr. Kim was a curator at the Paley Center for Media in the city.

"That's quite a collection." Ephraim didn't even recognize the titles of most of those shows, but he knew some of them from reruns he'd seen on cable at Nathan's, like *The Brady Bunch* and *Gilligan's Island.*

"Did you watch all these?"

"It's all my dad would let me watch when I was a kid. It grows on you. Sometimes watching TV is the only way for me to spend time with him."

Ephraim picked up a tape labeled "Bugs and Daffy."

"*Looney Tunes!*" he said. "I used to love these cartoons."

"Me too. They're classics."

He put the tape back and ran his hand along the rest of the shelf. "I'm glad we cleared things up," he said.

She nodded. "It's important to like the same cartoons. More important than anything else, I'd say."

"I meant—"

"Studies show that three percent of all divorces occur because the partners couldn't agree on what to watch."

"You're right. We'd have a serious problem if you liked Daffy Duck more than Bugs Bunny."

She put a hand to her mouth. "Oh no! I do prefer Daffy. We're doomed."

Ephraim was so happy he even let Jena drag him into the center of the living room, the makeshift dance floor, even though he didn't know how to dance. He just enjoyed being close to her finally—and due to the number of people crammed into the center of the living room, they were *really* close. Close enough that Ephraim smelled the soap she'd used as they danced. Close enough that he hoped she couldn't tell he didn't know what to do with his feet as he swayed back and forth in front of her.

He caught Mary and Shelley staring at them from the couch, which had been pushed aside to face the center of the living room. They had worn the same outfit but with reversed colors: Shelley wore a light-blue tank top and a yellow skirt, which at least made them easier to tell apart. He smiled over at Mary, but she didn't react.

"Um, is Mary all right?" Ephraim asked.

Jena glanced over at the twins. "I'd better check."

As Jena pushed through the throng of dancers, Mary got up and walked off. Jena followed her into the kitchen.

Alone on the dance floor, Ephraim edged back over to the snack table and grabbed himself a drink and a handful of stale popcorn. He went to sit on the couch next to Shelley.

"Shelley, right?" he asked.

"You want a gold star for getting my name?" Shelley said.

If he'd ever thought she and her sister were interchangeable, he wouldn't make that mistake again. Unsure of how to respond, he gulped his punch and quickly realized it had been spiked with alcohol. He just managed not to cough, but he stared into the bottom of the plastic cup, his eyes tearing.

He didn't know much about the twins, just that the two of them basically controlled the media at Summerside High: Mary was going to be a co-editor on the school newspaper next year, and Shelley pretty much ran yearbook. Jena spent time on the staff of both publications, and the group was as inseparable as Ephraim and Nathan were. More so, since Ephraim was at this party on his own. Ephraim fell silent, thinking about how Nathan would feel if he could see Ephraim talking to Shelley right now.

"She likes you," Shelley said.

Ephraim swallowed an ice cube and coughed. He felt the cold lump slide down his throat.

"Jena?" he asked.

"My sister, jerk. You were just flirting with her over there."

"I was? I thought she was just trying to be nice."

Mary liked him? Really? Come to think of it, Nathan had said Ephraim liked Mary—after his latest wish. He supposed the feeling could be mutual.

"I don't know what either of them see in you, but if you hurt my sister or Jena you'll regret it," Shelley said.

Ephraim laughed weakly. "Let me guess, you know a guy who'll teach me a lesson?"

Shelley scowled.

A shadow fell over Ephraim. He looked up and saw Jason Ferrer looming over him, blocking the light from a table lamp the way a mountain blocks the sunset. Jason played quarterback for the school team, the Summerside Badgers.

"Let's dance, Shell." He extended his thick hand toward her.

Shelley glared at Ephraim once more before turning a sweet smile to Jason. "I'd love to." She bounced up from the couch. She looked back and said, "And you should tell your little friend to stop stalking me. He's creepy." Then she and Jason moved off, and Ephraim was once again alone.

Aside from the dance with Jena, he'd spent most of this party by himself. He never had to worry about being bored or lonely or out of place with Nathan around. He'd underestimated how much having a best friend like Nathan made life at Summerside High bearable, even enjoyable. He'd made a big mistake not telling him about the party.

Ephraim glanced up and imagined he saw Nathan's face at the bay window in the living room. He decided his guilt must be getting to him.

No, it was really him. Ephraim pushed his way through the

dancing couples to the big window, but by the time he got there, Nathan had vanished. Had it just been his unconscious mind playing tricks on him? Or maybe the spiked punch, which was already giving him a pleasant buzz.

This was the second time he'd thought he'd seen Nathan someplace he didn't expect to. Was he following him? Shelley said he'd been stalking her, but then what had he been doing at the hospital the night Ephraim had brought his mother in? Why would he show up without saying anything?

Ephraim could barely see outside the window now, since the interior light was reflecting the living room in the glass.

If Nathan had found out about the party and decided to crash it, Ephraim had better apologize while he could—if it wasn't already too late. He left the house and found the window he'd seen Nathan at. The grass beneath it was trampled, but that could have happened anytime. He spun around slowly, but the only people outside were a couple of girls holding hands and sharing a cigarette under a tree. He made a circuit of the house.

"Ephraim!" Jena called from a second-floor balcony.

"Jena?" He looked up the side of the house at her.

"You aren't leaving already?" she said.

Ephraim checked his watch. It was already ten, and it was a long bus ride home.

"I probably should head out," he said.

"We didn't finish our dance," Jena said. She leaned over the railing, and he was suddenly reminded of the drama club's production of *Romeo and Juliet,* freshman year. She'd been Juliet, of course. He'd played one of the soldiers who didn't even have a speaking part—a good thing, since he couldn't have remembered his lines in her presence.

"I'll call you?" Ephraim said.

"I guess that'll have to do."

She turned to go back inside. He stared at her legs as she walked into the house. Just before she closed the door she waved and smiled shyly.

Ephraim reached the bus stop and discovered he'd missed the last bus by twenty minutes. He didn't know what to do—should he go back to Jena's house and beg someone for a ride? He could call his mother from a pay phone, or if he found Nathan maybe he could beg for a lift home while he apologized for being a crappy friend.

"Sucks, doesn't it?" A voice spoke from the bench behind him.

Ephraim turned and saw a shabbily dressed man sitting there. He couldn't make him out well in the dark, but the man had long greasy brown hair and a T-shirt that looked like it had once been white but was now gray and stained.

"Did the last bus go by?" Ephraim asked.

"Yup. Not your night, huh?"

Ephraim kicked the bus stop pole and considered his options. All he had in his pocket were two dollar bills for the bus.

Make that $2.25—and that extra quarter might make all the difference.

Ephraim pulled out the magic coin and considered his options. This was a frivolous wish, but it would be a good test of whether he even had any wishes left. And this was an emergency, after all. He had nothing to lose.

"I wish I hadn't missed the bus," he whispered, self-conscious about the homeless man watching him. He tossed the coin but lost sight of it in the dark. All he saw was a quick flash in the light from a streetlamp before he heard it hit the sidewalk. "Crap," he said.

He searched the ground frantically, but it wasn't where he thought it had fallen. If the coin had rolled even a short distance away, it would be difficult to spot at night. Ephraim was about to give up when the guy from the bench leaned over and picked something up—the quarter.

Ephraim eyed the coin, wondering if it was heating up and what the man might think of that. "Thanks, mister." He approached the man, wrinkling his nose at the sour stench radiating from his grubby clothes.

The man squinted at the quarter and rubbed his grimy fingers over it. "Hmmm." He raised it up to the light and turned it this way and that, pinched between thumb and index finger. When he saw the reverse side with the picture of Puerto Rico, he went "Hmmm" again.

Ephraim reached for the quarter. The man held it over Ephraim's open hand, poised to drop it. They locked eyes over the coin.

"Here you go, kid." The man finally lowered the quarter into his palm and pressed it there with a finger.

Vertigo swept over Ephraim. His stomach felt like it was dropping away from him, and then he was fine.

The man let his hand go and staggered away. He let out a loud belch. He seemed dizzy and started knocking his knuckles against the side of his head.

Ephraim stepped back quickly in case the man threw up. He checked the coin in his hand. It was tails up.

Suddenly they were illuminated by twin beams of light coming up the street. The man straightened. "Looks like another bus is here," he said.

Ephraim grinned with relief. There might not be a limit to the number of wishes he could make with the coin.

The bus stopped, and Ephraim climbed on. He fed his two dollars into the bill slot and took a seat at the front. The homeless man stepped into the bus too, and the doors closed with a whoosh.

"I don't have any money," the man said.

The bus driver sighed. "You can't keep doing this, old fella. This is a business, not a charity."

The homeless man turned to Ephraim. "I have to get home," he said. "You brought me here." His eyes were glassy and unfocused.

Ephraim pocketed his quarter. "Sorry," he said. "I don't have enough change."

"Change!" The homeless man chuckled to himself.

"You know this guy?" the driver asked.

"I don't know what he's talking about," Ephraim said. "I only met him two minutes ago."

"It's a real shame when someone gets like this. Well, what the hell," the driver said. "I'll take you anyway. *I'm* not losing any money over it and this is my last run of the night."

"*This* is the last bus?" Ephraim said.

"Yup. I'm thirty minutes late—trouble with the doors earlier. But I always finish my route." He shifted the bus into gear.

"Looks like it's your lucky night after all," the homeless man said as he shuffled past Ephraim's seat.

Ephraim stared after him. The man remembered their conversation from before Ephraim's wish for the bus. Why? Up until now, no one but Ephraim had been aware of the changes. So what was different this time from all the previous times he'd used the coin? It was either the man or something Ephraim had done.

He heard the unmistakable sound of the man vomiting in the back of the bus, and a moment later the acidic odor wafted toward him.

"Swell." The driver sighed. "That's what I get for being nice."

Ephraim turned and looked out the window as the bus moved down dark, empty streets. He kept his hand curled protectively around the coin in his pocket the whole time.

CHAPTER 7

Ephraim's mom wasn't home when he got back from the party. Instead of the lecture he'd expected for missing curfew, he found a note on the fridge telling him there were leftovers inside. It seemed she was back on the evening shift at the supermarket.

It bothered him that his wishes were causing unpredictable changes that he hadn't asked for. At least this time it had worked in his favor; because she wasn't home, his mother would never even know he'd been out so late, and he'd avoid spending the first two weeks of summer grounded. With the coin, it would be easy enough to put things right for his mother again. Or better yet, he could wish her into a job she might actually enjoy, one that paid more than her meager wages.

Ephraim hadn't eaten much at the party despite all his time near the snack table, so he nuked a plate of leftover meat loaf and mashed potatoes—a meal he didn't remember his mother cooking in the first place—and brought it to his room. As soon as he logged into his computer, an instant message from Nathan flashed on his screen with an accompanying tone that sounded wrong, distorted from usual. The last thing he needed was a busted sound card in his computer.

HEY. Where have you been? Nathan typed.

The cursor blinked at Ephraim accusingly. So that *had* been Nathan at the window.

Ephraim leaned back as far as his desk chair would go and passed the magic coin from hand to hand. Deep down he'd hoped that it had made it easier on him, changing things with his last wish so Nathan wouldn't know anything about the party, the same way it had affected his mother. His only choice was to come clean and apologize; if he lied about the party now, he would only seem like even more of a jerk.

Come to think of it, Ephraim could just wish for Nathan to forget he'd ditched him for the party, couldn't he? Nathan wouldn't even notice. It would spare him hurt feelings, and Ephraim wouldn't have to deal with the problem more directly.

Ephraim clenched the coin in his fist. He slapped the quarter down next to the keyboard.

Sorry, Ephraim typed. *I should have told you about the party earlier.*

Nathan loved it whenever Ephraim admitted a mistake, but his gloating response took a long time to appear.

What party? Nathan finally typed.

So he was going to make Ephraim work for this.

Jena invited me at the last minute. I should have mentioned it.

You went to a party without me? At Jena's house?

I'm sorry, Ephraim typed again. *It was a selfish thing to do.* He would have to say all the things Nathan wanted to hear.

I thought we were best friends.

"Ouch," Ephraim said. *Of course we are. I just didn't want to push my luck when I got the invite. I wanted to ask if you could come . . . I will next time, I promise.*

Was Shelley there? Nathan typed.

Ephraim didn't know why Nathan was playing dumb about the whole thing; he was fast losing his moral high ground. Nathan had seen Ephraim staring at him in the window just before he ran off, so he had to know he'd been spotted.

Yeah. She was in a bad mood, too. He didn't feel like explaining why right then.

Bastard.

Ephraim was done playing this game—if he had come clean, then Nathan should too. He typed, *Stop pretending. I saw you there.*

Where?

At the party. I saw you in the window.

Nathan didn't respond for a full minute. *I didn't even know about your stupid party. You really think I'm lame enough to follow you? How pitiful do you think I am? Never mind, I already know. THANKS.*

Ephraim shook his head. *I saw you.*

IT WASN'T ME.

As much as Nathan liked to prove Ephraim wrong, he hated to be caught in his own lies. But why was he keeping up this pretense? Trying to save a little embarrassment? Was it really possible that Ephraim's guilty conscience had made him think he saw Nathan's face at the window? Or maybe the coin had changed the way the evening had gone after all.

There was another option, one he'd considered before but still wasn't prepared to accept: there were two Nathans.

Whatever the case, Ephraim hadn't had to tell Nathan about the party at all. Now it was too late. He'd screwed up big time, and he wasn't sure what would make Nathan forgive him—aside from using the coin to smooth things over like they'd never happened.

Ephraim stared at the coin on his desk. Maybe it could help him out of this mess, after all.

Look. Ephraim typed quickly before he could change his mind. *I have something to show you. Something that can change our lives.* He hesitated only a moment before hitting the enter key.

Nathan's anger was matched only by his insatiable curiosity. He let Ephraim wait a while before responding. *What?* he typed.

Meet me tomorrow morning. 11am at the park fountain.

I'll think about it. Nathan's name went gray as he signed off. The usual closing door noise that signaled a user leaving the chat sounded more like a steel door sliding shut, like the bars in a prison. Maybe the IM service had changed up their familiar audio files.

Ephraim tapped the magic coin against his keyboard nervously. He hoped he wasn't making a mistake bringing Nathan in on this.

Well, it was worth a shot to salvage their friendship, wasn't it? He had been miserable on his own at the party. He was used to sharing everything with Nathan; things were always more fun with his best friend around. They could really have a good time with this.

And if it didn't work, if Nathan didn't believe him, he could still wish the problem away. It was a win-win situation. Ephraim flipped the coin and grinned. When you had magic on your side, anything was possible.

Ephraim was late the next morning. The Number 8 bus had taken an entirely different route than the one he expected. He'd had to get off and sort out the new bus schedule. He finally figured out he needed to transfer to the Number 5, which had never gone anywhere near the park.

Ephraim had still beaten Nathan there, at least. The fountain and its surrounding plaza served as the centerpiece of Greystone Park. The small area was paved with cobblestones and ringed by tall hedges. The Memorial Fountain was situated in the middle, marking the exact center of the sprawling park grounds. No one had ever been able to tell him what it was memorializing, though.

A bronze figure of Atlas—the Greek Titan who carried the world on his shoulders—decorated the fountain, facing north. Instead of a globe, Atlas supported a large bronze basin from which water cascaded into the larger granite pool below. Quarters lined the bottom of it, glinting faintly in the clear water and morning sunlight.

Ephraim wondered how much he had contributed to the fountain over the years since he had started coming there as a boy. And now just one coin was granting all his wishes.

Cold water sprayed across Ephraim's face as he sat on the rim of the fountain, trailing one hand in the water. The homeless man from the night before wandered from around the fountain into view and stared hard at him. Ephraim tried his best to ignore him. He focused on the coins in the fountain and started adding them up in his head.

"Spare some change?" the man said. Ephraim glanced at him but looked away quickly. The man's face was lined with dirt, and even on this hot summer day he wore a knit cap over his lanky hair. He had on a soiled gray thermal shirt with the sleeves rolled up. There was a tear in the seam over his right shoulder. The man reeked. Dried vomit crusted the front of his shirt.

Ephraim pulled his backpack onto his lap and held onto it tight. The bottom of the bag had gotten wet, and he felt water seeping through his pants.

"Sorry, no," Ephraim said. He stared at all the quarters on the bottom of the fountain. Why didn't the man just help himself?

"Hey! Get away from him!" Nathan came around the fountain from the other direction and glared at the bum.

"I'm just trying to get something to eat," the man said.

Nathan leaned over and swept a cupped hand through the water, splashing the homeless man and getting a fair amount on Ephraim as well. "Never mind food. You need a shower!" Nathan shouted.

Ephraim had never seen Nathan act like this before—by default he was mild-mannered, shy unless you knew him, which came from being bullied himself his whole life. Ephraim wondered if Nathan was taking his anger at Ephraim out on the wrong person.

The homeless man scowled and shambled off.

"Nathan, was that really necessary?" Ephraim said. "He wasn't hurting anything. I was just going to ignore him."

Nathan's camera flashed. "Heh. You wet yourself," he said. Ephraim looked down; the crotch and inner thighs of his jeans were wet.

"It's just water from the fountain. Thanks to you."

"Water. Sure it is." Nathan checked the picture, nodded to himself, then sat down on the other side of Ephraim's backpack. "Hey," Nathan said.

"Hey."

Thus a hesitant truce was formed.

"So, this party. You were actually at Jena's house?" Nathan asked, with no trace of bitterness in his voice. "How was it?"

"It was fine," Ephraim said.

"Did you get any action?"

"What?"

"Jena. Did you . . . you know." Nathan shoved him. "Did you at least kiss her?"

"I could barely handle *talking* to her."

"Chickenshit."

"I couldn't even get her alone for more than a couple of minutes. Mary Shelley pulled her away."

"There's a surprise. You know, if I'd been there I could have distracted the twins for you," Nathan said. "It would have been a sacrifice, but I'd do anything for you."

Ephraim sighed. "Because you're a better friend than I am."

"Exactly."

"You sure have mastered this whole guilt-tripping thing."

"I learned it from my mother. She comes from a long line of Jewish women trained in the delicate art of manipulation." Nathan shook his head. "So if you didn't get anywhere with her, what was the point in going?"

"I didn't say I didn't get *anywhere*. Jena did admit that she likes me," Ephraim said. Even now, remembering the night before still made Ephraim happier than he'd ever felt.

"Duh. Everyone in school knows she has a crush on you."

"I didn't know. She never showed any interest before."

"You weren't paying attention, you were so focused on Mary. What made you change your mind about her?" Nathan asked.

"That's the difficult part to explain. *I* didn't change. Everything else did. But I'm the only one who remembers what things used to be like."

"You're going to have to explain that."

Now that Ephraim was faced with the prospect of sharing the magic coin, he wasn't sure he wanted to. Things were probably fine between them now.

But a promise was a promise.

Ephraim reached into his pocket and pulled out the coin. He was carrying it in a small Ziploc bag, to avoid making any more accidental wishes while holding it. He'd tested it—the coin needed to be in direct contact with his skin for him to use it.

Ephraim slid the coin onto his palm. He held the quarter up between his thumb and forefinger and showed it to Nathan.

"It's because of this," Ephraim said.

Nathan frowned. "A quarter? What, get your allowance early this week?"

"It's not just a quarter. It . . . um. It grants wishes," Ephraim said.

Nathan glanced into the fountain. "Come on. Haven't you grown out of that yet?"

"I'm serious. This isn't like tossing a coin into the fountain. I've made a bunch of wishes and they all came true." *More or less.*

Nathan crossed his arms. "Really. What did you wish for?"

Ephraim paused. He didn't want to admit what his mother had done to prompt the whole discovery. Nathan knew she had some problems, but Ephraim had kept the worst of it a secret. Now that she was normal, it would make his story even harder to accept if he tried to explain how she had been before.

"Like I said, I wished that Jena liked me."

"Ephraim, Jena's liked you since forever."

"That's what I'm saying. Before I made the wish, she wasn't interested in me. You just remember her liking me, because the wish made it happen." He swallowed. "I've wished for other things too. Last night I missed the last bus, but I made a wish and then it came."

"That's just a coincidence, or dumb luck. If you have a magic coin, why didn't you wish yourself straight home instead?" Nathan leaned over and plunged his arm into the water up to his short shirtsleeve. He grabbed a handful of coins and held them for a moment, before letting them cascade back into the water with a splash.

Ephraim stared at Nathan. That was a good point—that would

have made a lot more sense, but he hadn't really been thinking clearly at the time.

"I'm still new at this, okay? Hey, I'm not joking." Ephraim's voice rose. He hadn't thought it would be this hard to convince Nathan, but it had taken Ephraim a while to believe it when he was actually seeing what it could do.

"But everyone would notice stuff changing around them. How could I miss something like that?"

"It's like . . . when the coin grants my wish, it changes people too, so they remember things differently."

Nathan scratched his forehead, considering.

"You mean the coin retcons the world to fit your wish? Like when lazy comic book writers make up a bunch of back story that never happened to justify their shoddy plotlines?" he asked.

"Um . . . you could put it that way."

"So I just have to take your word for it, because if you make a wish, I won't remember it. That's awfully convenient for you." Nathan snapped his fingers and held out his hand. "Let me see."

Ephraim reluctantly handed the coin to him and watched closely while he examined it.

"Okay, this is weird," Nathan said. He showed Ephraim the back of the coin, with the little frog and the palm tree. "Puerto Rico's not a state."

"Yeah, I know."

"But that doesn't make it magic." Nathan held the coin up and squinted at it. "Where did it come from?"

"From a dead body at the hospital. They mistakenly identified another boy as me, and they gave his stuff to my mom. I . . . kept the quarter, but that was before I knew it was magic."

Nathan's eyes widened.

Ephraim explained about the accident, and what he had found out—or hadn't found out—at the hospital. He wished he still had the other wallet and watch, not that they were conclusive evidence either. All he had from that night was the coin, a duplicate library card, and a few memories he'd rather he didn't have.

"That's a bit cracked," Nathan said. "You know how this sounds?"

"I would think my mother had imagined all of it, but there's the coin. And it *is* magic."

"How does it work?"

"You make a wish," Ephraim said. "Then you flip the coin."

"And how did you figure that out?"

"There was that note in my locker, remember? I showed it to you after the assembly. I thought you'd written it because it looked like your handwriting."

Nathan shook his head. "I don't remember. And I bet you don't have that anymore either." He smirked.

"No. That disappeared too."

"Yeah."

Ephraim wriggled a little. Water was soaking the seat of his jeans.

"Well, there's one way to prove this is magic." Nathan stood up. "I'll make a wish."

"Wait!" Ephraim grabbed Nathan's wrist.

Nathan scowled. "Stop acting. You and I both know it's not going to work. You're making this shit up, and it's a hell of a way to apologize."

"It's not that." Ephraim dropped his hand. "Every time I've changed something, people around me haven't even noticed. What if you use it and the same thing happens to me?"

Nathan shrugged. "Then I'll know about it. And I'll tell you what happened."

"And what if I don't believe you? I just . . ." Ephraim didn't want to give up his control of the coin. He was afraid if he let Nathan make a wish on his own, he would never see the coin again. Worse—he might not even know about it. He instantly hated himself for his suspicions, but the feeling didn't go away.

"You have another suggestion?" Nathan's voice had cooled.

"Uh." Seeing that homeless man had reminded Ephraim of what had happened last night, when his wish had apparently affected both of them. Was it because the man had held his hand when Ephraim touched the quarter? If the magic worked based on physical contact . . .

"Hold my hand," Ephraim said.

"Excuse me?"

"I think if we're touching while you make the wish, we'll both remember it even if everything and everyone else changes."

"You're just guessing that'll work."

"Call it a working theory."

Nathan sighed. He held out his hand. "Come on."

"Why are we standing?" Ephraim got to his feet and reached behind to pull the wet jeans from his skin. The back of his boxer shorts were damp too.

"It just seems like we should. It's more dramatic."

Ephraim grabbed Nathan's hand and looked at him, waiting.

"Don't get any funny ideas, either." Nathan closed his eyes. "I wish Shelley Morales were in love with me." After a moment he opened his eyes and looked at the coin.

"Is the coin getting hot?" Ephraim asked.

"No." Nathan flipped it in the air and caught it. He opened his fist and looked at the coin. "Tails."

Nothing happened. He tried it again and showed it to Ephraim. Heads this time.

"Very funny, Ephraim," Nathan said. He flicked his hand toward the fountain.

"No!" Ephraim turned and tried to see where the coin landed. He couldn't lose it—

"Relax." Nathan had the coin in his other hand. "Real magic is all about sleight of hand. Now you see it, now you don't."

Nathan tossed the coin to Ephraim, and he cupped his hands to catch it.

"I was just messing with you," Nathan said. "Like you were messing with me. You almost had me going."

Ephraim gritted his teeth. "I'm not lying. It's magic. Real magic. Not a parlor trick." He didn't want to entertain the thought that the coin's magic had simply run out, at the worst possible time. Didn't some spells break if you told someone else about them?

They stared at each other for a moment, neither one willing to budge.

"Maybe it only works for me because I found it," Ephraim said. "That's the only explanation."

Nathan's eyes rolled. "Not the *only* explanation."

"Look, let's try this again. I'll make the wish this time. If it doesn't work, I'll admit I was wrong. I'll toss the coin in the fountain and you can make fun of me about this all you want."

Nathan grinned. "You know I'll do that anyway." But he took Ephraim's hand, squeezing harder than he had to.

"I wish . . ." Ephraim said. "Are you sure you want this? It doesn't seem right."

"Come on," Nathan said. "You claim you got Jena interested in you the same way."

Ephraim sighed. "I wish that Shelley Morales likes Nathan."

"Love! I said love!" Nathan shouted. Ephraim flipped the coin and snatched it in mid-air.

The air shimmered. The hand holding Nathan's was suddenly empty.

Ephraim looked around in alarm and saw his friend a few feet away from him, now sitting on the fountain. Nathan glanced at him in surprise, then leaned over the fountain and gagged. Ephraim turned away. If he watched he would probably puke too. He didn't feel queasy at all anymore, though; he was definitely adjusting to the peculiar effects of the magic.

He opened his hand and glanced at the coin. Tails. If he was right about the sides affecting each wish, something bad was going to happen.

Nathan wiped his mouth and stared into the water. "This is kind of nasty." He lifted his camera with a trembling hand and took a picture.

"Gross," Ephraim said.

"Hey, where did all the coins go?" Nathan said.

"What?"

"The fountain's empty."

Ephraim leaned over the side and looked in the water. It was murkier than before, the bottom and sides streaked with green and brown, but Nathan was right—all the coins were gone. There had been hundreds of dollars in change inside, and now there wasn't a single penny.

"Now you see it, now you don't," Ephraim whispered.

Nathan slumped onto a park bench and pushed his long hair away from his forehead.

"So," Nathan said.

Ephraim smiled. "It worked."

"How do you know? Was it because I threw up or because the coins are gone?"

"Well, something happened. Didn't you feel it? How else do you explain the changes?"

Nathan scratched his chin, staring at the fountain. "What, um. What color's your backpack?"

"Red," Ephraim said.

"That's what I thought. It's green now," Nathan said.

Ephraim turned. His backpack still sat on the fountain where he'd left it, but Nathan was right—it was green.

"Crap. I hate green."

"Maybe we're imagining it," Nathan said. "Like a group hallucination. Do two people count as a group?"

"It's a side effect of using the coin. I've seen it before. Little things change along with the big ones."

"Hoo boy, that's some trick. It changed the color of your back-pack! It stole money from a park fountain! That's really special. And as an added bonus, it makes people hurl."

"It does more than that," Ephraim said. He heard a distinct whininess in his voice that embarrassed him. "We were holding hands right next to each other and then after the wish we were a few feet apart."

"Damn, that's useful. Better not let that coin fall into the wrong hands." Nathan closed his eyes for a moment and pressed his hand against his stomach. He belched loudly.

Ephraim stuffed the coin back into his pocket. "You just saw *magic*. It was small, but something still happened—"

"I'm not even really sure the color changed. Maybe it was always green."

Ephraim couldn't believe that Nathan was treating this . . . *miracle* like it was some common parlor trick. He didn't know how he could convince Nathan that he was telling the truth. Then it came to him.

"Your camera!" Ephraim said.

"What about it?" Nathan frowned and held up his hand, the camera dangling from a strap around his wrist.

"You took a picture of me not five minutes ago. Let's check it. If my bag's a different color, then that proves the coin is magic."

Nathan made a show of slowly switching on his camera and nav-igating to the picture he had just taken. He hesitated for a moment before looking up at Ephraim. He checked the screen on the back of the camera again.

"Well." Nathan handed the camera to him. The screen showed a picture of Ephraim sitting on the fountain. The cascading water was frozen behind him, and sure enough, his pants were wet around the crotch, as though he had pissed in them. But it was the backpack Ephraim was interested in—it was sitting just behind him, a little out of focus, but clearly red.

"Ha!" Ephraim said. There was something else odd about the photo. In the background, behind the fountain, it looked like someone was crouching behind a tree. He thought he saw a face and a tuft of blond hair, the same shade as Nathan's. He zoomed in on the figure, but the poor resolution blurred the image.

Ephraim glanced over at the same tree, but there was no one there now. He didn't mention it to Nathan, not wanting to confuse the issue further.

Nathan's brow creased. "This is a hoax, isn't it? But I don't know how you pulled it off."

"It's magic." Ephraim kicked at a rock by his foot.

Nathan fiddled anxiously with his camera. Instead of being excited, he was anxious all of a sudden. Ephraim hadn't done him any favors dumping this on him.

"You know what? Never mind." Ephraim smiled. "I felt bad about ditching you yesterday, so I wanted to make it up to you. I know how you enjoy a good prank."

Nathan held up his hands in surrender. "Hey. It's cool, dude. Don't worry about it. I knew you were just fooling."

They sat in silence for a while, then Nathan abruptly jumped up. "Come on, we're near the library. I have some new pics to show you. Maybe Shelley will be there and she'll want to make out with me in the stacks, thanks to the 'wish.'"

Ephraim smiled, pretending to go along with the joke. He should just let it rest—they were talking again, they were still best friends. And the coin was still just his. Besides, he didn't mind spending the afternoon at the library. It was another chance to see Jena.

CHAPTER 8

"What the hell is this?" Ephraim said.

"Easy," Nathan said in a low voice. "You don't want her to hobble over here on those crutches, do you?" Mrs. Reynolds hated it when kids used the computers for anything but research, but she accepted it as a necessary evil to get them in the library doors where they might accidentally pick up a book. Ephraim was sorry to see she still had a sprained ankle, thanks to him.

Ephraim turned his attention back to the screen. He remembered this picture: one of Michael Gupal in the weight room, resting after hoisting a 200-pound barbell over his head. His eyes were closed, fluorescent light shining on his sweaty forehead, arms draped over the side of the exercise bench with his hands grazing the floor. A moment after this picture was taken, Michael had tossed a damp towel at Nathan and called him queer.

Nathan had altered the image: a small dark hole had been added to Michael's forehead. Red lines dribbled down his face and pooled on the floor below him. The towel under his head was drenched with a crimson stain that Ephraim could practically see spreading. It was so realistic, it sent a shiver through him.

"Holy crap, Nathan."

"It looks good, doesn't it? I did it in Photoshop."

"Okay. Why?"

"It felt good. Cathartic. Kind of like a little revenge. It doesn't hurt anyone." The look on Nathan's face told Ephraim that Nathan wouldn't have minded if it did.

Nathan clicked through a slideshow of horrors. Images of their teachers and classmates scrolled by, each one more graphic than the last—each one a macabre work of art. There was a picture of Mr.

Morchauser with a gory hole in his stomach, like it had been blasted out with a cannon. He could actually see the blackboard with their homework assignment through the dark tunnel in his shredded flesh. There was a picture of the football team with their eyes gouged out. A cheerleader that Nathan had virtually flayed, her pompoms sprayed with blood.

Nathan had talent, though its usefulness was dubious.

"You could get into some serious trouble if anyone finds these," Ephraim said. School officials were paranoid these days about anything that suggested their students were thinking of violence.

"The images aren't public. Is that all you can say about them?" The excitement faded from Nathan's face, with anger lurking just behind it. Ephraim wondered if there were any pictures of *him* that Nathan wasn't showing him.

"I'm really . . . impressed," Ephraim said. He also felt a little nauseous, which he couldn't blame on the coin this time around. "You must have worked on these for a long time."

"It was fun. Next time you come over I'll show you how I did some of them," Nathan said.

"Yeah. Cool."

Nathan glanced behind Ephraim and hurriedly closed the browser window. Ephraim turned and saw Jena standing there.

"Hi, Ephraim," she said. She looked upset. Had she seen the pictures on the screen? "Hey, Nathan." Nathan nodded to her.

"Sorry if I'm interrupting. Can I talk to you for a second, Ephraim?" she said.

"Sure." Ephraim stood up. "I was just on my way out. I'll see you later," he said to Nathan.

Nathan waved him off, already turning back to the computer.

Ephraim followed Jena. It looked like she was leading him to the stacks. He thought of Nathan's comment about making out back there and felt his face flush.

She veered off into a private office. It looked like this was where they did book repairs. There was a long workbench lined with mending tape, pieces of string, bottles of glue. Books in varying states of damage were piled up, cloth covers scattered everywhere.

"Is this where you've been hiding?" he asked. He'd looked for her when they came in and figured she just wasn't at work today.

"Just trying to catch up on all this work." She seemed nervous, or maybe distracted. "Thanks again for . . . you know."

"Yeah." Smooth, he thought.

She looked like she wanted to say something else, but instead she opened a drawer and pulled out a small rectangular package wrapped in a copy of the school newspaper. She handed it to Ephraim.

"This is for you."

"A gift? For me?" It was hard on the wide flat surfaces, and the wrapping gave a little on three of the narrow sides. A book.

"It's nothing." She looked embarrassed. "It's not even new. I just thought you'd like it."

"Thanks." He didn't know what to say or do. "We should hang out again soon, if you want. Go out, I mean. Together."

"I'd love that." Her face fell. "But, I don't think now is a good time, with everything that's going on. I'll have to let you know."

"Sure." What had happened? Her mood had changed abruptly—was it something he'd said or done?

It was the coin. It had to be. That last wish had changed something with Jena.

"Well . . . I should get back to work," Jena said.

"Yeah. Um, thanks again for this."

They looked at each other awkwardly. Ephraim hesitated, then opened his arms and leaned forward. At first Jena was startled, but she returned the hug. She rested her head against his shoulder and pressed closer to him.

Ephraim was glad he was still holding the gift, otherwise he was sure he would have left sweaty handprints on the back of her shirt. As nervous as he was, he suddenly felt more relaxed with her. She was warm and soft, and if he held her for too much longer she would find out this was really turning him on.

He moved to pull away and was surprised when she squeezed him even tighter before finally letting him go. They held each other at arm's length and looked at each other. Before he could lose his nerve, he kissed her on the cheek. She didn't even flinch. Instead she smiled, but he thought it was a sad smile.

When he got home his mother was in a fancy red dress, her hair was pinned up and away from her neck, and she was wearing makeup. Apparently she was no longer on the evening shift. It was like the coin was playing with him. How could Nathan's wish possibly have affected his mother's job?

A pizza box rested on the kitchen table. It was from Pete's Pizza, a place he'd never heard of; they'd always been loyal to Sam's. He put his hand on the box—it was still warm.

"Where are you off to?" he asked as he sat down and opened the lid. He lifted a slice out and lowered a dangling strand of melted cheese into his mouth. It tasted the same as what he was used to.

"Are you still giving me a hard time about this?" she said.

"About what?"

"Jim's taking me to dinner. Is that all right with you?"

Ephraim froze, the pizza still held over his mouth. A drop of hot tomato sauce and grease splashed onto his lip, and he dropped the slice back into the box.

"You have a date?" he said.

"I don't need your permission," she said.

"You have a date?"

"Are you stuck, Ephraim?" She slapped him in the back of the head, lightly. "How's that?"

"You have a—" He smiled. "So who's Jim?"

"An accountant at my office." *Office? What office?* "You've met him, actually. We ran into him at that Mexican restaurant on your birthday."

"You like this guy?"

She smiled. "He likes me. I'm still making up my mind." She tousled his hair. "There's nothing to freak out about. It's just a date."

Ephraim turned back around in his seat and bit viciously into his pizza. She watched him sedately.

"Good pizza," he said finally.

"Thanks. I slaved over a hot phone."

He swallowed the bite, then chased it with a swig of Coke. "Have a good time tonight."

"I'll make a deal with you. You don't make a fuss over my dates, and I won't make a fuss over yours. Probably."

Ephraim blushed. "Mom." But that reminded him. He wiped his palms off on his jeans and pulled out Jena's gift. Too late, he realized his mistake.

"Oh, what's that?" his mother said.

"None of your business."

He put it down on the table next to his plate as though it were a suspicious package that might explode at any moment. He'd been putting off opening it all the way home.

"Aren't you going to open it?" she said.

Well, why didn't he? He picked it up and glared at his mother while he pried away a corner of the thin newsprint.

His mother rolled her eyes. "Here we go. This is why I don't wrap your Christmas and birthday presents anymore," she said. "Life is too short, honey."

He ignored her, wanting to prolong the moment as long as he could. When the final piece of tape was pulled free, the paper blossomed open. It was a book, just as he'd thought.

"*The Wonderful Wizard of Oz*," she said. "Interesting choice."

"It's from Jena," Ephraim said. He flipped through the pages.

"Your father read that to you when you were younger." His mother hadn't mentioned his father in years.

"I don't remember. Is it like the movie?"

"It's a little different," she said.

He put it down.

"You don't like it?" she asked.

"It's a nice gift," he said. "She reads a lot of that fantasy stuff. Fairies. Tolkien."

"And you like sci-fi more. You come from two different worlds. You'll obviously never work out." She laughed and picked up the book. "Ephraim, it's an incredibly intimate thing to share one of your favorite books with someone else. I think so, anyway."

"How do you mean?"

"Your father gave me a book on our second date, the first gift he ever gave me." She turned to the front page and studied it. "When you give someone a book, it's like saying: 'I'm trusting you with something that means a lot to me.' It doesn't matter whether you like it or not, though it helps if you do. What matters is that you understand why she likes it. Why she gave it to you." She closed the book and handed it back to him. "You should read this. Particularly the title page." She stood and picked up her purse.

Ephraim opened the book and flipped to the title. There was an inscription, written in pink sparkly ink: "For Ephraim. This book opened up new worlds to me. I hope it does the same for you. Love, Jena." She had drawn a little heart next to her name.

He closed it.

"You have a very silly grin on your face," his mother said.

"Mom! Don't you have a date to get to?"

"I'm meeting him downstairs."

"You don't want to bring him in to meet me? Maybe I should make sure he's good enough for you."

"I don't want to scare him off. I'm sorry, but if we get married, we're going to ship you off to boarding school."

The intercom for the lobby door buzzed.

"That'll be him." She pressed the button and yelled, "I'm coming down." She came back to the table. "Okay, hon, I'm going."

He kissed her on the cheek and she made a face. She picked up a napkin and made a show of wiping grease from her cheek. "Don't wait up," she said.

"Ew. Mom."

She flashed him a mischievous smile. It had been a while since he'd seen her this happy. He didn't know who this Jim guy was, but she obviously liked him. Did he look that way whenever he thought of Jena?

"What are you smiling at?" his mother asked. He shook his head. He followed her to the door.

"What book did he give you?" Ephraim asked. "Dad?"

"*One Hundred Years of Solitude* by Gabriel García Márquez. I read it cover to cover after he dropped me off. It's the only reason I agreed to a third date, when he gave me another book. Your dad had me pretty well figured out back then." She smiled and tousled Ephraim's hair.

Ephraim locked the door behind her, then sat back down at the kitchen table with a fresh slice of pizza. He thumbed through the book, careful to avoid getting any grease or sauce on its pages. He started reading.

When the phone rang, he answered it distractedly.

"Hey, Eph." It was a girl's voice, but it wasn't Jena.

"Who's this?" he said.

"It's Mary Shelley." Two voices spoke, in perfect synchrony.

"Oh, hi. What's up?"

"Just wanted to confirm we're still on for tomorrow night." Just one voice this time, but he didn't know which sister it was.

"Tomorrow?"

"We have a reservation for four at Louie's, the Italian place on Central Boulevard."

Four? "Right, of course," he said. He had no idea what she was talking about. Could Jena have arranged this after their talk this afternoon? He would have preferred a more private first date, but maybe she'd feel more comfortable in a group with her friends. And a guy would have to be crazy to not want to go out with three beautiful girls. Then he remembered Nathan and their wish. This was the perfect opportunity.

"Listen, would it be okay if my friend Nathan came along? He really likes Shell—uh, fish. Shellfish." Ephraim grimaced.

The girls laughed. "Well, yeah," one said. "That's the whole point of a double date. Shelley's been looking forward to this all week."

"Mary!" Shelley squealed. Ephraim jerked the phone away from his ear.

"I've been looking forward to it too, of course. Ephraim?" Mary said.

Ephraim felt like he'd been broadsided by a truck. What was going on? "Yes. I'll see you both tomorrow," he said. "I can't wait."

"Don't forget our presents!" they said in unison before hanging up.

This must be the coin's doing; Nathan was getting his wish. Ephraim dialed him up.

"We have a double date with Mary and Shelley on Friday night," Ephraim said.

Nathan was silent.

"Say something," Ephraim said.

"I don't know what to say."

"How about, 'I'm sorry, Ephraim. You were right about the coin.'"

"You're still playing with me."

"I'm not."

"You better not be lying about this. If you are, our friendship is over. I mean it," Nathan said.

"You're going out. With Shelley. Tomorrow night. I just got off the phone with them." Mary had called it a double date. If Nathan was paired with Shelley, that meant . . .

"Holy shit, Eph. This is completely amazing. This is going to be the best night of my life."

Ephraim looked at the book Jena had given him. Even though they weren't properly dating yet, this felt kind of like cheating on her. He didn't want to lose the progress he'd made with her, even to help Nathan, but he did owe his friend. He should just call Jena, explain that this wasn't really a date. She would understand.

Unless she already knew about it. Mary was her best friend; she would surely have told Jena about her big double date by now. And Jena had seemed sad when he last saw her. Ephraim closed his eyes. He was screwed.

"Hello? Ephraim?" Nathan said. Ephraim had completely tuned out Nathan's excited babbling.

"What?"

"I was asking you if we should get them something. Flowers? Candy?"

"They want us to bring them presents. Is that normal for a first date?" Ephraim asked.

"Oh, of course! Saturday's their birthday."

"How do you know that?"

"Never underestimate the value of Internet research."

"I think that's more commonly referred to as stalking."

"This is huge. This isn't just dinner—this is their birthday dinner. They must be really into us."

So now Ephraim had to buy presents for Mary and Shelley, and he was already practically broke. He was tempted to wish for some money, but he didn't know what other mischief that might get him into.

"Aren't you psyched?"

"Yeah," Ephraim said. "This is going to be something."

CHAPTER 9

Louie's was a two-star restaurant with four-star aspirations. The white linen tablecloths and little candle bowls at every table confirmed Ephraim's fear that this dinner was going to bankrupt him. Fortunately, now that his mother had an office job she was apparently giving Ephraim an allowance, and she'd advanced him a couple of weeks' worth for tonight.

"I'm glad I dressed up," Nathan said. He was wearing a suit, complete with a red and blue striped tie, gray jacket, and matching slacks; he looked like his father. Ephraim had gone more casual with a brown sports jacket over his faded blue t-shirt, corduroys, and black Chucks. Yet somehow Nathan carried off his look without effort, while Ephraim still felt like he was trying too hard. Ephraim had taken a long time with his appearance—too long, considering he wasn't out to impress Mary.

"So which twin do you want?" Nathan said. "I think we should work that out before we sit down."

"I don't want either of them. I like Jena, remember? Besides, I thought you wanted Shelley."

"I have dibs on the thin one."

Ephraim gaped at him. "There is no thin one. I mean they're both thin. They're the same . . . width."

"Then I suppose we could just flip a coin." Nathan winked. "Hey, where is it, by the way? Do you keep it with you all the time?"

Ephraim slipped his hand into his pocket to check on the coin. It was still in its plastic bag.

"You're with Shelley and I'll take Mary," Ephraim said.

"I knew you liked her."

"Just for tonight. To help you out."

A maître d' led them to the rear of the restaurant. Mary and Shelley sat at a table, sipping soda from wine glasses.

"Happy birthday," Ephraim said. He offered them a box wrapped in SpongeBob SquarePants paper. "Sorry about the wrapping paper. It's all they had."

"It's perfect! We love SpongeBob SquarePants," Shelley said.

Ephraim winced.

"So do I," Nathan said. "It's from me too, by the way." Ephraim clenched his jaw. He was doing this for his friend, he reminded himself. He'd let Nathan share the credit, even if he never paid Ephraim for his half of the present. As long as it made Shelley like Nathan, and got Nathan off his back.

Ephraim sat down across from Mary, and Nathan slid into the booth next to him.

"Should we open it now?" Mary asked, patting the present on the table between her and Shelley.

"If you want," Ephraim said.

Each girl took a corner and tore at the wrapping paper, their pink lacquered nails flashing in the light from the mini crystal chandelier above the table. Beneath the wrapping was a plain gray cardboard box. They opened it in tandem, looked inside, then frowned.

"You got us statues of . . ." Shelley said.

". . . naked men?" Mary said.

Nathan coughed, spraying bread crumbs over the tablecloth. "What?" he said.

"They're Castor and Pollux," Ephraim explained. "The Gemini twins. Because you're Gemini, and . . . uh, twins."

"Actually, we're Cancers," Shelley said.

"Oh," Ephraim said.

"But we're on the cusp," she added.

"You know what they say about Cancers," Nathan said.

"What?" Shelley asked.

"They have a way of growing on you."

Shelley giggled, but Mary rolled her eyes. Ephraim exchanged a sympathetic glance with her.

Mary and Shelley each lifted out one of the statues. They were actually made of plaster, painted to look like granite. The Roman men wore laurels in their hair and small loincloths. Each of them bore a torch: the one on the left had one in his left hand turned downward, while the one on the right held his slung over his right shoulder.

"They're bookends," Ephraim said.

"Thanks, Ephraim," Mary said.

"Nathan helped me pick them out," Ephraim said. "In fact, they were his idea." He smirked when Nathan shot a look at him, his cheek still bulging with bread. He looked like a blond hamster.

The twins packed up the bookends and moved the box and torn wrapping paper to the bench beside them.

"We love them," Shelley said. "That was very thoughtful." She sat up straighter in her seat, which pushed her chest out and over the table. Nathan choked and reached for his water glass.

"Nice outfits, by the way," Ephraim said. They each wore a light-blue shirtdress with the top two buttons undone. *They probably couldn't fasten them even if they wanted to*, he thought.

"We always get new clothes for our birthday," Mary said.

"So they're kind of like your 'birthday suits'?" Nathan said, his voice scratchy. Ephraim gave him a withering look.

"Why do you still dress alike?" Ephraim said. "Do you like it when people can't tell you apart?"

"Some people can tell us apart," Shelley said. "Our parents can. Jena can." She shrugged.

"If someone really knows us, they won't have any problems with it," Mary said.

"Plus it's fun to mess with people's heads," Shelley said.

"Are you two completely identical?" Nathan said.

Mary wrinkled her nose. "Oh, like we haven't heard that one before."

Shelley batted her eyelashes. "Maybe you and Ephraim can compare notes later," she said.

Mary shoved her. "Don't encourage him," she said.

Shelley actually seemed to like Nathan. If that wasn't proof of magic, Ephraim didn't know what was.

Nathan leaned forward. "I've always wondered—"

"Shut up," Ephraim whispered.

"But—" Nathan said.

"Trust me," Ephraim said.

Mary and Ephraim exchanged sympathetic glances again.

"You're no fun," Nathan and Shelley said at the same time. They glanced at each other in surprise then giggled.

Then Mary surprised Ephraim by winking at him. "We aren't *completely* identical," she said in a soft voice. At his shocked expression she wiggled the fingers of both hands at him. "Different fingerprints."

Ephraim laughed.

The waiter swept in. "Ready to order?" he said, pen poised over a little pad.

Ephraim knew Mary and Shelley were different people, but it was still unexpected when they each ordered something different: fettucini with alfredo sauce for Mary, and chicken parmigiana for Shelley.

"And if you couldn't tell already," Mary said, looking at Nathan pointedly. "We have pretty different tastes too."

Ephraim got the spaghetti carbonara, and Nathan ordered chicken parmigiana, even though Ephraim knew he hated cheese.

Nathan raised his eyebrows at Shelley. "I guess we're food twins."

Mary sighed heavily.

"So you're taking Jena's job at the library, Ephraim?" Shelley said. Mary jabbed her elbow into her sister's side.

"Ow! Sorry, I forgot—" Mary elbowed her into silence.

Nathan smiled. "Hey, since you're twins, do you feel each other's pain?"

"Shut up, Nathan!" Ephraim said. He turned to Shelley. "What? I'm doing what? Where's Jena going?"

There was silence, broken only by the waiter bringing their plates of food over. Ephraim pushed his pasta around his plate with his fork.

"Where's Jena going?" he asked again.

Mary looked down at her plate. "We thought you knew. She told us you agreed to fill in for her job. We just didn't want to bring it up at dinner, since this is a happy occasion." She glared pointedly at Shelley.

"Why is she leaving?" Nathan asked.

"Mr. Kim just got a job in California."

"California?" Ephraim felt like a long thread of spaghetti was caught in his throat. He couldn't get enough air.

"L.A. It's a big promotion for him. They're moving next week."

"Bummer," Nathan said. "Isn't she like your best friend?"

Mary stared like she was trying to burn him with her eyes.

"That won't change because of a few thousand miles," Shelley said.

"Well, you can always hang out with me," Nathan said. "Us."

Ephraim lowered his head.

"Are you all right?" Mary stretched her hand across the table to him.

He pulled his hand out of reach. "Yeah." He rested it in his lap, pressing his fingers against the coin in his pants pocket.

Shelley quickly changed the subject, turning her attention to Nathan. Ephraim suffered silently through dinner, listening to Nathan's stupid attempts at humor and Shelley's giggled responses. He'd made that wish and given up Jena as a result . . . for this?

Mary didn't seem to have much fun either, picking at her food and stealing quick glances at Ephraim. He felt bad that he was likely ruining her birthday, but he didn't have anything to say. He didn't feel up to forced conversation. He had only two thoughts on his mind.

Jena was going to leave.

He couldn't let her go.

CHAPTER 10

Ephraim woke up on the couch, his head wedged between the cushion and the back. He rubbed his face and felt the texture of the couch cushion mapped onto his cheek.

"'Morning." A male voice spoke softly by the front door.

Ephraim bolted up and felt a stab of pain in his stiff neck.

A man stood by the front door, slipping his right foot into a black Oxford. A bald spot glinted on the top of his head as he bent to tie the laces.

The man looked up as he crammed his other foot into its shoe. "I'm Jim. You must be Ephraim." Horn-rimmed glasses slid down his nose, and he pushed them back up. He looked like a flabbier, balder Clark Kent. "This is awkward, huh?"

"Hi," Ephraim said. Jim didn't look like his mother's type at all, not that he knew what that might be. He'd expected him to be more like his father, but since that hadn't exactly worked out he couldn't blame her for going for someone different. Completely different.

Jim stood up and straightened his tie. "We can talk about this if you want."

Ephraim shook his head. "No, no. It's none of my business." He was too confused to process all this right now. He didn't want to think about his mother bringing a guy home.

"I don't think that's true."

"I'd really rather not know, thanks."

Cartoon gunfire drew Ephraim's attention to the television. Bugs Bunny ran across the screen, bullets flying after him.

"I hope you don't mind, I changed the channel," Jim said.

Ephraim had come home after dinner and zoned out in front of the television, his thoughts running in circles. They hadn't had cable before

Ephraim's last wish—maybe it was a benefit of his mother's new job, whatever it was—so he'd just channel-surfed until he fell asleep.

"You still watch cartoons?" Ephraim yawned.

"Constantly. You don't? There's fresh coffee in the pot, by the way. Looks like you need some." Jim slung a laptop case over one shoulder and his suit jacket over an arm. "Are you allowed to drink coffee?"

"Allowed? It's mandated. Thanks. So, I guess I'll be seeing you around?"

Jim grinned. "That's up to your mother."

"I'll put in a good word for you, for what it's worth," Ephraim said. He'd seen how happy that date had made his mother, and it had obviously gone very well—Ephraim wasn't going to think about that—and so far Jim seemed like a decent guy.

"Your opinion is worth quite a lot with Maddy," Jim said. "She talks about you frequently. Well, I should be running off to work now."

"But I thought you two worked together? Why don't you—oh. Yeah."

Jim nodded. "I already have to explain wearing the same suit two days in a row, but I think I'll pick up a cheap new tie on my way in. It's been a long time since I did this kind of thing. Really. I don't make a habit of it."

"Bye, Jim." Ephraim smiled.

Jim let himself out of the apartment with a friendly wave.

Ephraim hopped into the shower and changed into mostly clean clothes quickly. While he was helping himself to coffee, his mother wandered into the kitchen in a loose satin robe over a red lace slip, which was sliding down dangerously.

"Mom!" Ephraim averted his eyes.

"Oh, Ephraim." She closed her robe and staggered toward the coffee pot.

"So. I met your . . . friend," Ephraim said.

She blinked. "Honey, I'm sorry about that. I wanted to introduce you two properly." She leaned against the counter. "Now I'm embarrassed. I'm the worst mother in the world."

"No, Mom. You're far from it." He'd seen her at her worst.

"This is some lesson I'm teaching you—"

"Don't worry, I'm not going to start bringing guys home."

"I was wondering about you and Nathan for a while." She smiled.

"Mom." Ephraim sighed. "I like girls, but I'm not going to bring one home with me anytime soon." Especially since Jena was about to move across the country.

"Good, because if you do, I'll ground you forever."

"That's much better parenting. Thanks."

"Jim's gone? I didn't even hear him get up." She looked at the clock over the refrigerator and groaned. "Oh no, I'm going to be late for work."

"You like him, then?" Ephraim tried to sound casual.

She took the mug out of his hands and sipped from it. "So far, I do." She lowered the cup and looked at him thoughtfully. "When did you get in last night? There may be a grounding in your future after all."

"I have to go," Ephraim said.

"Oh?" She looked at the clock again. "Right, you're starting at the library today. Nice of you to fill in for your friend. Looks like we'll both be late for work. I suppose we can grill each other on our love lives later." She emptied the rest of the coffee from the pot into her mug and padded out of the kitchen with it, trailing the sash from her robe behind her.

"You're late," Jena greeted him.

"I'm sorry," Ephraim crossed his hands on the circulation desk and looked across at Jena. She should have been happy he'd shown up at all, considering he didn't even remember agreeing to work there.

She looked at him over her glasses. Black secretary frames today. He would have found them sexy if she weren't so annoyed.

"Look, are you serious about this job or not?" she asked. "I could have asked anyone else to fill in for me, but you volunteered. Mrs. Reynolds trusts my recommendation and I don't want—"

"It won't happen again." She was pretty high-strung this morning. He supposed that if he had to uproot his life on short notice, he'd be stressed about it too.

Her face relaxed.

"Okay," she said.

"So where do I start?"

"There are a ton of books to re-shelve. Usually we try to do it at night before closing, but I saved them so I could show you first thing."

Ephraim shrugged out of his backpack. "Sounds like fun."

Jena smiled. "You obviously haven't done it before. Do you do the Dewey?"

"That's a very personal question," Ephraim said.

"I mean, do you know the Dewey Decimal system?" she replied. "Guess not. That's all right, you'll figure it out. It's pretty obvious where most of the books go."

She showed him where the book trolleys were and taught him how to decipher the labels. She helped him shelve the first few before she had to return to the desk. It took him over three hours to put all the books away. By that point, Ephraim was exhausted and sore from pushing the carts, reaching up to high shelves, and crouching down to the floor to reach the lowest ones. But when he glanced over at Jena, he often caught her monitoring his progress, so he didn't show how tired he was.

The last book he shelved was a copy of *Through the Looking Glass*, by Lewis Carroll. It looked like the same copy he'd checked out of the library when he was seven. He thumbed through it, remembering the soothing sound of his father's voice as he read it to him.

Jena indicated a free chair for Ephraim when he returned to the circulation desk. He collapsed into it and stretched his arms.

"That was pretty fast," Jena said. "It usually takes me a lot longer to get through them." She tapped the book open in front of her. "But I get distracted easily."

"No problem. They get shelved alphabetically by the author's first name, right?"

"Ha ha."

"Oh, no!" Ephraim said, feigning alarm.

"You are kidding. Aren't you?"

"Sure I am." Ephraim rubbed his hands together, then wiped them on the legs of his jeans. "Ugh. My hands feel disgusting."

Jena opened a side drawer of the desk and pulled out a packet of HandiWipes. She passed it to him.

"Dirt comes with the territory," she said. "Please, no dirty librarian jokes."

Now that he was closer to her, he noticed that her eyes were bloodshot. Had she been crying?

"So, um. Thank you for the book," he said. "I've always wanted to read *The Wizard of Oz*."

"Oh yeah. I just needed to get rid of some stuff, you know? So there's less to move." Jena looked away from him and started piling books onto a cart behind the desk.

"Oh." Ephraim scratched at a peeling library sticker on the spine of a book, focusing on the numbers so he didn't have to look at her. 702.11 B. "Right. Your father's job."

Jena shoved a book onto the cart, and the books on Ephraim's side domino-ed over. "How was your date last night?"

"Date?" His voice went too high. He cleared his throat. "It wasn't a date." Ephraim tilted the books upright on the cart shelf and slid them over to Jena's side, then tucked in a metal bookend to hold them in place. "It was a celebration. A birthday celebration. As friends."

"Shelley thought it was a date," Jena said. "Mary thought it was a date." The cart jerked away from him, its wheels squeaking angrily. It rolled a couple of feet to his left, and Jena stood to pile more books on the top shelf.

He rose and grabbed onto the handle of the book cart.

"I only agreed to it because Nathan wanted to spend time with Shelley," Ephraim said.

"They liked your present."

"They practically ordered me—us—to bring one."

"It was appropriate, too. I didn't know you liked *The Patty Duke* show," she said.

"Yeah," he said. He didn't know what she was talking about. "No. I haven't seen it. What?"

She sang, "'A pair of matching bookends, different as night and day.' That's the theme song. The show's about two identical cousins."

"Identical cousins? That sounds unlikely."

"Well, their fathers were twins . . . It's improbable I suppose, but it's kind of fun once you forget about the logic of it."

"That's right. Your dad likes all that old stuff."

"It's pretty good, actually. I should show you some." Her hands dropped from the cart like a puppet's strings being cut. "At least, I would if I weren't moving away. God, this isn't fair. We didn't even have a chance to . . ."

"You're not happy about it, are you?" Ephraim asked.

"It's a good opportunity for my father," Jena replied. "It's good for the family."

"Sure." Ephraim gripped the cart handle tighter. "It's okay to think of yourself, you know. It isn't just about your father. Your whole life is here. What about school? Your clubs?"

"They have schools in L.A., Ephraim. It's perfect timing really. I'm going to college in a year; it doesn't make sense to stay just for me when I'll be leaving anyway. And the extra money will help pay for tuition." She shrugged. "I'd be crazy to not want to move to an exciting place like L.A. over a sleepy town like Summerside. I mean, there's all that . . . smog. You can't get that quality of smog in New York City. And I'll fit right in there, as long as I pretend to be someone else."

"You could dye your hair blonde," Ephraim said. "Get a tasteful tattoo, a couple of piercings. Yeah, I can see that."

Jena squinted at him over her glasses. "That's, like, totally making me feel so much better."

"Look, you could come back east for college, couldn't you?" Ephraim said. "You're probably looking at some of the Ivys, right? There's Columbia, Yale, Princeton. Your friends will still be here when you get back."

"I'm not so sure about that."

"Come on. It's only a year. Mary and Shelley have been your best friends since forever."

"I think they'll get by without me," she said. "If they even wait until I'm gone."

Ephraim frowned. "You're upset because I went out with them last night?"

"You're cute, but you're kind of slow sometimes, Ephraim." She turned away and pulled the cart with her. Ephraim held onto it and pulled back, bringing her to an abrupt stop.

"Ow," she said. She spun around and rubbed her wrist. "I have work to do. *We* have work to do."

"I'm cute?" Ephraim said.

"Like I said: slow." She sighed and rested her arms on the cart, leaning over it to look at him. "But it doesn't matter, because I'm leaving. And my 'friends' will probably be better off."

"I'm not interested in dating Mary," he said. "I told you, I only went on that double date for Nathan's sake."

"See, it was a date!"

"Jena—"

"You don't have to make excuses. I know I'm probably being silly. Maybe I'm overreacting. I just feel like when I leave, we'll make plans to stay in touch, but I won't really be missed. It'll be like I never existed. Life will go on, my friends will make new friends, I'll make new friends. It'll be a different life." Her voice shook. "But I don't want a different life. I like the one I have. I want to graduate with the people I grew up with."

"You wouldn't change anything in your life if you had the chance?" Ephraim asked.

Her eyes searched his face. "What do you mean?"

"There's all sorts of things in my life that I've wished were different, you know? My dad left, and my mom . . . well, she has issues. Had issues."

They always said you were supposed to count your blessings, but Ephraim had always cataloged his problems. Even though he wasn't the only person to grow up without a parent, all of his friends seemed to have happy, stable families. He didn't know anyone else with an alcoholic mother who worked at a supermarket.

He got decent grades, but he didn't like school much, and now that Jena was leaving, he wouldn't even have that one bright part of his life to get him through senior year.

"Ephraim? What's wrong?"

Ephraim closed his hand around the coin in his pocket, squeezing it in its plastic bag. "Never mind. It'll all work out."

"I know," Jena said. She straightened and took a deep breath. "It's out of my control. There's no sense stressing about it." She tugged on the cart again, and this time Ephraim let it go. She walked backward, pulling the cart along with her. She smiled brightly, her eyes shining. "If you're ever in L.A., look me up, will you?"

"When are you leaving?"

"In a week."

Ephraim nodded.

Not if I can help it.

CHAPTER 11

When Ephraim got home, Nathan was lying on the floor by his bed, leafing through a stack of the old *Playboy* magazines Ephraim had rescued from the trash after his father left.

"How the hell did you get in here?" Ephraim asked.

"Madeline let me in," Nathan said. "These are so awesome." He was looking at an article that promised to teach "32 Surefire Ways to Put a Woman in the Mood." Presumably, none of those included the aid of a magic coin.

Ephraim dropped his bag on the floor and noticed a plate of oatmeal cookies on his desk beside an empty glass of milk. "My mother gave you cookies?" She never let Ephraim snack on junk food before dinner, especially in his room. He popped a cookie in his mouth whole.

"She lured me in with them," Nathan said. "I couldn't resist."

"Don't make that sound naughty. She's my mother." Ephraim slumped into his desk chair and woke his computer up from hibernation. "Where is she, anyway?"

Nathan closed the magazine and put it aside. "She went out. And I have to say, she looked really hot."

She must have another date tonight.

"You didn't take a picture, did you?"

"What do you take me for?" Nathan asked.

"Hand over your camera."

"There's no picture!"

"Nathan," Ephraim said.

"How was work? Have fun with Jena?" Nathan asked. Everything that he had said sounded suggestive. He was being more of a pervert than usual.

"Why did you come over if you knew I wasn't home?" Ephraim asked.

Nathan's eyes were glued on a platinum blonde who was leaning over with her breasts cradled in her arms.

"I wanted to thank you for last night." Nathan wiggled his eyebrows.

"Okay, you have to cut that out."

Nathan tossed the magazine on the floor and picked up another one. "Mary really likes you," he said. "Why'd you have to ignore her like that?"

"I just couldn't think about anything but Jena leaving," Ephraim said.

"Why do you suddenly like her more than Mary?"

"I just do. Why do you like Shelley?"

Nathan grinned.

"Okay, besides her obvious assets."

"What's wrong with liking someone because they're attractive?" Nathan flipped over onto his back and held an open magazine over his face.

"Because there's more to them than that. Why do you like Shelley instead of her sister? They look the same."

"Because she likes me." Nathan lifted the magazine and looked at Ephraim. "Thanks to you. I guess she probably wouldn't be as interested in me without your coin."

Ephraim smirked. "So you believe me now."

"I think I might need more proof. What's our next coin trick?"

"What?"

"Well, this was just the start. We can have anything we want," Nathan said.

"I still feel bad enough about what we did to Shelley."

"What we did to her?" Nathan sat up and dropped the magazine into his lap.

"Hey, be careful with those." Ephraim went over and began stacking the magazines neatly.

"You don't think she could like me without the coin?" Nathan asked.

"I didn't say that. But we made her like you, so we'll never know, will we?"

Anger flickered over Nathan's face. "You did the same thing to Jena."

"That was different."

"Of course it was." Nathan jumped up from the bed then flopped into the desk chair. Ephraim left the magazines on the floor and sat on the edge of the bed facing him. "It was an accident when I did it."

"But you didn't feel bad about it when you realized what had happened, did you? Do you?"

Ephraim drew in a breath. "No."

"See?"

"I don't think we should use it to manipulate people anymore. It doesn't feel right."

Nathan laughed, a harsh sound that Ephraim wasn't expecting.

"What?" Ephraim asked.

"Because it's me who's getting the girl?"

"No, that's not—"

"I thought we were going to share the coin."

"I never agreed—"

"If I had found it first, I would share it with you." Nathan crossed his arms.

"I *am* sharing," Ephraim said.

"Look, what do you think this coin is for? What do you think we should wish for? World peace?"

"Something like that." Ephraim frowned. He'd been too preoccupied helping himself to consider that he could use it for some greater good. Maybe Nathan was right and he shouldn't keep this to himself. "But we don't really know how the coin works. I think we should take it slow, and try to figure out what its limits are. It hasn't always done exactly what I expected; if we wished for world peace, we could just as easily wipe out everyone as get them to stop fighting. It's like the coin makes arbitrary trade-offs when it gives us what we want." Like how Nathan's wish had led to Jena's impending departure from Summerside.

Nathan nodded. "Okay. We'll take it slow for a while. Stick to small wishes."

"And we won't use it to change people's feelings or force them to do anything they wouldn't want to do," Ephraim said.

Nathan snorted. "Whatever. People manipulate each other every day without the benefit of a magic coin, but if you want to play it safe . . ."

Ephraim took out the coin. "We also have to make sure we're touching when I make the wish."

"Now who's being pervy?" Nathan asked. "So what's it going to be this time, boss?"

"I'm going to wish that Jena doesn't have to leave."

Nathan coughed a word: "Hypocrite."

"This doesn't count as manipulating her feelings. It's true that I don't want to lose her, not now that things are starting to work out. But she doesn't want to move either."

Nathan yawned. "Well, let's do it."

Ephraim grabbed Nathan's left hand with his and made his wish.

"I wish that Jena didn't have to move away," he said.

Ephraim told himself that he was doing this for Jena, not just for himself. He flipped the coin in his right hand and caught it.

"Tails," he said.

Ephraim felt a sideways lurch, like he was on a train that had braked abruptly. The air around him rippled, and a moment later he wasn't in his room anymore. He was sitting in a booth at a diner. And Mary was across from him holding his hand instead of Nathan.

"Uh," Ephraim said.

CHAPTER 12

Mary jumped in surprise and blinked at him. Ephraim covered the coin in his hand.

"Whoa," she said.

"How did I—" Ephraim closed his eyes and opened them again. He was still in the diner. Ephraim looked around, but Nathan was nowhere in sight. "What . . . what was I saying?" Ephraim asked as he casually slid the coin into his pocket. Whenever he thought he'd figured out how the coin worked, it always threw him for another loop. Why had it transported him to the diner this time? And where had Nathan ended up?

"Um. Weren't you wearing a blue shirt a second ago?" Mary asked.

Ephraim looked down at his T-shirt. It was black, the same one he remembered picking out that morning. "I don't think so."

"I thought . . ." Mary frowned.

Ephraim didn't know what she'd seen, but he knew the coin was involved. He snapped his fingers. "I wore that shirt yesterday," he said. "It looks just like this one, but you know . . . blue. Dark blue. Almost black."

"Yeah, I guess that's it." She popped a french fry into her mouth and chewed it thoughtfully, staring at his shirt.

"Hey, have you seen Nathan around here?" Ephraim asked.

"Nathan? Shelley's out with him." Mary sniffed. "We don't have to do everything together. No matter how many times Nathan asks."

Ephraim gripped the edge of the table. "She's out with Nathan? Right now?"

"What's wrong?"

Ephraim looked at their plates and saw Mary had already finished her burger. Half of one remained on his plate, but he wasn't hungry.

"I'm not feeling well," he said.

"Oh no! Was it the food?"

He feigned a pained expression. "I think so. Would you mind if we called it an early night?"

"Oh. Of course." She looked disappointed.

"I'm really sorry. I just don't think I'll be very good company like this." He had to find Nathan right away.

He signaled for the check. Mary picked at the fries on her plate and didn't look up.

"I'm . . . glad we did this," he said.

Mary perked up. They were obviously on a "real" date, and strangely enough, it seemed to have been going well up until he ruined things. The coin had dropped him in the middle of an awkward situation. It had actually moved him from his bedroom to the diner, which he hadn't even known it was capable of doing.

He was still missing something important. Flipping a coin implied a random outcome, heads or tails. The coin had landed on tails when he made his last wish. It had also been tails when Mrs. Reynolds sprained her ankle so he could talk to Jena.

What had happened when it turned up heads? He thought back to his earlier wishes. It had been heads when he wished his mother out of the hospital, and again when he wished she were a better parent, with good results each time.

Had it been tails when he wished Shelley liked Nathan? He thought so. And that was when he found out Jena was moving, the worst outcome of all.

"When's Jena moving?" he asked suddenly.

Mary frowned. "At the end of the week."

So that was still the same. He'd wished that Jena weren't moving, and the coin hadn't done a thing about it—it had just pushed him deeper into some relationship with Mary. He couldn't piece this together at all.

"Ephraim, what's going on?" Mary asked.

"That's what I'm trying to figure out," he replied.

"What?"

"I'm sorry. I need some air. How about I walk you home?" Ephraim asked.

He set the last of his money down on the table and held the door for Mary as they left. As they walked together, his head buzzed with discovery. The coin hadn't granted his wish, at least not yet. Jena was still going to move, but other things had obviously changed. If something bad happened, that would support his hypothesis that getting tails on the coin flip meant trouble.

Some of the shops they passed looked different from what he remembered, but stores were always closing and new ones opening in this section of town. He knew he was getting paranoid about the extent of the coin's alterations to the world, but it was important to understand the magic before they messed with it again.

"Hey, can I ask you a personal question?" he said.

She glanced at him sidelong. "Sure."

"This has been bugging me for a long time. Why Mary and Shelley? How could your parents do that to you?"

Mary laughed. "It's not so bad. Most people don't even get it, until teachers make a point of bringing it up in class. But the responsibility lies with my father. He's an English professor with a fondness for his work. Mama never would have let him get away with it, if they hadn't met in a Lit class on the Shelleys as freshmen."

"That's romantic," Ephraim said.

"Gothic, actually," Mary replied.

Ephraim groaned.

"If you liked that, imagine hearing it over and over again for your entire life. That probably did more psychological damage than the weird names. Though, try telling that to my brother Dorian."

Mary stopped walking. "This is me," she said. They had already arrived at her house.

"Do you think Shelley and Nathan are back yet?" he said.

"Our window's dark, so I don't think she's home."

"Right. What would they be doing in a dark room?" he asked innocently.

She batted him lightly on the shoulder. "Hey! That's my sister you're talking about." Her hand lingered on his arm. He realized with sudden certainty that she expected him to kiss her.

"So, I'll call you," he said as he took a backwards step.

"If you're feeling better, you could come in for a little bit. My parents are out. This is their bridge night."

"No, I'd better not push it. I should go home and rest."

Suddenly she leaned up and kissed him. Her lips were cool, but then they opened and he felt her hot tongue slip into his mouth. Now he really felt dizzy.

She pulled away, her hands on his chest. "I know you're shy, it's adorable, but really—I've been wanting to do that since our first date. Not that it isn't good to take things slow," Mary said. "I see how fast Shelley and Nathan are moving and I wonder if it's me . . ."

"Well, that's Nathan for you."

"And my sister. She becomes attached really easily."

Mary walked up her driveway then whirled to face him. "It would be nice if you asked me out instead of the other way around, for a change." She turned and walked up the path to her door. She stopped again and looked over her shoulder at him. "Was that too obvious?"

"You can never be too obvious for a guy," Ephraim said. His head buzzed with shock and pleasure. Then feelings of guilt began creeping in.

"That's what Shelley says. Take care, Eph."

"Good night."

He still felt her lips on his. He had never kissed anyone that way before.

He wondered what it would be like with Jena.

Ephraim's mother jumped up from the couch as soon as he entered the apartment. "Finally! Where have you been?" she said.

"What's wrong? Who died?"

"Don't make jokes like that."

Uh-oh.

"I have something to tell you," she said.

Ephraim followed his mother into the kitchen. She filled the tea kettle with water and put it on a burner but forgot to switch on the flame. She leaned against the counter and looked at him somberly.

Ephraim sat down at the table. "What is it, Mom?" He was getting scared.

"Linda called," she said.

"Linda?"

"Linda Kim, Jena's mother."

"Oh." Ephraim gripped his knees, digging his nails into the warm denim. "Is Jena . . . is everything all right?"

"Her father's at the hospital. He's had a heart attack."

Ephraim started breathing again. "Is it serious?"

"Of course it's serious. It was a heart attack. He's in the ICU. The doctor says he has a fifty-fifty chance."

"Oh God," Ephraim said.

"Jena's obviously upset. She's still at the hospital, just in case . . ." At the expression on his face, his mother put a hand on his arm.

"Should we go there?" he said.

"I don't think there's anything we can do there except get in the way."

Ephraim put his hand into his pocket.

A fifty-fifty chance. Might as well flip a coin.

His hand twitched. It was his fault. If he hadn't made that wish, none of this would have happened.

"Do they know what caused it?" he said.

"It's hard to say. He's been under a lot of stress. The new job. The move."

"I guess . . . they won't be leaving, then." He stared down at the table.

"Not anytime soon, I imagine. If at all, after this. Are you all right, Eph?"

He stood. "I'll be in my room."

His mother nodded. Then she remembered. "Oh, don't you want tea?" She turned to the stove and realized she hadn't turned on the burner under the kettle. "It'll be a minute."

"No, that's all right." Ephraim stood. "I need some time alone." He walked to the door, then turned, struck by a thought. "How do you know Jena's mother, anyway?" he asked.

His mother looked at him, one hand still on the handle of the tea kettle. "We're on the PTA together."

"Since when?" His mother had never shown any interest in his school. It was just the place he went to every day, the way she went to work. As long as he stayed out of trouble and got decent grades, she didn't care to know more. But this was a new mother—the one he had wished for.

For the first time he missed his old mother, the one who'd raised him. He loved her, flaws and all. There was so much he didn't know about this woman. What had their life been like together until now?

"For over three years. We've had the Kims over for dinner plenty of times. Honey, I know this must be hard for you, after what happened to your father—"

Ephraim stepped back. "What?" he said.

"Ephraim?"

"What happened to Dad?"

His mother's eyes teared up. "I know what you're thinking. But Mr. Kim is in much better shape than your father was when he died. John Kim doesn't drink, for one." She shook her head.

Ephraim's father was *dead*? Even though his parents were divorced, he still liked knowing that his father was out there somewhere, thinking that one day he could be a part of their lives again. He wasn't supposed to be dead.

"You look pale. I'm sorry, I shouldn't have said anything," she said.

"I'm worried about Jena, that's all."

His mother nodded. "He'll make it," she said. "I know he will."

Ephraim shut himself in his room and sat on his bed. He turned the coin over a couple of times. Heads then tails. Heads. Tails.

It was too risky to keep using it.

Every wish brought other changes that he didn't ask for, things he didn't know how to handle, like Mary liking him, and his father . . .

Why did that bother him exactly? His father was barely in his life at all before. What did it matter if he was alive or dead? He wasn't a good man—he probably got exactly what he deserved for hurting his mother. For hitting her.

Ephraim had made a mistake. He needed to make one more wish to fix it, then he would stop.

He had also made a promise, he remembered. Nathan was sharing the coin with him now; he'd come with him this far, and he had to be included in it. Ephraim rolled the coin over his fingers. But there wasn't time. If he waited too long, Mr. Kim could die. Besides, if he made the wish now, Nathan would never know.

Ephraim sighed. He put the coin down. He'd told Nathan about the coin to make up for betraying their friendship. He couldn't do that again. He would find him, and they'd make this last wish together. Once he explained what he'd figured out, he was sure Nathan would understand why they shouldn't make any more wishes.

"I don't understand. Why do you want to stop using it?" Nathan stabbed a french fry into a glob of ketchup.

"It's too dangerous. It's unpredictable."

"What's unpredictable? You make a wish, you flip the coin, you get your wish. Am I missing something?"

Ephraim tried to stir his straw in his black-and-white milkshake but the ice cream was too thick.

"Bad things keep happening, things we didn't ask for. Whenever the coin lands on tails."

"Nothing bad happened last night," Nathan said. He had reported a similar experience to Ephraim's after their wish: he'd appeared in a movie theater with Shelley. But he'd taken to the abrupt shift with more enthusiasm. "If Mary is anything like Shelley, you'll see the coin is the best thing that ever happened to us."

"Charming. I don't want to hear any more about it. And I don't want to see any more pictures." Ephraim nervously separated the layers of his paper napkin. "Listen, we don't know anything about the way this magic works," Ephraim said. "I found those instructions, and I followed them without thinking it through." That excuse only worked for the first time, though.

"It just doesn't seem that harmful to me."

"I gave Jena's dad a heart attack." Maybe he should try a different tactic. "It's not just changing things. It's changing *us*. Doesn't that scare you?"

"You're right, Eph. You weren't always this selfish."

"Selfish? I want to help Jena's dad. You're the one who's changed. You didn't always have such a bad temper. You used to care about other people more."

"I still care. But from what I'm hearing, you want us to stop using the coin, except when you really want to. If you didn't want to share it with me, you shouldn't have told me about it in the first place."

"This next wish has to be our last. Just to set everything straight again."

"No," Nathan said. "I like things the way they are. Don't take that away from me."

"I just want to wish for Jena's father to be all right. Even the coin can't mess that one up." He wished he was more confident about that. If the coin landed on heads, they would be okay. If not, things might get even worse.

"You just spent the last half hour trying to convince me that the coin is unpredictable. If you're right, I might lose Shelley with the next wish. You can't promise otherwise."

Ephraim squeezed the coin. He couldn't believe Nathan was going to put his stupid crush ahead of someone else's life.

"If this wish changes that, we'll figure out how to get her back, all right? But safely, after we know how it works," Ephraim said.

Nathan glared. Then his shoulders drooped. "Okay, Ephraim. I trust you." He shoved their plates aside, and Ephraim stared at the coin, concentrating.

"I wish Jena's dad were healthy again," Ephraim said. *Heads*, he thought. *Please be heads.* He flipped the coin and caught it.

Heads!

Ephraim grinned.

Too late, Ephraim realized he hadn't taken Nathan's hand before he flipped the coin.

CHAPTER 13

Ephraim blinked, and he was suddenly alone in his bedroom. He was beginning to adjust to the coin's abrupt changes; the diner was gone, but the french fries he'd eaten there weighed heavily in his stomach. He wondered where Nathan had ended up this time, and what state he might be in.

He tried Nathan's house first and was relieved when he answered.

"Nathan! Are you all right?" Ephraim said.

"What? Who is this?" Nathan sounded groggy, like he'd just woken up. It confirmed Ephraim's fear that he'd left his friend behind with that last wish. Maybe there was a chance he would still remember, since he'd actually been a part of Ephraim's wishes before.

"It's me. Ephraim."

"Ephraim . . . Ephraim Scott? What do you want?"

"Stop playing around. Look, I made a mistake. Please tell me you remember the quarter." Ephraim squeezed the handset of the phone.

"What quarter? What are you talking about?"

What have I done? Ephraim thought.

"You have to remember it." *You have to remember me.* "The coin. Come on, think about it. Just a couple of minutes ago we were at the diner—"

Nathan groaned. "I was asleep a couple of minutes ago, and I wasn't dreaming about you. Whatever you're on, save some for me, dude. Later." The line clicked and went dead.

Nathan didn't remember the magic coin. He barely seemed to remember Ephraim, for that matter. On the one hand, Ephraim's accidental exclusion of Nathan could be for the best: he wouldn't have Nathan pressuring him to use the coin anymore.

On the other hand, Ephraim might have a bigger problem to worry about. He might have lost his best friend.

Jena checked the time on her cell phone pointedly when Ephraim rushed into the library.

"Late, for the second day in a row," she said.

"Sorry. Rough morning," he said.

So he still worked there. He'd hoped that would change, considering he'd taken the job because Jena was leaving. But that didn't mean his wish hadn't been granted. The coin had landed on heads, so her father should be all right. That's what was important. The fact that Jena was at work today was probably a good sign.

She hadn't changed much either. Maybe she looked a little tired, but that was understandable with her father in the hospital.

"Why are you staring at me like that?" Jena asked.

"I'm not."

"Okay." She patted a cart by the desk. "This cart's ready for shelving. If you're ready to do some work."

"Yeah," he said. Jena's appearance was the same, but her personality had been altered. She seemed colder than before. Maybe she was still worried about her father.

"Hey, is your dad okay?" he asked.

Jena's expression softened. "He's going to be fine. It was a false alarm. How'd you know he was in the hospital?"

"My mom mentioned it. A false alarm? That's a relief, but I'm sure it was scary."

Jena nodded.

"I guess you're still moving then? After he recovers," Ephraim said.

Jena stopped scanning the stack of books in front of her. "I'm not moving anywhere. What made you think that?"

"Uh. Then why am I working here?"

"What? Mary said you wanted a summer job for your college applications next year. If you're having second thoughts—"

"No. I want to work here. I do. Sorry, I didn't get much sleep last night. I'm not making a lot of sense."

She narrowed her eyes.

"I'll put those carts away," he said.

She gave him a tight-lipped smile. "You do that." She picked up the scanning gun and turned away from him. "Let me know if you have any questions."

"Yeah." All he had were questions.

Jena barely spoke to him all morning, except to give him orders, correct a mistake, or make sarcastic comments intended either as insults or humor, he couldn't tell which. She wasn't the girl he had fallen for. He worried that he'd lost her friendship too, before he'd ever really had it.

Mr. Kim wasn't going to die, at least, but that pretty much discounted his ideas about the coin flip determining the outcome of the wish. Which meant Ephraim knew very little about the coin at all.

As the clock ticked toward twelve o'clock, he tried to figure out how to ask Jena to join him for lunch. But at the stroke of noon, the wide glass doors of the library slid open, and Mary and Shelley walked in. Of course she would already have lunch plans.

"Hi, guys," Mary and Shelley said in stereo.

"Hi," Jena said. She smiled for the first time all day.

Mary sidled up to Ephraim. "Hey, sweetie," she said. She put a hand on his arm and leaned in for a kiss. Ephraim froze.

"Hi, Mary," he choked out.

He disengaged himself and grabbed onto another cart half-full with books. "I'll be right back. Just have to finish this up."

He tried to ignore the hurt look on her face and the annoyed one on Jena's. He pushed the cart dangerously fast and ducked behind a shelf, knocking some books to the floor. He could still see the front desk through the gaps in the books on the shelf. He leaned on the cart, his heart pounding.

"You ready for lunch?" Jena said to the twins.

"You bet," Shelley said.

"Is it all right if . . ." Mary darted a glance toward where Ephraim had disappeared.

"Sis wanted to have lunch with Ephraim," Shelley said. "She was going to *make* him lunch until I talked her out of it. I mean, it's the twenty-first century, right? Do we really want to perpetuate those outmoded stereotypes?" Speaking of stereotypes, that was the longest sentence Ephraim had ever heard Shelley say at once. Had everyone changed with that last wish?

Jena darted a glance over her shoulder and lowered her voice. Ephraim practically shoved his head through the bookshelf as he strained to listen.

". . . creeping me out," Jena whispered.

Jena didn't sound jealous of Mary like he'd assumed. More like she hated him.

Ephraim pulled out the coin. "You caused all this trouble," he said to it.

"Who are you talking to?" Mary said. She had just come around the corner. He concealed the coin in his fist.

"I was just . . . working." His eyes fell on the book cart. "I like to read the titles aloud as I put them away."

"'You caused all this trouble'?" Mary said.

"It's a self-help book." Ephraim shoved the coin in his pocket and stepped around the cart.

When they reached the library entrance, Ephraim saw Nathan standing there, and he couldn't believe his eyes. Nathan had really changed—physically. His usually floppy hair was short and spiked, pointing in every direction. He wasn't as thin as he should be, either; his shoulders were broad, and tight muscles showed through a thin Summerside Badgers football jersey. Nathan hated football.

"You've met Ephraim, Nat?" Shelley said.

Nat?

"Ephraim? Hey, what did you want this morning?" Nathan's voice sounded deeper than normal.

"Nothing. I dialed the wrong number," Ephraim said. "Sorry about that."

"You know, I think I'll pass on lunch," Jena said. "I didn't expect it to be a big group thing."

Mary drew Ephraim outside with them. He pulled his arm away from her at the top of the stairs. "I can't come either," Ephraim said.

"Why not?" Mary asked. A lock of curly brown hair stuck to her sweat-dampened forehead.

"We're just busy today," Ephraim said. He glanced over his shoulder back into the library. He saw Jena at the circulation desk, head bent down toward her computer screen.

"You'd rather hang out with the bookworm?" Nathan laughed.

Ephraim stared at Nathan in shock. He felt Mary's eyes on him, and he shriveled up inside under her gaze.

"It's my job," Ephraim said.

"Do you want to meet up later?" Mary said softly.

"I can't. I have   plans tonight."

"We don't need him along to have a good time," Nathan said. He grabbed for Mary's arm, but she jerked it away from him.

"Actually, I think I'll go home then," she said. "Three's a crowd."

"Suit yourself," Nathan said.

Shelley pouted. "See you later, sis."

Mary stalked off down the street.

"Nice ass," Nathan said. He winked at Ephraim. "That's the best thing about dating Shell. She can't get upset if I compliment her sister's looks."

"Is something going on with you and Jena?" Shelley said quietly to Ephraim.

"No." Not anymore, anyway.

She looked like she wanted to say something else, but Nathan pulled her arm.

"Ow," she said.

"Come on, *chica*," Nathan said. "I'm hungry. Let's get some wedges."

Ephraim trailed after Mary, trying to think about what he could say to make things better, but coming up short.

He caught up with her in front of the post office. "Mary!" She finally slowed and leaned against a mailbox. He put his hand on her shoulder, and she flinched away. She wouldn't turn around, so he moved in front of her.

She glared. "Were you just playing with me?" she said.

"Mary, I'm sorry. I've just been a little preoccupied—"

"I see that." She spat her words at him now. "You're interested in my best friend. Why not chase my sister while you're at it?"

"Nathan would kill me." The levity didn't disarm her the way he'd hoped.

"You don't want to go out with me though, do you?"

"It's not that," he said. "You're terrific. I like you."

"But?" She stood up straighter.

"You're very attractive . . ." Ephraim said.

"Just admit that you'd rather be with Jena." Mary squared her jaw, and she put both hands on either side of the mailbox, clenching it so tightly he wasn't sure if she was bracing herself on it or trying to tear it out of the ground so she could hit him with it. An elderly man approached with a handful of letters, glanced at them, and turned around to head into the post office.

Ephraim plunged his hands into his pockets. His fingers grazed the magic coin. He didn't have to hurt her, he thought. She didn't deserve this. *I wish*—

He withdrew his hands. "You don't really like me," he said. "It's hard to explain, but what you're feeling . . . it isn't real."

"I should know who I like and don't like." She took a step away from him. "I think you're the one who's confused. You've changed somehow, Ephraim."

"*I* seem different?" *What about all of you?* He laughed.

"See, the Ephraim I know wouldn't find this funny. You should have been honest. You aren't being fair to me. Or Jena."

"It's more complicated—"

"I'm sure it is. But that doesn't mean it's better to feed me bullshit just to make it easier on you." She took in a deep breath. "I thought you were a nice guy. But you're just a different kind of jerk, the kind who pretends he isn't."

Ephraim swallowed. "That isn't fair either. I just didn't want to hurt your feelings. I'm being honest now."

"Thanks. Good job." Mary let go of the mailbox.

She walked past him. Ephraim thought about stopping her, but he couldn't say anything that wouldn't make things worse.

Well, you handled that well, he said to himself. He could do something about this, but there was no guarantee the coin wouldn't make it even worse.

In the meantime, breaking up with Mary might at least make things less awkward with Jena. Unless, of course, she sided with her best friend. Maybe things would become even more of a mess from here.

Either way, Ephraim had to try to figure out how the coin worked before he dared to use it again. Then he would find a way to fix everything.

CHAPTER 14

Ephraim returned to the library and settled himself at a computer terminal. He typed search terms into the library catalog database: "magic quarter," "wishes," "coin flip," "Puerto Rico."

Zero hits.

Well, he hadn't really expected it to be that easy. He tried again, cutting out "Puerto Rico," and a short list of books scrolled onto the screen. He printed the list and hunted them down.

Ephraim was dismayed to find most of the books were children's books, collections of fantasy stories, or academic essays on fairy tales. He collected them all and sat down to look through them anyway.

Jena followed his actions from her desk while he hunted for his books. Every now and then he picked his head up from his reading and caught her watching him.

He stacked his books and belatedly realized he couldn't just leave them on the table for someone else to put away—it was his job now. None of them had turned up anything useful. He had run across references to cautionary tales about wishes: variations on a story called "The Monkey's Paw," stories about genies and lamps, *Doctor Faustus*, and an amusing kids' novel about a sand fairy. They all seemed to agree that it was impossible to make a wish and have it turn out the way you intended. In story after story, the wishers tried to trick their way to what they wanted and inevitably failed. That wasn't very encouraging.

Jena appeared at his side. "How's it going?"

"I'm sorry, I know my break is over. I'm just putting these away."

"Your break ended an hour ago, but you were so focused I didn't want to interrupt you. Don't worry. It's really slow this afternoon. I can handle it." She gestured at the books on the table. "This looks pretty important."

Ephraim hesitated. "It might be."

She picked up his stack of books. "Keep doing what you're doing. If it picks up, I'll call you. You're done with these?"

He nodded.

"I'll put them away."

"Thanks," he said.

"Sure." She wandered away with his books, and he realized she probably just wanted to know what he was researching. At least she was talking to him again. He would take curiosity over animosity any day.

He spent the rest of the afternoon typing in different search strings on the computer, but he didn't come up with much of anything new. Jena caught his eye once and smiled encouragingly. What was going on with her? He hadn't made another accidental wish with the coin, had he? Her frosty demeanor had thawed considerably over the course of the afternoon.

She snuck up behind him again but had the courtesy not to lean over his shoulder. "Can I help?" she said. "You look stuck."

"It's kind of . . . personal," he said.

"I understand. But I saw the books you were reading. I read a lot of fantasy, so I'm something of an expert on magic and fairy tales . . . are you writing a paper? I didn't know you were taking summer classes."

"I'm not in summer school," he said. "This isn't an assignment. I was just curious."

"Just, in general?" She put a hand on his shoulder. "What are you looking for? I think I can speed up the search a little." She stood up straighter. "I am a librarian after all. In training."

Maybe the coin could help Ephraim without him needing to make a wish. This was his chance to take some action of his own, make things happen without the use of magic.

He took a deep breath. "Okay," he said. He turned to face Jena, her face close enough to kiss. "I'll tell you about it—over dinner."

She stepped back.

"Is that such a horrible prospect?" Ephraim asked.

"I can't," she said. She twisted her thumbs in the belt loops on her jeans.

"I'm not dating Mary, if that's what you're worried about," he said.

"She told me. That's the problem. It wouldn't be right for me to go out with you so soon."

"I can honestly tell you that I'm not interested in Mary. Despite what she might think, what happened between us, I never was. I can explain it all tonight, I promise. Don't look at it as a date. You're just helping me with a research project."

She tilted her head, considering. Then she smiled.

"You're on," she said.

CHAPTER 15

"This wasn't exactly what I had in mind when I asked you to dinner," Ephraim said.

They were sitting in Jena's living room. The last time he'd been here was for her party, which already seemed ages away even though it had been less than a week ago. This time it was just the two of them, which he much preferred, though he knew they weren't truly alone. Mrs. Kim was skulking around the kitchen, and Jena's father was resting upstairs.

"I thought it made more sense to meet here, since we're doing research," Jena said. She patted the MacBook on the couch beside her. "I have my computer and wireless Internet, and all the books in my room."

Ephraim wondered what her bedroom was like, but Mrs. Kim's close monitoring made it clear that it was off-limits. Not that it seemed likely Jena would invite him up there anyway.

"And this way you can truthfully say that we didn't go out together," Ephraim said.

"Bingo," she said.

She was acting normal, friendly even, though he wasn't sure if she saw him as a potential boyfriend anymore or if her curiosity was simply piqued. Returning to her house reminded him that she had liked him once, and he hoped she would again.

"So, tell me what you're looking for." Jena bit into her chicken taco and leaned back. She propped her bare feet on the coffee table beside the take-out containers.

Now that he was here, he was afraid to tell Jena about the coin. How would she react? As much as she liked fantasy books, was she capable of believing in real magic?

"Come on, Ephraim," she said quietly. "Let me help."

He put down his burrito and rubbed his hands clean on his denim shorts. He retrieved the wishing coin from his pocket and placed it on the glass tabletop.

Jena leaned forward to examine it. "A quarter. You want to find out if it's rare or something?"

"No, I'm already pretty sure it's rare. It's . . ." He took a deep breath. "It's magic."

"Magic?"

He nodded.

"A magic . . . quarter?" she said.

"I'm not sure it is a quarter really, but it looks like one."

Jena stared at him. "You aren't kidding."

"No."

Jena picked up the coin and turned it over and over in her small fingers. She stared at the reverse side. She rubbed at it with a thumbnail, then held it up to her face and squinted at it with first one eye, then the other. She smiled, and Ephraim was worried that she thought it was all a joke.

"'The Enchanted Island,' huh?" She glanced at it one more time before closing her fingers over it. "Well, where else would you get a magic coin? So, what does it do?"

"That's what I hope we can figure out," Ephraim said. He told her about how he'd found it and the first time he'd used it: about the dead body that everyone had thought was his, the note in his locker telling him how to make a wish, and the changes he'd seen in his mother. Jena listened silently while he explained, wiggling her toes from time to time. He couldn't read her intent expression, but he knew how it must sound.

Jena looked him in the eyes. "You know that's all a bit hard to accept," she said.

"Yeah."

"But I always try to be open-minded."

"You believe me?" Ephraim asked.

"I didn't say that. I think you're either telling me the truth or you believe you're telling me the truth," Jena said. She examined the coin again.

"So it's magic, or I'm crazy? Thanks for the vote of confidence." She didn't seem to hear him.

"You never saw this other body at the hospital?" she asked.

"No, but my mother did. And Mrs. Morales confirmed it was there, before my first wish. After that, no one remembered it but me."

"You don't have that note anymore, either. Which means there's nothing and no one to corroborate your story."

He shook his head. This was just how it had gone when he told Nathan about the coin. Then he remembered.

"Wait. I still have these." He pulled out his wallet and showed her the two identical library cards. She examined them carefully side by side.

"Not to be a stickler, but you could have printed a second card at work," she said. She passed them back to him. "Sorry."

"With the same barcode?" he asked. "The system wouldn't let you do that."

"You're right. But those cards have different barcode numbers."

He checked them again. She was right. He'd never compared them, just noted that his name was printed on both.

"That doesn't matter. The coin rearranges things when I make a wish." He squeezed his fingers around the cards, the plastic edges digging into his hand. "It changes things . . . and people. I know I can't prove any of it—"

"Now, don't get all defensive. I'm just trying to reason this out. So, if you made a wish about your mother being out of the hospital, why would it make your body disappear?"

"Jena, I'm not dead. That body wasn't mine."

Jena frowned. "Obviously you're not dead yet, but he is. The other Ephraim, I mean."

"The other . . . ? What are you talking about? There's only one me! And what do you mean by 'yet'?"

Jena slapped the quarter down on the glass top of the coffee table. "Calm down, Ephraim. You seem really certain of what's possible and what's impossible, for a guy who's trying to convince me he has a magic wishing coin."

Ephraim sighed. "Point taken."

"I'm just working this through, okay? That's why you asked for my help," Jena said. "If you want me to believe you, you have to keep an open mind, too. Anything is possible if we're talking about magic. Or whatever power this coin has."

"I just don't see how there could be two of me." Ephraim said.

"The simplest solution is usually the truth. It seems like you had a twin, so you probably did."

"*That's* the simplest solution? How about it was just some poor kid who looked a little like me?"

"Consider all the other clues: the wallet, the library card, the watch. I see at least two possibilities. Maybe he was from the future." She tapped the back of the coin. "A future where Puerto Rico is part of the United States."

"He can't have been much older than me, if the hospital and my mother confused the two of us. Besides, the date on the coin says Puerto Rico became a state in 1998—which it didn't. That's historical fact. It'll be true in ten years as much as it is now."

Jena pouted. "That doesn't necessarily invalidate my theory. But it would mean you were going to die pretty soon, after wishing yourself back in time to give yourself the quarter. Which also implies that *you're* the reason you have the coin, which just opens this up to all kinds of temporal paradoxes. Okay, let's set that aside for now. Too messy."

"Sounds good to me. I don't want to have to worry about dying anytime soon, and I'm having a hard enough time buying into magic without throwing time travel into the mix," Ephraim said.

"Still, the coin came from somewhere. Some place where magic works, assuming that it's really magic." She sat up straighter and tucked her feet under her bare thighs, momentarily distracting Ephraim from the problem at hand.

"Well," Jena said. "If not the future, then what about a parallel universe? One where magic works, where the US has fifty-one states." She turned the coin over. "This Washington head is facing the wrong way, too. And if the coin's from a parallel universe, maybe that's where the other Ephraim came from, too!" Her words were coming faster as she got taken with the idea.

"A parallel universe? That's just stuff for comics and movies." He'd read stories about alternate universes: worlds where heroes were villains, or had never gained their super powers, or where history had unfolded differently.

Jena took out her cell phone and snapped pictures of both sides of the coin.

"What are you doing now?" Ephraim asked.

"Checking to see if anyone has one of these," she said. She tapped at the screen a couple of times and shook her head. "If they do, they haven't uploaded a picture to the Internet. So for now, I'll assume that means no others exist."

"Right. Because it doesn't exist if it isn't on the Internet."

"Hold on," she said. "The image scan did get a couple of hits." She scrolled through the text on her screen. "The bust of George Washington on your quarter matches a design by a woman named Laura Gardin Fraser. She won a contest and it was supposed to be used on all quarters starting in 1931, but they ended up going with the design we're used to instead. Anyway, the only time it's ever been used in American currency is on the commemorative half eagle in 1999."

She tipped her phone toward Ephraim and he looked at the picture of the gold-colored Washington coin. The right-facing Washington head was identical to the one on his quarter.

"So you think a Wikipedia entry proves the coin's from a parallel universe where . . . what? They went with a different coin design in 1931?" He passed the phone back to her.

"Multiple worlds isn't science fiction, it's a legitimate theory. I'll get our physics textbook."

"I don't remember studying anything like this in class," Ephraim said.

"Like you were even paying attention. I read ahead in class when I'm bored. Which is often. There's a brief overview on the subject in the back, and I found some amazing books in the library. You know, learning doesn't end in the classroom."

He leaned forward. "Just summarize."

She pushed her hair back and braced her hands on her knees.

"It isn't easy to explain, but I'll do my best. Okay. So, lots of physicists believe in what they call the 'many-worlds interpretation of quantum mechanics.' There are several different theories about parallel universes, but the most popular suggests that for every decision we make, for every observable event, there are multiple outcomes. Each of those outcomes occurs in another world just like ours, and all those worlds exist in a collection of multiple universes—a multiverse—rather than a single universe."

"I . . . didn't follow any of that."

"I barely understand it myself." She looked around the room for inspiration. "Here."

Jena opened her computer and typed in a Google search. As she read the screen, he munched on a cold burrito.

"Let's try this," she said. "You've heard of Schrödinger's cat? Everyone's heard of Schrödinger's cat."

"Yes!" Finally, something sounded familiar to Ephraim. "That's the experiment where they put a cat in a box with a gas pellet that either killed it or didn't."

"That's right, basically. It didn't really happen, it's just an imaginary way of illustrating a theory. According to quantum physics, until someone opens that box, the cat is both dead and alive at the same time."

"That sounds impossible."

"As impossible as a magic coin?" Jena crossed her arms. "Remember what I said about keeping an open mind. In quantum physics it's not only possible, it's *probable*—and it only gets weirder. The theory of multiple universes—a multiverse—suggests that even after you open the box, the cat is simultaneously dead and alive, but in different, parallel universes. In one reality, the cat is dead. In another, similar reality, the cat is alive. It all depends on the perspective of the person observing the outcome."

Jena picked up the coin from the coffee table.

"Here's another way to look at it." She flipped the coin before he could stop her. He tensed, even though she hadn't made a wish, and he was pretty sure the coin wouldn't work for her given what had happened when Nathan tried it. "When you flip the coin, you observe that it lands on either heads or tails." Jena opened her hand and showed him it had come up heads. "In this universe, as far as you know, it was heads and that's the only outcome. But in a parallel universe, another version of you might be just as sure that it had landed on tails. And you'd both be right."

Ephraim nodded slowly. "I think I'm starting to get it," he said.

"But there's one more twist: that second universe—the one where the coin landed on tails—didn't exist until the moment you flipped the coin. At the moment you observed the outcome, another quantum reality split off from this one." She tilted her head. "Or the other way around. There's no way for us to know whether we're in the original reality or the branched one." She put down the coin.

"But which is the real universe?" Ephraim asked.

"They both are," she said.

Ephraim put his hands to the sides of his head. "I'm getting a massive headache."

"I won't bother getting into string theory then." Jena grinned.

"So you think the coin could have come from one of those alternate realities?" Ephraim asked.

"In an infinity of other universes, a lot of them could be just like ours but with different physical properties. Maybe in some of them, magic actually works." She leaned back and smiled, like a content cat. "But it's only a theory. It's just as hard to find evidence of multiple universes as it is to demonstrate the existence of magic." She slid the magic coin along the glass table toward him with her foot. "Maybe harder. But since you claim to actually have a magic coin, show me what it can do."

This demonstration had ended disastrously with Nathan, and he was in no hurry to repeat that with Jena. Not when all he had were wild theories about where the coin had come from.

"You want me to use it? Now?"

"Make a wish," she said.

Ephraim licked his lips. "Like I said, I don't know how it works, not completely. I don't want to use it again until I know it's not going to cause any more harm. And now you're talking about other universes and everything, and it sounds even more dangerous than I thought."

"Wait. Any *more* harm? What harm has it done so far?" Jena asked.

"It gives me what I wish for, but sometimes . . . sometimes bad things happen, too. Things I didn't intend. Things you can't predict."

"Which is why you were looking through all those books on fairy tales. Bad things like what?"

Like your father having a heart attack.

Ephraim swallowed and kept his mouth shut. He wasn't ready to tell her everything.

"Maybe we should leave this for now," he said. It all suddenly seemed less important. Jena was talking to him. Her father was okay. He was getting things back on track without the coin.

The only problem was Nathan. He wasn't the friend Ephraim

remembered, and he didn't know if they could be now. They hardly had anything in common anymore; Nathan was a popular football jock, and he was dating Shelley Morales. He didn't have room for Ephraim in his new life. He didn't need Ephraim the way he always had before.

"No way," Jena said. "If you stop now then I'll have to assume you're lying about the coin."

"I wouldn't lie to you." Ephraim picked up the coin. "All right. But you have to hold my hand when I make the wish."

Jena blinked. "Is this some attempt to put a move on me?"

"We have to be touching or you won't remember the way things were before the wish. It worked that way with Nathan."

"Nat Mackenzie?"

He nodded.

"What does Shelley's boyfriend have to do with this?" she asked.

"Before all this . . . we were best friends. He was different then. I told him about the coin, we shared a few wishes. But so far the coin only works for me, and I forgot to grab his hand the last time we used it, so he doesn't remember it or our friendship now," Ephraim said.

"Who else did you tell about the coin?" Jena asked.

"No one," he said. "Nathan was the only one. I swear."

"Not even Mary?"

"Why would I tell her?" Ephraim said.

Jena smiled. "Forget it."

Jena held out her hand, and Ephraim gripped it lightly, worried she would notice how sweaty his palm was. Her skin was cold. She stared at their clasped hands for a moment and then met his eyes.

"You were dating my best friend," she said.

"That was a . . . side effect of a wish I made for Nathan." He swallowed. "I've only ever wanted to go out with you, Jena." There, he'd said it.

She pursed her lips but squeezed his hand.

"So what should we wish for?" she asked.

"Something small. Something harmless, but noticeable. That should minimize the possibility of things going wrong, or changing too much. I hope." Ephraim eyed the take-out containers on the coffee table. "I have an idea," he said.

He balanced the coin on his thumb, ready to flip it. "I wish we'd ordered Chinese instead of Mexican." He raised his eyebrows, and Jena nodded. He flipped and caught it a moment later.

Heads.

He felt his stomach flop as though it had just been turned inside out, and the room shimmered. He realized he and Jena were now sitting on opposite ends of the couch, no longer holding hands. After a moment of obvious disorientation, Jena clapped a hand over her mouth and ran for the kitchen.

Jena came back a few minutes later wiping at her mouth with a damp paper towel. Her face was pale.

"Um. I should have warned you about that," Ephraim said.

"You knew that would happen?"

"It only happens the first time. What's wrong now?" She was ignoring him, looking at the coffee table.

Ephraim suddenly noticed the little white cardboard containers. Jena tucked her hair behind her. "Chinese food," she said.

The aluminum containers of Mexican food were gone, replaced by tins of egg foo young, cartons of white rice, dishes with chicken in brown sauce. Jena's plate was empty, but food still sat untouched on Ephraim's plate, the sauce gelled on top.

"There's no way you could have switched all that while I was in the kitchen, is there?"

"Not without magic." He grinned.

"Okay, hold on. When you came over I asked if you wanted Mexican or Chinese. And you said Mexican. That's how I remember it." She furrowed her brow the way she did during exams, when she was concentrating really hard on a question.

"And I just changed that with my wish." Ephraim said.

"So now it's like we had ordered Chinese in the first place. But what I just threw up in the kitchen was definitely Mexican food." She put her hand over her stomach. Ephraim made a face. "So why didn't it change the contents of my stomach too?"

"Because you were included in my wish." It seemed that Jena believed in the coin now.

"Because I was an observer . . ." Jena muttered. She collapsed onto the couch and toed the Chinese food plate away from her with a grimace.

"It's just Chinese food," he said. He picked up his own plate and poked at the thick gel with the end of a chopstick. "It's not radioactive or anything."

"How do you know? Do you have a Geiger counter?" She shook her head. "I just don't have much of an appetite anymore."

Jena picked up her laptop and started typing. Then she shrieked and closed the lid.

"What the hell, Ephraim?" she said.

"Huh?"

She showed the laptop to him, close to tears. "My MacBook. My beautiful MacBook. What have you done?"

The laptop was still silver, but it was clearly a PC.

"Oh no," Ephraim said.

"If this is a joke, it isn't funny, Ephraim. Give me my Mac, and I won't kill you."

He swallowed. "I didn't do that. It was the coin." He shrugged. "Random stuff like that happens whenever I use it."

"Well, wish it back then."

"It's not that easy. The next wish could make things worse."

"I don't know what could be worse than this," she muttered. She took a breath and opened the lid again, poking around sullenly at the mousepad. "All my files seem to be here, at least. Probably some nasty viruses too." She glared at him. "All right, we'll fix this later."

She started typing, more slowly and with an occasional curse. "We should go over this. Scientifically. It would be better if we had some actual equipment, access to the labs at school."

"You really want to test it with a Geiger counter?" He hoped the coin wasn't radioactive; he'd been carrying it around in his pocket every day.

"Well, we could at least weigh it, compare it to a regular quarter. But let's start with what we do know about it," she said.

"One: it's probably not from our world, because of the Puerto Rico thing and the different bust of Washington."

"Not to mention the magic thing," Jena said dryly.

"Right. Two: you have to flip the coin to make a wish," Ephraim said.

"Actually, stop right there. That's interesting. What's the purpose of the coin flipping? Some magical ritual?"

Jena picked up a Pepsi—had it been Coke before?—and sipped. She frowned and examined the can distrustfully.

"It starts getting hot as soon as I make a wish, and it cools after I flip it," Ephraim said.

"So it's like making the wish activates the coin, or charges it. And flipping it completes the process," Jena said.

"That makes it sound like it's mechanical."

Jena shrugged. "I'm just trying to be logical. Does it matter if it's heads or tails?" she asked.

"I've been wondering about that. I've tried to remember each of my wishes, and I think when it's heads I get what I asked for, more or less. When I get tails it still grants the wish, but something bad happens along with it."

"Like a Monkey's Paw," Jena said.

"Yeah. That's what I thought." He'd found the story in library research. In it, a magical monkey's paw twisted every wish its owner made so horribly that the owner regretted ever making it. "But I guess it seems more like a mixed bag after each wish, regardless of how the coin comes up. I can't account for every change it's made, just the ones I've noticed."

"Was that last coin toss tails?" she asked.

"Heads," he said. "I prefer PCs."

She grimaced. "No one's perfect. So the outcome of each wish is essentially random. Tricky."

"That's what really has me worried."

"In stories, magical items often aren't the blessing they seem. People usually get in trouble when they start to abuse them, or think they can outsmart the magic somehow. Of course, until today, I didn't think magic existed."

"You read all those fantasy books, but you didn't actually believe in magic?" Ephraim asked.

"I read to escape the real world. I never thought magic could be real, no matter how much I wanted some in my own life."

She typed some more; Ephraim enjoyed watching her. It was comfortable being with her like this. It was what he'd always wanted, right from the beginning. Maybe the coin was still granting that early wish of his.

Jena shot him a glance over the top of her screen. "If I hadn't been holding your hand when you made that last wish, would I have realized that we'd had Mexican before, or would I have just thought we'd gotten Chinese?"

"You wouldn't have remembered things were ever any different," he said.

Jena's nails clicked against the keys for a moment.

"Ephraim." Jena looked at him somberly.

"Jena?"

"You said that dating Mary was just a 'side effect' of Nat's wish. What did you mean? What did he wish for?"

"*Nathan* wanted me to wish that he and Shelley were dating. Somehow that made Mary like me. I didn't want that or anything, it just happened."

"When did you make that wish?"

Ephraim thought back. "Four days ago."

"But you two have been dating for the last month. You've gone out three times already."

"I don't remember going out with her before the other night, aside from the birthday dinner with her, Shelley, and Nathan."

Jena drummed her fingernails against the laptop case. "You said it yourself. You remember things differently because you made the wish."

"But why would it change things that far back?" he asked.

Jena shook her head. "Four days ago . . . that's when you kissed Mary, isn't it?"

Ephraim's palms began to sweat. He'd known girls talked to each other about stuff like that, but he was still shocked that Jena knew about the kiss. "I was confused. One minute I was by myself, the next I was out on a date with her. She kissed me, if you want to get technical."

"You kissed her back."

"No, I—"

"Ephraim. Did you ever use the coin on me?"

"What?"

"Have you made any wishes that affected me directly?" Jena asked.

He sighed.

"That sounds like a yes," she said.

"I was going to tell you."

She closed her eyes. "Tell me now."

"It was just an accident. I wasn't used to the coin yet, didn't even think it worked really, and I sort of wished . . . that you liked me."

"I don't remember ever not liking you." She opened her eyes. "Damn."

She slid the laptop onto the couch and pulled her legs in so she was sitting Indian style with her hands on her knees. "What else? You said that was 'the first time.'"

Here it was. He had to tell her. "I was just trying to help,"

Ephraim said. "But the coin is so unpredictable. That's why I stopped using it, to figure out how to get control over it."

"What did you wish for?" Her voice was flat.

"You don't remember it, but you and your family were going to go to L.A."

"Oh. That's why you thought I was moving. My father was being considered for a promotion, but he didn't get it." She narrowed her eyes. "Was that your doing?"

"He got the job before. I didn't want you to leave, because it seemed like we were finally getting to know each other." He paused, but he didn't remind her that was only because of his previous wish. "So I wished that you didn't have to go. The coin landed on tails. And . . . your father had a heart attack."

Jena didn't say anything.

"As soon as I realized what had happened, I used the coin to make him better," Ephraim said. "I tried, honestly. But every time I use it, I don't know what else is going to change. It just gets harder to fix. That was going to be my last wish."

She wouldn't look him in the eyes. "I thought you were a good person. I liked you, Ephraim."

"After that last wish, I was afraid you hated me."

"I was jealous, Ephraim. I've always liked you too, but Mary got you first. So I stepped out of the way." She sighed. "It's stupid, I know. I hated the way it made me feel when I saw the two of you together. I thought I should be happier for both my friends."

"Then why did you act like you hated me?"

"I was angry with myself for never telling you how I felt. But I guess I took it out on you, because I didn't want to lose my best friend, too." She sighed. "It was easier to be around you if I pretended that I didn't like you. The thing is, right now I'm not sure if I'm pretending anymore." She spoke quietly.

"Jena, it turned out all right though. Your father's fine. *We're* fine. Aren't we?"

"Don't make any more wishes about me, even if you think you're helping me. I mean it. I know I can't enforce it, I guess I probably wouldn't even realize if you change things around so that I love you or we're dating or whatever. But if there's a tiny sense of decency in you, you won't do it."

"I wouldn't do that! Of course I wouldn't."

She slammed her laptop shut and ran her fingers over the black Tandy logo, where the Mac apple had been.

"In fact, don't make any more wishes, period. It's obvious you don't know what you're doing. You can't control what the coin changes." She lowered her head, her bangs falling over her eyes. "I think you should go now. We're done here," she said.

He stood up and waited for a moment, hoping she would say something else. Hoping she'd ask him to stay.

"Thanks for all your help," he said.

"You should take tomorrow off from work, Ephraim." Jena pulled her legs up and hugged them to her chest, staring at the coffee table.

"Right."

He'd made it to the front door when she called after him. Ephraim returned to the living room, hoping she had changed her mind.

"You forgot your coin," Jena said.

He picked up the quarter from the coffee table and left.

The evening had started out so well. Not only had he been making progress with Jena, he thought they had come really close to figuring out where the coin came from. He knew if they could work as a team they would solve it together. Had that last wish somehow messed things up? No, he couldn't blame the coin. It had all been his fault; he'd made all those wishes, all those choices, on his own. It'd only been a matter of time before Jena found out about them, once he told her about the magic coin.

He deserved every bit of her resentment. He took some comfort in the idea that there might be a parallel universe out there where he hadn't so completely screwed up, where maybe he'd made different choices and he and Jena were still friends, or even a couple.

There was a way Ephraim could make it up to her—to prove that he could be responsible for his actions. All it would take was one more wish.

CHAPTER 16

Since Ephraim wasn't welcome at the library while Jena was there, and he couldn't hang out with Nathan, he spent the day reading in Greystone Park. He also hoped he might run into Jena there. He knew she walked to work every day, and the fastest route required cutting through the park, past the memorial fountain.

Eventually the skateboarders and the mothers with strollers left the park, and Ephraim was alone. Jena hurried into the plaza just a short while before the park closed at dusk. When she spotted Ephraim, she veered around the fountain, away from him. Ephraim rose and held his hands out, palms open.

"Can I talk to you?" Ephraim said.

"I don't want to see you right now. I can't believe you followed me."

"I didn't. I was waiting for you."

"Like that's much better."

"I just need to say something. It's not an excuse, not an explanation."

"I don't want to hear it. I need some time to process all this," she said.

"This can't wait. I have to do this before I change my mind." Ephraim flashed the quarter at her, tucked between his first and middle fingers, like he'd seen magicians do after pulling a coin from behind someone's ear.

Jena looked frightened. "What are you doing?" she asked.

"I'm going to fix things," he said.

"No, Ephraim." She bit her lower lip and stepped toward him, her eyes focused on the coin. She was close enough to see that it was the same coin. "You said it was unpredictable. Too dangerous to use."

"It is," he said. "I keep hurting people, and it has to stop."

"Give it to me, Ephraim. I'll bury it somewhere. Or we can try to melt it down . . ."

"It isn't the One Ring," he said. "And where are we going to find a volcano in Summerside?"

"Huh?" she asked.

"You know, like in *The Lord of the Rings.*"

She had never heard of the books or movies, and she wasn't messing with him. He swallowed.

"Uh, never mind then," he said. "Jena, I'm sorry. I really am. Even if you don't want to hear it, even if you don't believe me. I only used the coin because I—I wanted to get to know you. I didn't think I'd have a chance with you otherwise. You don't remember, but you didn't always like me the way you do now. The way you did, anyway."

He shook his head.

"It was wrong to use the coin to make you interested in me," he continued. "I may have ruined the possibility of friendship, but I needed you to be here for this." He clenched his hand. "I'm going to make one last wish."

Jena took another step toward him.

"Don't worry," he said. "Trust me."

"I can't."

Jena grabbed for the hand holding the coin. He jerked it away, and while she held onto his arm he said the words in a rush, "I wish this coin would go back to wherever it came from!"

Jena stared at him in surprise. The coin was getting uncomfortably hot in his fist.

"I have to flip it," he said.

Jena nodded.

"But don't let go of me," he added.

She held onto his other arm as he flicked the coin into the fountain like a skipping stone. It actually bounced on the water once before it ricocheted off Atlas's left foot and sank. Heads or tails, it didn't matter anymore.

Ephraim and Jena looked into the water fountain. He couldn't spot where the quarter had ended up; now it was just one quarter among many, unless it had—hopefully—disappeared.

Jena sat down right on the cobblestones of the plaza.

"Wow," she said. "You got rid of it."

Ephraim felt a sense of loss mixed with relief. "What did you think I was going to wish for?" He leaned against the rim of the fountain. "I meant what I said. I'm sorry. I wanted to show you that I'm done with messing around with other people's lives. At least, magically."

"I'm impressed," Jena said.

"Can you forgive me?" Ephraim asked.

"I don't know. This is a good start to that," she said.

"That's all I'm asking for."

"I appreciate the grand gesture, but it's not enough to make me feel better."

"Uh . . . what would make you feel better?" he asked.

She climbed to her feet and drew closer to him. She leaned in to him, eyes half-closed. Surprised, he closed his eyes and leaned toward her. Jena put her hands on his shoulders.

She shoved him hard, and he sprawled backward into the fountain.

He thrashed around in the shallow water then sat up, coughing. Icy cold water showered down on him from the basin on Atlas's shoulders, and he gasped as he climbed to his feet. His soaked jeans dragged heavily and his sneakers squished. He had the nasty metallic taste of the water in his mouth.

Jena crossed her arms. "See you at work tomorrow, Ephraim. Don't be late."

CHAPTER 17

Ephraim ventured into the library the next day. Jena didn't even mention what had happened at the fountain; if he hadn't known better, he might have thought she'd forgotten all about it. Instead, she put him back to work, which was better than her avoiding him.

Without the coin, Ephraim was forced to accept his current situation—the situation he'd created. Over the next few days, he was relieved not to have to worry about the sudden, sporadic changes initiated by the coin. He was busy enough getting used to life as his wishes had left it.

It wasn't all bad. His mother was much happier working at an office job in the city and continuing to date Jim. Nathan was inseparable from Shelley Morales, like he'd always dreamed. Ephraim had made the right decision to part with the coin. Any changes he could have wished for would have been selfish ones. He still hoped he might be able to put his friendship with Nathan back on track eventually.

And as for Jena   she remained friendly but distant in their interactions, which was disappointing but not discouraging. So he was surprised when she offered him her spare ticket for the July Fourth matinee of the Broadway musical *Wicked*.

Jena made things very clear from the start: "This isn't a date. I just don't have anyone else to ask on short notice." She'd ended up with an extra ticket because Mary had canceled on her at the last minute; their friendship had been strained since Ephraim had broken up with Mary and turned his attentions to Jena. Ephraim felt guilty enough about the whole situation, which he knew was basically his fault, to scrape up enough money for the ticket, even though he didn't even like musicals. It was still an opportunity to spend an afternoon with Jena. He hoped that with time and luck he might get her to like him again one day—without any magical shortcuts.

Ephraim bicycled to the Summerside train station, once again missing Nathan and his old car. He almost wished he'd gotten a car of his own out of the coin before getting rid of it. He arrived a minute before the train was scheduled and raced down the platform to meet Jena.

Ephraim tugged at his tie and tried to scratch at an itch along the side of his neck, where sweat was trickling down his starched shirt collar.

"Where's your top hat and cane?" Jena laughed. She was in a yellow sundress that fit her perfectly, though she kept pulling the front up surreptitiously and tugging at the hemline.

"Did I overdo it?" Ephraim asked. He'd never been to a Broadway show before, but he thought he should dress up. He had also wanted to impress Jena. Maybe making her laugh was almost as good.

"You look handsome," Jena said. She closed the tattered paperback of *Wicked* she'd been reading while waiting for him.

"Thanks. You look great," he said.

They crowded together onto the packed Metro-North train headed for New York City. There were no available seats, so they stood in the middle of the car. Jena leaned against the train doors and stared out at the Hudson River as the train raced along it.

"It's too bad Mary couldn't make it," Ephraim said. He knew it was the wrong thing to say as soon as the words left his mouth.

"You didn't have to come."

"That's not what I meant. I meant . . . I guess she's still upset. About us."

Jena bit her lip and stared at the back of her book. She opened the back cover and looked at the last page.

"There's no 'us,' Ephraim. We're just friends."

"Right. Maybe I should talk to her?"

"At some point you have to stop blaming yourself for everything. Not all of this is your fault." She worried a page between her fingers, turning it back and forth, curling the corner of it over.

"Isn't it?" Ephraim asked.

"No. A lot of it is, of course. You screwed up, big time," she replied.

"Well, that does make me feel better," he said.

"But. You did the right thing in the end and you regret your mistakes. So stop beating yourself up over it. If you can't forgive yourself, how can you expect me to?"

Ephraim stuffed his hands into his pants pockets and stared down at his shoes. He'd shined them before he left, but they were already scuffed and dusty. He fiddled with the loose change in his pocket, but he still missed the comforting feel of the coin in his hand.

"Please stop acting like I'll break if you look at me the wrong way," she said.

He looked up. "Okay."

"I'm still angry with you, but I'm getting over it. We wouldn't be having this conversation otherwise."

"I just feel like I should do something. Now that I don't have the coin, I feel kind of . . . powerless."

"The coin wasn't the answer to your problems." Jena lowered her voice as a stout train conductor approached them. "You know that. It only made things worse," she said.

"Tickets, please," the conductor said. He sounded like one of the carnival barkers at the Westchester County Fair.

Jena tucked her book under an arm and rifled through her purse.

"Shoot," Ephraim said. "I didn't have time to buy one at the station."

The conductor thumbed through a yellow pad of tickets. "Fare's five dollars extra on board the train."

"*Five dollars?*" Ephraim said.

"Extra. The total is twelve dollars."

Jena handed over a small paper ticket. "You can use this for both of us," she said.

"Thanks," Ephraim said.

"Very generous. You're a lucky guy," the conductor said. He punched two holes in the ticket and handed them a torn strip of cardboard with zones marked on it. "Happy Fourth of July," he said, then moved off.

The train lurched into the Marble Hill station, and two seats opened up. Ephraim and Jena grabbed them. Jena turned to look out the window as the train pulled out.

"I'll buy the return ticket," Ephraim said.

She nodded, as though distracted. They rode in silence for a minute before she turned to him.

"Ephraim, you can't fix everything. You have to accept that you aren't responsible for anyone's decisions but your own." She leaned forward conspiratorially. He forced his eyes up to her face and looked at her lime-green cat-eye glasses. "But if you really want to help, there might be something you can do," she said.

"What's on your mind?"

She twisted her fingers together in her lap. "Look," she said. "I think . . . I think Nat's been hurting Shelley. I saw a bruise on her arm; she tried to hide it with makeup."

"She plays tennis, doesn't she?" Nathan had dragged Ephraim to the courts to watch more than one doubles match with the twins. He'd even convinced Ephraim to join the club with him in junior high, until they were practically driven out. Ephraim knew how hard those tennis balls hit off a powerful serve.

"Then why would she try to hide it?"

"Vanity? I don't know. I just wouldn't automatically assume that her boyfriend's abusing her without any proof."

"You've seen the way she acts around him. She hangs on his every word, does whatever he tells her. Sometimes I swear she acts like she's afraid of him."

"She may just really like him."

"If that's how you think someone acts when they like someone, you might be hopeless after all," Jena said. She faced the window again. "I know her, and something's wrong. I don't trust him. I know he was your friend, but . . ."

"That Nathan wasn't my friend," Ephraim said. "If he's hurt Shelley . . . shouldn't we just ask her?"

"She denies it."

"What does Mary think?" he asked.

"She hates Nat. But she hasn't seen him hurt her, either."

"So what do you think I can do about this?"

"Guys talk about girls, don't they?" Jena said.

"I assume about as much as girls talk about guys," Ephraim replied. "But Nathan barely talks to me now. Certainly not about Shelley. Maybe you should ask one of his football buddies." The thought of Nathan hanging out with Michael Gupal sent a shiver down his spine. It highlighted just how much Ephraim had messed things up.

"You know him better than anyone. How long were you friends?"

"Ten years. But that might as well have been someone else."

"Still. If you spend some time with him, you could bring her up. You were dating her sister, after all; compare notes or something equally disgusting. Do you know him well enough to tell when he's lying?"

Ephraim nodded. "I think so," he said.

The truth was, he'd been afraid to try to strike up a friendship with Nathan again. Seeing him so changed only made the loss of his friendship hurt more. It deepened his guilt. He was in no hurry to force the issue.

"What are we going to do if it turns out he is hitting her?" Ephraim asked.

Jena scowled. "I'd start by figuring out how to break them up," she said.

"And if he isn't hurting her?"

"Don't you see? If they break up, Mary gets her sister back, you have a chance to get your friend back"—she wrinkled her nose—"and I get both my best friends back. And maybe if you help, that'll convince Mary that you aren't such an asshole too. We all win."

"Seems like you have other reasons for resenting their relationship. Even if we could end it, I don't know if we should. Especially if Shelley's happy with him." If he still knew Nathan at all, he was happy with her, and Ephraim didn't want to take that away from him. He hoped that Nathan was innocent.

"So you won't help?" she asked.

Ephraim loosened his tie. "I'm just being cautious, that's all. I'm trying not to force people to change—as you know, that only causes trouble. But I'll try. I'll talk to Nathan, for what good it will do. If I have the opportunity."

Jena turned to him again. "Thanks, Ephraim. I appreciate it."

Her face brightened. "Hey, after the show you should come over for the *Twilight Zone* marathon. They run it every year on the Syfy Channel."

"Haven't you seen them all?" he asked. He'd noticed rows of DVDs of the old series on the shelves in her living room.

"I have, but that's not the point. I haven't seen them with *you* yet," she said.

Jena didn't mention Ephraim's promise again, which he thought was a sign that she at least trusted him to take care of the situation. It wasn't that he'd forgotten about it, he was just putting it off. Soon a week had passed, and he still hadn't come up with a plan to broach the subject with Nathan. Then Nathan made it easier for him—he came looking for Ephraim first.

That morning, Ephraim got off the bus at the stop in front of Greystone Park and found Nathan seated in the shelter. Nathan hadn't ridden a bus since he could drive, and he made no move to get on the bus now. He just sat there with his legs spread out and his arms crossed over his chest. It was obvious that he'd been waiting for Ephraim.

Nathan seemed less imposing than the last time Ephraim had seen him—less like a jock and more like his old friend. Was it possible the effects of the coin could wear off with time? The idea filled Ephraim with hope. Nathan's long blond hair was flat, with strands plastered to his sweaty forehead and neck. He wore his familiar wire-rimmed glasses, perched on the end of his nose. The one big difference was about two days of stubble that made him look a little older than his sixteen years.

"Hey, Nathan. Nat. How's it going?" Ephraim said.

Nathan's eyes bore into him. "Ephraim. It's good to see you again."

"I've been hoping to catch up with you."

"Yeah. I've been around."

"So, uh . . . how are you and Shelley doing?" Ephraim said.

Nathan blinked. "Mary Shelley's . . . fine," he said hesitantly.

"I know you fantasize about both of them, but I was referring to your girlfriend." Nathan must have been really out of it today. Usually he couldn't shut up about Shelley.

Nathan laughed. "Oh, yeah. Of course. You know how it is, I think of them as one person sometimes. But *Shelley*. Yeah, she's great."

Ephraim swallowed. "It's just that Jena said she saw a nasty bruise on Shelley's arm. Do you know what caused it?"

Nathan cocked his head back and eyed Ephraim. He laughed. "You think I hit her," Nathan said.

"Did you?" Ephraim asked.

"Why would I? I love her."

"I don't know."

Nathan's eyes widened. "What if I did hurt her? What would you do? Punish me? Use your magic coin?"

"Don't get so defen—" Ephraim stared at Nathan. "I thought you didn't remember the coin."

Nathan laughed again, but it sounded hollow. Mean. "You haven't been using it lately."

How did he know that? "We don't need the coin," Ephraim said. "You have what you want. I have what I want." Or at least a chance at getting it, if he didn't screw things up again.

"But I want more," Nathan said.

Nathan stood and advanced toward Ephraim. Ephraim stumbled backward.

"Friends share things." Nathan paced back and forth. "Friends help each other. Aren't you my friend, Eph?"

"I used to be. I'm not sure anymore," he said. "Not since that last wish."

Nathan's eyes looked half-crazed. "No time for me now that you have Jena."

"I don't 'have' her. She barely tolerates me. And you're one to talk, the way you've been spending all your time with Shelley." Nathan hadn't even remembered his friendship with Ephraim before, but now he had that memory back too. Unless he had just been pretending not to remember for some reason . . .

Nathan paced inside the three walls of the bus shelter like a caged animal, constantly in motion. If he was trying to intimidate Ephraim, it was working.

"You replaced me first. You intentionally excluded me from your wish when you told Jena about the coin," Nathan said.

How did he know what had happened after he was left behind? He shouldn't have realized things were ever any different. Ephraim stared straight at Nathan. Something wasn't right.

"So? I told her about the coin," Ephraim said. "I decided to be honest with her, the way I should have been from the beginning. The wishes we made . . . they affected more than just the two of us. We were wrong to make them."

"You betrayed me, Ephraim. Abandoned me." Nathan leaned close. Sweat beaded on his face. A drop hovered there for a moment then fell from his bristly chin.

"What happened to you, Nathan? I want my friend back," Ephraim said.

"No you don't. I know you pitied me. You think you're better than me. I was your *sidekick*," Nathan replied.

"What do you want me to say?" Ephraim asked.

"It's not what I want you to say. It's what I want you to do." Nathan looked around. "I'm getting bored here. I want you to make one more wish for me."

Ephraim balled his hands. "I can't."

"Don't fuck with me, Ephraim."

"It's not that I won't help you. I can't. The coin is gone," Ephraim said.

Nathan's face contorted with anger. "Gone where?"

"I got rid of it."

"You wouldn't throw away the only thing you had going for you. The only thing that makes her interested in you." He jerked his head at the library. Ephraim saw Jena through the glass doors, reading at the circulation desk.

"I wished it away." Ephraim stood and tried to push past Nathan but Nathan grabbed his shoulders in surprisingly strong hands and held him fast.

"You couldn't have. Don't lie to me. Not to *me*. Not again. Where's the coin?"

"It's gone back wherever it came from," Ephraim said quietly. Nathan stared at him, his face an inch from Ephraim's, then finally let him go.

Nathan stomped the length of the bus shelter, then whirled around again. "I don't believe you," he said. He fumbled in his back pocket and pulled out a folded piece of paper. He flung it at Ephraim's feet. Ephraim picked it up and opened it.

It was a grainy digital printout of a photograph. It showed a body on a metal cart with a sheet pulled down from his face. The face was torn and bloody, but familiar—very familiar. Ephraim was looking at himself.

"What?" Ephraim asked. The paper fluttered in his shaking hand.

"It isn't my best work. I didn't have time to get an artistic shot—I was in a hurry. The lighting was poor in that hospital morgue."

"This is the body they found? The one they thought was me?"

How could Nathan have taken this photograph when he hadn't even known about the body until Ephraim told him about it, *after* it had disappeared?

But Ephraim *had* thought Nathan was there that night, right by the door to the morgue. Why would he have gone down there? Why would he have pretended he didn't know anything about it until now?

"This is just another one of your faked Photoshop pics," Ephraim said lightly.

"It was you, Ephraim. And it will be again if I don't get what I want," Nathan said. "But it doesn't have to happen that way. I'd like us to be friends again instead. We make a good team."

"Threats aren't very friendly."

Nathan smiled. "Eph, you know I couldn't—wouldn't—hurt you." He put his hands in his pockets and started walking into the park. "Your friends, on the other hand . . ."

"What are you implying?"

"If you told Jena everything about the coin, I'm betting she knows where you're hiding it. And I won't take no for an answer from her. Think about that." Nathan turned on the path and disappeared from view.

Ephraim had to warn Jena. He ran toward the library.

He used to think he could beat Nathan in a fight if it ever came to it, but since the coin had rearranged his life, he couldn't be sure of anything. Nathan had managed to take down Michael Gupal, so he was anything but a pushover.

Nathan was right, too—Ephraim had looked down on him. If he hadn't been embarrassed of their friendship, he would have brought him to Jena's party when all of this started.

Worst of all, he was beginning to regret giving up the coin. It was the only thing he could have bargained with—but more importantly, it was probably the only way he could have returned Nathan to normal. If his friend weren't gone for good already.

Jena looked up as he rushed into the library.

"You're early," she said.

He took a moment to catch his breath and steadied himself by holding onto the circulation desk. His hands were shaking.

"Ephraim, what's wrong?" Jena asked.

"Everything," he said.

CHAPTER 18

Jena made Ephraim sit behind the desk until he calmed down. He waited for her to check out books for a few patrons, growing increasingly impatient and uneasy. He kept his attention on the sliding glass doors at the entrance. Though he doubted Nathan would confront them at the library in the middle of the day, he still jumped every time someone came in.

Jena finally came back from assisting an elderly woman with a computer and sat beside Ephraim.

"What happened?" she said. "You're a mess."

"I just spoke to Nathan," he said.

"And?"

"He says he isn't hitting Shelley. He loves her."

Jena frowned. "Do you believe him?"

"No. But I actually think we have a bigger problem right now. Jena, he asked me about the coin."

"That's strange," Jena said. "I thought he forgot about it because you weren't in contact with him during that wish?"

"He did. He couldn't have been pretending all this time. So what made him suddenly remember it?"

"Whatever the reason, isn't this a good thing? That means he's your friend again, right?"

"He might remember our friendship, but he's definitely not normal. Not the way he used to be. I've never seen him like that," Ephraim said.

He had never been afraid of his friend before. It was disturbing to see him so different . . . so angry. Nathan's reckless movements and body language seemed to hint at barely controlled violence, and had Ephraim worried for him. What had happened to Nathan?

Ephraim was less afraid of Nathan hurting him than he was of what Nathan might do to Jena if he didn't get what he wanted.

"He gave me this," Ephraim said. He handed Jena the folded picture of his body in the morgue. She stared at it for a long time, her eyes wide. Then she put it on the counter face down and slid it away from them.

"So it really happened like you said," she said. "I mean, I believed you before, but now we know there was another you."

He nodded.

"Is this picture a threat?" she asked.

"What else could it be? But that's not what worries me. He threatened you, too. I'm sorry to drag you into this, Jena. I won't let him hurt you."

She took a deep breath. "I appreciate the protectiveness, but don't you worry about me. He's just trying to get to you because he knows you have a hero complex. What's he after, anyway?"

"The coin," Ephraim said.

"Didn't you tell him you wished it away?"

"He thinks I'm lying. He said I'd never get rid of it because . . ." He looked at her. "Because it was the only way I could get you to like me."

"See? He doesn't know what he's talking about," she said. "Getting rid of it was the only way to get me to like you." Jena smiled. And just like that, Ephraim felt a little better already.

"Even so, I think we should be careful for now. There's really no telling what he might do."

"He's a coward, Ephraim. That picture is the worst he can do to you, and he knows that. That's why he's trying to scare you."

"Trying? He succeeded," Ephraim said.

"I'll keep looking over my shoulder if it will make you feel better."

"I'd like to work the circulation desk today . . . I could use the practice." He would feel better out in the open where he could see

Nathan and Nathan could see him, rather than in the back some-where putting away books, worrying about Jena's safety.

She searched his face. "You just want to get out of reorganizing the periodicals, I bet." She stood up and looked toward the entrance. "Thanks for watching out for me."

He smiled.

"On the bright side, now I have good reason to warn Shelley to stay away from him," Jena said. "If Nat's starting to threaten people, he's definitely not good boyfriend material."

By the end of the day, Jena was as worked up as Ephraim was. She hadn't been able to get hold of Shelley or Mary all afternoon.

At closing, they locked the entrance, and Ephraim shut down the computers while Jena checked all the rooms and turned off the lights. He jumped when someone pounded on the glass doors. He glanced over, praying it wasn't Nathan. Instead, he saw Mary and Shelley standing outside.

He hurried over and saw that Mary had her arms around her sister, practically holding her up. Shelley's eyes were red and puffy, her face splotchy and streaked with dark smudges. He fumbled the lock and stepped back as the automatic doors slid open.

"Are you all right?" Ephraim asked. He noticed a purple and yellow bruise on her forearm. It didn't look like a tennis ball had done that.

Mary looked at him. "Nat," she said. "He . . ."

"Did he do this to you, Shelley?" Ephraim said.

She closed her eyes. "Nat's dead."

Ephraim felt something cold clench in his stomach. "No. I just spoke to him this morning."

"So did I." She let out a choked sob. Ephraim took a helpless step toward her, uncertain of what to do. He waved them inside and led them over to a large table where Mary settled Shelley into a seat.

Ephraim sat across from them, stunned.

Nathan was dead. It seemed impossible. Ephraim ran over their last conversation in his mind. He hadn't known it would be the last time he'd see him. "Tell me what happened," he said, overriding his own feelings.

"He was shot," Shelley said.

"Shot? As in murdered?"

She nodded.

Ephraim took a deep breath. Given Nathan's erratic behavior, he'd thought he might have committed suicide. Somehow, this was easier to accept.

"He was shot from behind—" It was hard to understand her. She was practically gasping her words in between heaving sobs. "In . . . the . . . head . . ."

Ephraim stood up and walked around the table, because he couldn't just sit still. "Who would shoot Nathan? Why? He's never hurt anyone." He glanced at the bruise on her arm. He had to remember that this wasn't the same Nathan he'd grown up with. Who knew what this Nathan was mixed up in, or what he'd been capable of?

Jena emerged from the stairs behind the circulation desk. "Mary? Shelley? I tried to call you. Oh my God, what's wrong?"

"We've been at the police station all day," Mary said. She got up and pulled Jena away. They whispered together by the desk, glancing back at Shelley with concerned expressions. That left Ephraim with Shelley. He sat back down next to her.

Her head was bowed, and she was crushing the hem of her skirt in both hands. "He called me this morning," she said. "He wanted to meet at the bleachers behind the school after lunch."

"The bleachers? Why?" There was no game scheduled today.

Shelley swiped tears away from her face and avoided looking at him. "It was the only place we could be alone . . ." Oh. She meant *under* the bleachers.

"So you went to meet him."

She shivered. "It was horrible."

She'd been the one to find him, Ephraim realized. From recent experience, he knew how it felt to find someone you cared about near death.

"I'm so sorry," he said.

Shelley smoothed her skirt in her lap, then crushed the fabric again.

"Was anyone else around?" Ephraim asked. Sometimes there were joggers on the school track, and different sports teams always trained over the summer.

"I didn't see anyone," she said.

"So the question is, was he just unlucky, or was someone waiting for him there? A robbery?"

Summerside had its fair share of crime for a small city, but this didn't sound like a random act of violence, especially considering Nathan had seemed so agitated during their talk. But if it had been premeditated, how would the killer know where to find him? Unless he'd simply followed Nathan.

"They don't think it was a robbery. They found his wallet in his pocket, with cash and cards inside. His cell phone, too."

"Was he mixed up in anything bad?" Ephraim asked. "Drugs or something?"

"Of course not!"

Mary and Jena looked over in alarm. He held a hand up to show them it was all right.

"I'm sorry, Shelley. I don't mean to accuse him of anything. I want to know who did this as much as you do."

She sniffled and nodded.

Still, Nathan must have been worried about something. Maybe he even knew someone was after him. That could explain why he'd come to Ephraim for the coin that morning. If only Ephraim had been able to help Nathan, with or without magic.

"I can't believe he's gone," Ephraim said.

"I want him back," she said.

"Me too," he said.

Shelley leaned over. Her face was serious. "Then do something about it."

Ephraim stared at her. "Like what?"

"He said that if anything happened to him, I should come to you. That you'd know what to do. He told me to show you this." She reached into her purse then put something on the table. It was a quarter.

He picked it up and looked it over carefully, his pulse racing. It was just a regular coin as far as he could tell, not even one of the state quarters.

"That means something to you?" she said.

"It's just a quarter. You didn't think that was a strange thing for him to say?" Ephraim asked.

"Nat's a strange guy." She swallowed. "Was. But I cared about him."

"When did he tell you this?" he asked.

"That's the weird thing. The other weird thing." Shelley pulled out a crumpled up tissue and blew her nose into it. "The cops said that Nat died this morning. Between nine and eleven."

Ephraim nodded. "So?"

"He phoned me *this afternoon*. That's when he told me about the quarter. I have the record on my phone." She flipped open the screen and showed him. Sure enough, it showed a call from Nathan's home phone at 12:23 p.m. that day.

"So they got the time wrong. I'm sure it happens." They had to be wrong, because Ephraim had been talking to Nathan at just before ten in the morning.

"I don't think so. It didn't take me long to get to the school, and he was already dead when I got there." She heaved a sigh. "Something's going on, Ephraim."

"Nathan couldn't have called you after he died," Ephraim said.

"Of course not. I don't know why, but he thought it was really important that I talk to you. Like his life depended on it." She closed her eyes. When she opened them again, they were bright and fierce. "So if there's any chance you can do something, anything, you have to do it," Shelley said.

"That's crazy," Ephraim said. He considered the coin she'd given him. He didn't know what else to say. "I can't help him anymore."

"Bullshit." Shelley straightened. "Nathan didn't believe that and I don't either. When I pulled out that quarter you reacted to it. What does it mean?"

"Nathan's dead," he said.

"I know that!" Shelley took a breath and crossed her arms. "What if it had been Jena?"

"That wouldn't change the situation."

Ephraim curled his fingers around the quarter. But Shelley was right. He would do anything to save Jena.

He put the coin down on the table and looked Shelley in the eyes. "I'll try," he said. "That's all I can promise. But it might be too late."

"Try then. I don't need to know the details, but do whatever you have to. I know you won't let him down."

Mary and Jena came over. Ephraim met Jena's eyes as he gave his seat to Mary. He went to the circulation desk. He fiddled with Shelley's quarter, his mind spinning.

Ephraim lowered his head to his hands. None of the pieces seemed to fit in any way that made sense. If Nathan's time of death was sometime that morning, not only couldn't he have called Shelley in the afternoon, he should already have been dead during—or shortly following—his conversation with Ephraim by the park, clear on the other side of town from where his body was found. The cops had to be wrong about that much.

Which didn't alter the fact that Nathan was dead, whatever the circumstances. Ephraim could only think of one crazy solution to the crazy problem at hand.

Jena came over and stood behind him, her hand on his shoulder. He looked up. Mary and Shelley were gone.

"I'm sorry, Ephraim." Jena sounded like she'd been crying; her voice wavered as she spoke.

"Me too," he said.

Tears hadn't yet come for Ephraim. Nathan's death was slowly sinking in, but now that he had a plan, however unlikely, he wasn't quite ready to accept it.

She sniffled. "I know what you're thinking."

"What am I thinking?"

"That this is your fault."

"This is completely my fault. Maybe not directly, but it's all because of those wishes." He'd traced it all back, and he figured it out: he'd traded his mother's life for his best friend's.

"You don't know that for sure. Stop pitying yourself."

He showed her the quarter. "Shelley gave me this."

"She knows?"

He shook his head. "Nathan just sent it with her to give me a message only I would understand. He told her I could save him." He tapped the quarter against the counter, hitting it harder and harder. Jena put her hand over his to still it.

"That isn't an option."

Ephraim sighed. "I wonder."

"You sent it away. It disappeared. There's nothing you can do."

Ephraim flipped the quarter. "Whenever I made a wish, if I didn't flip the coin immediately, it got hotter. Like it was being 'activated,' like you said."

He scratched his chin with the edge of the quarter. He'd just remembered that night at the bus stop, when the homeless man had picked up the coin right after Ephraim made a wish and dropped it. The wish had been granted when the man handed it back to him—when it made contact with Ephraim's skin. "If the wish isn't granted until I flip the coin, and touch it, it could still be in the fountain."

"So maybe you have to touch the coin a second time to complete the wish? Ephraim, I don't know."

"You're right, I don't know that for sure. I don't really know anything about it. But I have to touch other people to include them in the wish too. Maybe the coin is contact-sensitive."

"That kind of makes sense. But even if it's still there, it'll be impossible to find. There are a lot of coins in that fountain."

"But there's a chance . . ."

"Ephraim, think about this. Really. Is this a good idea? You said you weren't going to change anything anymore. You promised. That's how you get trapped; there's always one more thing that you have to fix. What will you do if something happens to your mother again, or to m—you could just make things worse. Remember the monkey's paw!"

"I know. But none of this would have happened if I hadn't used the coin in the first place. I have to try," he said.

"Then I'm coming with you," she said. "It'll be faster if we both look."

CHAPTER 19

There was still half an hour of sunlight before the park closed. It was completely deserted, the tall columns lining the path cast long shadows over Ephraim and Jena. The fountain of Atlas loomed before them ominously in the plaza. They stood at the base and looked up into the bronze statue's face.

"I have a bad feeling about this," Ephraim said.

Jena gaped at him. "I can't believe you actually said that. What's wrong with you?"

"Sorry." He slipped out of his sneakers and peeled off his socks. Jena kicked off her yellow sandals. She climbed over the side of the fountain and sat on the edge, dipping her feet into the shallow water. She shrieked.

"It's cold!"

Ephraim followed her. It *was* cold. It froze his toes and lapped against his calves as he waded in. The bottom was slimy, and coins pressed into the soles of his feet. He walked gingerly halfway around the fountain, feeling on the verge of slipping the whole way. He pointed to an area near the platform at the statue's feet.

"I threw the coin over there and it bounced back . . ." He waved his hand over a rough arc near the center of the pool. "Kind of around here?"

They crouched in the water, sweeping their hands along the bottom of the pool and coming up with dripping handfuls of silver and copper coins. From a distance they'd always made him think of pirate treasure at the bottom of the sea.

"We should be organized about this," Jena said. She picked through the coins, scrutinizing each one and dropping the rejects into her open palm. She sloshed over to the side of the fountain and

167

dumped the handful over the side before returning for more. "If only we had some buckets," she said.

Ephraim blinked as a spray of water hit him from above. His shirt was already soaked. He looked over at Jena and saw that her dark-blue tank top was wet through, too. She caught him staring at the clinging fabric and splashed him in the face with water.

"Next time that'll be a handful of coins," she said.

"Right."

"I almost wore a white shirt today, too," she said, pulling the shirt away from her skin with a grimace. "You can wipe that smile off your face."

"I wish we could turn that water off," Ephraim said.

The gurgling water suddenly stopped, and the fountain sputtered off. "Well, how about that." He slicked his hair back and grinned.

"Ephraim! Don't wish for anything while we're handling coins. Get it?" Jena flicked her own damp hair away from her eyes. She rubbed her speckled glasses uselessly against her wet shirt. "I think that was just a coincidence. They turn the fountain off at night. Keep looking."

"Hey, do they have security in here at night?"

"The police are supposed to check the park, but I don't know how often they come by."

The man who had built Greystone Manor and the surrounding estate in the late 1800s had spent his fortune frivolously, then lost it all during the Depression. When he went bankrupt, the city took over his estate and turned it into a public park. It was on extended loan to the Summerside Public Library, which maintained the grounds. Kids still explored the abandoned buildings, and there'd been reports of weird rituals in the middle of the night—thus the prohibition against being in the park after dusk.

They continued methodically sorting through the quarters in the fountain, piling them out of the way on the side. If cops did catch them there, it would probably look like they were stealing.

After an hour they were working in twilight. They had cleared a good amount of coins from the base of the statue but still hadn't found the one they needed. Ephraim's fingers were numb from the cold, and the tips felt raw from scraping against the cement floor.

Ephraim called a break and sat on the edge of the fountain.

"My fingers are all wrinkly," Jena said. She pulled one foot into her lap and examined it. "My toes too."

"You're lucky. I can't even feel my toes anymore." Ephraim sighed. "Maybe the coin did disappear. We're wasting our time."

"Aw. Don't give up now," a voice said behind them.

Ephraim turned and saw a dark shape separate from the shadowed hedges around the fountain's plaza.

"Who's there?" Ephraim asked. He recognized the voice, but it couldn't be . . .

"My body's not even cold in the ground yet and you've forgotten me already. Then again, I can't say I blame you, considering the distraction. That's Jena, isn't it? Looking good." A wolf whistle cut through the darkness.

A flash went off, and Ephraim flinched. A bright green blob floated in his field of vision.

Nathan stepped into the circle of moonlight illuminating the plaza. He lowered his digital camera. Jena gasped.

Ephraim stared. "Nathan?"

"But you're dead," Jena said.

"I've come back to hauuunt youuuu . . ." Nathan grinned. He stuffed the camera into a back pocket of his jeans. "Just kidding. I wouldn't want one of you to piss yourselves in the fountain. That wouldn't be sanitary."

"He tricked me," Ephraim said to Jena. "He sent Shelley to tell me that he was dead, hoping that I'd bring him to the coin." He kicked some water out of the fountain.

"You're close, Eph," Nathan said.

"Did Nat have a twin?" Jena whispered. She stood behind

Ephraim now, one hand on his arm. Her palm was hot against his cold, wet skin.

"No, not that I know of. Why?"

"That isn't Nat," she said in a low voice. "He moves differently. His body isn't quite as built up. His hair's too long. Nat had short spiky hair, and it can't have grown to shoulder length in a day."

Now that Jena mentioned it, he saw it too: this couldn't be the same football player that Nathan had become thanks to the coin. He was leaner, for one—those broad shoulders and thick biceps couldn't disappear overnight. The angles of his cheekbones made him look meaner too, especially when he looked over his glasses at them. He wore a thin silver chain around his neck, a fitted black T-shirt, and black jeans. Ephraim had noticed the difference this morning, but he'd hoped Nathan was just gradually changing back to the way he used to be.

"Who the hell are you?" Ephraim said.

"I'm disappointed, Ephraim," Nathan said. "You're slower than your counterpart."

"What do you mean, my 'counterpart'?"

"It looks like Jena's figured it out, but then she's always been smarter than you." His eyes raked over her. "No luck finding it?" Nathan asked.

"Finding what?" Ephraim asked.

"You expect me to believe you guys are raiding the fountain for ice cream money?" he asked. "I want your 'wishing coin.' More specifically, I want you to use it to make a wish for me."

"We went over that this morning. That was you, wasn't it? The coin's gone," Ephraim said.

Ephraim eyed Nathan, wondering if he could take him down if he caught him by surprise. Or maybe they should just run. He tensed, waiting for Nathan to get close enough for him to jump him. Nathan caught the movement.

"Don't try anything," Nathan said. He reached back behind him and drew a pistol. Moonlight glinted off its dark barrel.

"Oh God." Jena's hand tightened around Ephraim's arm. Her fingernails dug into his skin. "That's real, isn't it?"

"Would you like to find out? If you don't get that coin and make a wish for me, you're going to end up just like this universe's Nathan."

Jena drew in a sharp breath. "I knew it!" she said. "There were two of him."

Ephraim stared at the other Nathan. "Why would you kill your own double?"

The other Nathan shrugged. "I asked him about the coin, but he said he didn't know anything about it. He was more useful to me dead."

"You killed him . . . then you called Shelley and told her about the coin and asked her to meet you, so she would find the body." Ephraim said, putting the pieces together.

"Knowing that once she told Ephraim, he would come looking for the coin." Jena groaned.

"This was a set-up." Ephraim said.

"I knew you would go after the coin, for the sake of your best friend," Nathan continued. "And here we are." .

"I wasn't lying before. I wished it away."

"If you really believed that, you wouldn't be searching for it." Nathan said. He leaned against a lamp post and swept the gun out in a wide arc. "Please, keep at it. But if I hear the words 'I wish' coming out of your mouth, I'll shoot you. Trust me, I have fast instincts and I'm a good shot. I've had a lot of target practice."

"I hope he's referring to video games," Jena muttered. Nathan chuckled. Ephraim and Jena stepped back into the fountain and scooped up more coins.

"Jena?" Nathan said.

She turned and glared at him.

"Your shirt's wet," he said. "I wouldn't want you to catch a cold. Why don't you take it off."

When she didn't move, Nathan pulled back the safety hammer of the gun and calmly leveled it at her. She glared, but she pulled off her shirt. Ephraim looked away and stared down into the water, silently fuming.

"Victoria's Secret?" Nathan pulled out his camera in his left hand and flashed a picture one-handed.

Jena threw her wet shirt at him, but it fell short. "Asshole," she said.

"Just be thankful I'm only shooting pictures." He held up the gun in his other hand.

She hunched over, trying to hide her breasts with her arms while she awkwardly groped around for quarters. A bra strap slipped down over her shoulder, and she cursed.

"How could there be two Nathans?" Ephraim whispered to her. The camera flash went off again.

Jena bit her lip. "He's a doppelganger," she said.

"A doppelganger?"

"It's like a double, a twin. They can be ghosts or shadows or invaders from a parallel universe. Classically, they're a sign of bad luck. Or death."

"The gun tipped me off on that one. So the kid in the morgue, the photo that Nathan showed me . . . that really was me. It was my doppelganger?"

Jena nodded. "That nixes my time travel theory, at least."

"This second Nathan showed me that picture of my dead . . . doppelganger. So he's probably been hanging around since he died." Ephraim had even seen him at the hospital that night. Suddenly Ephraim had an explanation for all the times he had spotted Nathan where he couldn't have been, sometimes in two places at once. This Nathan was the one who beat up Michael Gupal while Ephraim's Nathan was trapped in the locker. This Nathan had been spying on Ephraim at Jena's party. "I wonder if they're both from the same universe, the same place the coin came from."

"Hey. Enough talking," Nathan called.

Jena nodded. She reached up and straightened her bra strap. Ephraim averted his eyes again.

"Why didn't I see it before? We even got a picture of him in the park!" he said. He splashed his hand into the water. "Dammit! I bet he's been following me ever since I found the coin."

"If he's actually from a parallel universe, there is no 'real' Nat. They're all real—just different from each other." Jena pushed her wet glasses up her nose excitedly. "This is really big. We have evidence that the multi-world hypothesis is true!"

"I said shut up!" Nathan shouted.

"What's the matter, are your ears burning?" Jena said.

"Don't *taunt* him," Ephraim said. He turned to Nathan. "We're trying our best, but there are a lot of coins in here. They all look the same."

They moved around the fountain, sifting through coins with increasing desperation. Ephraim knew their time was running out. When they drew close again, Jena whispered.

"Are you thinking what I'm thinking?" she said.

"That we're screwed?"

"Besides that. The coin comes from a parallel universe, right? At first I thought it might be from a world where magic works like science, because of different physical properties in its universe. But now I don't think it was granting your wishes at all."

Nathan cleared his throat. "I can see I'm going to have to break you two up. Jena, come here."

Jena stood up and crossed her arms over her chest. "I'm *not* taking my bra off."

Nathan shrugged. "Nothing I haven't seen before."

Jena waded to the edge of the fountain and glared at Nathan. "What's that supposed to mean?"

"Ephraim," Nathan said. "The sooner you find that coin, the less fun I can have with your girlfriend."

Ephraim increased his speed, picking up quarters and shoving them into the pockets of his shorts when they turned out to be ordinary. When they filled to overflowing, he walked with leaden legs to dump them over the side of the fountain.

Five minutes later he noticed a warm current of water as he swept his hand along the slimy bottom. He moved his hand back and forth, palm flat like a metal detector over a patch of sand. Yes, it was definitely warmer over there.

He advanced inch by inch toward the source, his hand outstretched. He was getting closer.

Nathan yawned. "What are you doing, Ephraim?"

"I'm trying!" Ephraim said.

"You aren't stalling, hoping someone will discover us, are you?"

"No!"

"Maybe you just need more motivation." He pointed the gun at Jena.

"Nathan, don't—"

A gunshot rang out and Jena's body jerked. Ephraim flinched.

She couldn't have been hit. Nathan wouldn't really kill her. That was only a warning shot, or the gun was loaded with blanks. It had to be a replica, one of those movie props, to psyche them out into giving him what he wanted.

This wasn't happening.

Jena spun around and looked at Ephraim, her face white as the moon. Blood ran down between her breasts. She lifted a hand to the wound in her chest and opened her mouth, then pitched face-forward into the water.

"Jena!" Ephraim dropped the coins he'd been cupping in his hands and stumbled toward her. Nathan stepped up to the fountain edge and aimed the gun at him.

"Stop right there, Ephraim."

"But Jena . . . she still might be—"

"She's gone, buddy. The only way to save her is to find that coin. Then *maybe* I'll let you 'wish' her back to life." He laughed.

Ephraim waited for Jena to move, but she didn't. Her body floated in the shallow water, with a red cloud spreading around it. The damp air was tinged with a metallic scent that nearly made him gag.

Nathan's camera flashed against the water's surface.

"You bastard." Ephraim tensed. "You didn't have to—"

"Find it, Ephraim. Or I'll shoot you next."

Ephraim clenched his fists and held his arms straight at his sides, his eyes locked on Jena. He couldn't move even if he wanted to. He watched for the slightest sign that she was still there, that she was just pretending, so she could surprise Nathan, or. . . . He willed her to be alive. She had to be.

But Jena couldn't hold her breath underwater for this long, and there weren't any air bubbles as the water around her grew darker and darker and slowly billowed toward him. The numbness in Ephraim's submerged feet froze every part of his body.

Nathan cocked the gun again, a sharp sound that broke Ephraim's paralysis.

"You won't kill me," Ephraim said hoarsely. He swallowed the lump in his throat. "I know I'm the only one who can use the coin." His Nathan hadn't been able to before, at least.

"I'll shoot your knees so you can't walk. How's that sound?"

"Go ahead." Ephraim's voice trembled. He breathed in and out. In and out. He spoke the next words strong and clear. "You've already killed my two best friends. You can't hurt me any worse than that."

"Oh, have you forgotten about Maddy? I haven't."

Ephraim snapped his attention to Nathan and took a step forward. Nathan didn't even flinch. His gun was trained on Ephraim's knees, his left hand bracing his right wrist the way he held the controller when they were playing a shooting game. The psychotic grin on his face told Ephraim that Nathan would do it. He was vicious enough to shoot Ephraim's mother. If Ephraim were going to rush him, he'd better be sure he could win the fight without getting himself incapacitated or killed.

"Shit," Ephraim said.

He turned away from Jena's lifeless body, but he could still see her drifting in front of him, even through the tears blinding his vision. He wiped his eyes with the palm of his hand, pressing so hard he saw bright spots flare. But he still saw Jena.

Ephraim crouched with his back to Nathan and pressed his hands to the fountain's bottom with renewed urgency. The water was so hot in this spot he was surprised it wasn't boiling. He patted around as if he were looking for a lost contact lens. He must be close.

He squinted through the dark water. George Washington's head wavered before him like a mirage, luminous in the moonlight. The coin had landed on heads after his last toss. Ephraim smiled.

"I have it," he said.

"Bring it here," Nathan said.

"I don't think so." Ephraim picked up the coin, wincing as he closed his hand around the burning metal. He stood and turned to face Nathan.

Ephraim felt a twinge in his stomach. The air rippled around him.

"What's—?" Nathan started. He launched himself at Ephraim. They collided and fell backward in a tangle of limbs.

And slammed into hard concrete.

In an instant everything was different. Ephraim was lying on the now dry bottom of the fountain, his back screaming with pain. He was too winded to move.

Nathan groaned and dragged himself to his feet beside Ephraim. "Ow," he said. "Fuck." He retrieved his gun and kicked Ephraim in the side. Ephraim twisted over and curled to protect himself.

Nathan pulled out a cell phone and flipped it open as he stumbled out of the fountain.

Ephraim lay there for a while, trying to force air back into his lungs. Finally he sat up painfully. Water dripped from Ephraim's wet clothes, forming a brackish puddle around him. His face was wet too, but not from fountain water.

The granite bottom of the fountain was cracked and pitted; instead of coins it was filled with garbage, crushed soda cans, cigarette butts, and broken glass. The statue of Atlas was nearly black with tarnish.

Nathan was gone. So was Jena's body.

Ephraim stood shakily and leaned on the rim of the fountain for support.

"Ephraim!" A voice shouted behind him. It was a very familiar voice, the one he wanted to hear more than anything in the world. But it couldn't be. He turned and saw Jena running toward the fountain with a wide grin on her face. She was alive!

"I knew you'd be back," she said. Before he could speak, she planted her lips against his, and he didn't think about anything else.

She pushed him away and put her hand against her mouth. "You're not him." She had been on the verge of tears, but now anger flashed across her face.

"Jena, it's me," he said.

She scowled. "*Jena?* Shit."

"What? What's wrong?"

"My name is Zoe. Zoe Kim."

She wasn't Jena. Her hair was long, loose around her shoulders. She wore dark red lipstick and a white tank top. She had a tiny silver stud in her nose, but even more striking than that was seeing her for the first time without glasses. He suddenly noticed her eyes were blue, not brown. She must be Jena's doppelganger in this universe.

Ephraim was in a different universe.

"What happened to my Ephraim?" she said.

"Huh?"

"If you're here, where did you leave him?"

"It's a long story." Ephraim glanced around the park, suddenly paranoid. Every shadow seemed menacing. An image flashed in his mind of Nathan watching them from the bushes. "Can we discuss this somewhere else?"

"Not until you tell me what happened." She crossed her arms.

"Nathan's probably not far from here, and he's armed."

"Nate." She spit the word out then actually spit onto the dirty and cracked cobblestones. "He came back? Ephraim was going to ditch him in another universe."

"He hitched a ride on the wish that brought me here." She looked puzzled. "He's trying to get the coin, to get me to use it for him. He just killed . . ." He choked on the words and sat on the edge of the fountain. He couldn't tell Zoe that he'd just seen her, or even someone who looked like her, die right in front of him while he did nothing. He stared at the puddle of water forming around his feet. Surely he was imagining that it had a reddish tint. He shuddered.

Zoe's face sobered. "You can tell me about it on the way to my place," she said.

Ephraim dropped the coin into the fountain, crossed his arms over his knees and doubled over. He couldn't move, he was exhausted of all this. He kept seeing Jena's body. He shouldn't have brought her along with him. He should have listened to her when she told him not to go after the coin. He'd been trying to help Nathan, and he'd ended up losing two friends.

"Hey." Zoe crouched and picked up the coin. She brushed it off and looked at it with a concerned frown. "I know you're confused. You've obviously been through a lot."

"You have no idea," he said.

"But you really don't have time for a breakdown."

"Just give me a minute."

"You're stronger than this, Ephraim." She pressed the coin into his palm and closed her hand over his. Her grip was firm and reassuring. She gave him a tender look then stood, pulling him up with her.

He looked her in the eyes. Her *blue* eyes, reminding him that she wasn't Jena no matter how much she resembled her. "How do you know? We don't even know each other."

"I know because my Ephraim wouldn't take all of this sitting down. Now let's go." She looked down at his still bare feet. "Don't people wear shoes where you come from?"

CHAPTER 20

Ephraim followed Jena—no, *Zoe*—in a daze. She seemed to be sticking to darkened side streets. It was only ten at night, and downtown Summerside was completely deserted.

"Where is everyone?"

"It's after curfew," Zoe said.

He stared at her blankly.

"Kids here aren't allowed out after sundown." She stopped him on a street corner, and they waited for the light to change. "We have to be careful."

"That seems a little extreme."

"We're at war. They say it's for our own safety."

"Um. Who are we fighting?"

"Iraq, Iran, North Korea. The USSR is getting in on it, too."

"You mean Russia?"

"And the rest of the Soviet Union. Which means China probably won't be far behind." That sounded like the beginning of a third World War.

Ephraim stepped off the curb into the street—

Zoe grabbed his arm and pulled him back just as a car sped past from his right, barely a foot in front of him. Its horn blared, and it squealed to a stop half a block away, its brake lights glowing like red eyes.

"Are you trying to get yourself killed?" Zoe said. The car door opened, and someone shouted after them.

"Hell. Come on!" Zoe said.

She grabbed his hand, and they ran across the street to duck into the shadowed entranceway of a building. Ephraim grunted as he stepped on broken concrete. Running in bare feet on pavement hurt.

"That car came out of nowhere!" he said.

"Didn't your mother teach you to look both ways before crossing the street?" Zoe asked.

"I did look, but that car was on the wrong side of the street," he replied.

"You still don't get it? This isn't your universe. Things are different here," Zoe said. She sighed. "Just be more careful."

She started moving again, and Ephraim followed her down the sidewalk, nervously darting looks to his left and right. He saw another car pass them, also on the wrong side of the street. The driver was behind a wheel on the passenger side of the car, like in Europe.

Ephraim tagged along silently, chewing her words over and over in his mind. *This isn't your universe.* Jena's multi-world theory was right, then. He was in a parallel universe where cars drove on the other side of the street, and there was a city-wide curfew, and the United States was stuck on the losing side of a war. And Jena called herself Zoe.

He stared at her as they walked, wondering what else was different here. This universe had another Nathan—Nate. And there'd been another Ephraim, too.

"Here we are," Zoe said.

Zoe's house looked more or less like he remembered it, perhaps a bit more weather-worn. The front lawn was parched and dead, her mother's prized flowers long overrun by weeds. Zoe pulled out a key ring and started unlocking the door. It looked like there were four separate sets of locks.

Zoe put a hand on Ephraim's chest. Her fingernails were short and unpainted. "You have to be quiet. My dad's girlfriend is over tonight." The silver stud in her nose flashed in the porchlight. It was kind of sexy.

"His girlfriend? What happened to your mother?"

Zoe's face crumpled.

"Oh no. I shouldn't have said—"

"Never mind. You didn't know. We'll sort all of this out in a minute. Just be quiet. We're going up to my room, and my dad doesn't like it when I bring boys home."

"How often does that happen?" Ephraim asked.

"Well. He doesn't like it when I bring *you* home. Ever since he caught us . . ." Zoe looked away.

"Um." Ephraim clamped his mouth shut and followed Zoe upstairs. He felt so lost in this universe.

Ephraim halted at the bottom of the steps, struck by a disturbing thought. If the coin was powerful enough to transport him to a parallel universe, maybe it had done it before.

Maybe it had done it every time he made a wish.

That's what Jena had been trying to tell him just before she was killed.

"Crap," Ephraim said. He felt a bit dizzy.

"Shhh," Zoe said, her hand on his arm.

As they crept around the landing on the second floor, Ephraim heard a woman giggling in a room by the stairs. Zoe rolled her eyes and pushed him past the door to her bedroom at the end of the hall. She closed and locked her bedroom door behind them.

"I've only seen his new girlfriend once," Zoe said. "I think she teaches art classes at a community college in the city. Or maybe she *takes* classes there. She doesn't look much older than me." She wrinkled her nose in disgust.

Zoe flopped down on the bed, and Ephraim stood, wondering what he should do. She stuck her foot out and pointed at the desk chair with her toes.

He looked around the room, wondering if it was any different from Jena's room, since he'd never seen it before. From the books piled up on every available surface, most of the stacks almost as tall as him, he saw that Zoe had something in common with her counterpart.

"Have you read all of these?" Ephraim said.

"Not yet. But I'm working my way through them." She pointed

to one stack and smiled. "That's August." She pointed to the one next to it. "September." Her hand swept around the room in an arc. "October, November, December. Not much else to do around here these days, especially since Eph took off." She cleared her throat.

"Did you rob a bookstore?" Ephraim said.

"The Summerside Public Library ran out of funding. I rescued those before they closed. Like an extended loan." She looked at him soberly. "I know you have a lot of questions, but I have to ask one first. It's important."

Ephraim nodded.

"Do you know what happened to my Ephraim? If you're here, he must have come to your world and given you the coin."

Ephraim lowered his eyes. "I never actually saw him in person, but . . . I'm sorry."

Zoe closed her eyes and tears welled up under her long eyelashes.

"He was hit by a bus," Ephraim said.

"That's so stupid," she said. "He'd been to so many different worlds. He knew how to survive."

"I guess you two were . . . close."

She only nodded.

"Jena, I—"

"It's *Zoe*." Her voice was hard. She swiped the back of her hand across her face and with one last sniffle she composed herself. "Don't call me that again."

"You just look so much like her. I have to remind myself you're a different person."

"I know what you mean." She scratched her nose, just above the tiny silver piercing. "My dad was going to name me Jena, but my mom preferred Zoe. She died during labor, so."

"I didn't know." Maybe he should stop talking. Everything he said only seemed to make her more upset.

"You're going to have to get used to a lot of new things in this universe."

"I don't plan to be here long enough for that."

Ephraim pulled out the coin. He was shocked to see that the metal surface of it was blank. He turned it over. It was smooth on both sides. It wasn't a coin anymore, just a thin metal disc, though it retained its reeding, the grooved lines along the edge.

He felt like his heart had stopped. "It's game over," he said.

"What?"

He showed her the coin.

"Oh, right," she said. "I noticed that when you appeared in the fountain."

"So it's gone blank like this before?"

"Not that I've ever seen."

Ephraim squeezed the coin. Maybe it didn't have unlimited wishes after all. If he'd used the last one, he was stuck here.

"But I only got a good look at it a couple of times," Zoe said. "My Ephraim . . ." Her voice caught and she swallowed. "Ephraim and Nate never let me into their little boys-only club. It was always a coin when I saw it."

"So why does it look like this now?"

"Your guess is as good as mine. It could be out of juice. They used to talk about charging it up."

He turned it over in his hand. Maybe a better question was why it had looked like a quarter in the first place. "Is Puerto Rico a state here?" he asked.

Zoe shook her head. "Just a territory. We don't even have quarters like that, with the war going on and all."

That meant the coin probably didn't originate in this universe either. But then why did it bring him here when he wished for it to go back where it had come from?

"I wish I were back home," Ephraim said, wishing harder than he ever had before. The coin didn't even heat up. He flipped the coin and caught it, but as he expected, nothing happened except for Zoe gaping at him.

"Out of power," he said. "Or broken." He didn't even want to think about that. Maybe it had been underwater for too long, or been damaged when he and Nate crashed into the fountain.

"Why did you flip the coin?" Zoe asked.

"That's how I was told to use it. To make my wish come true."

Zoe laughed. "You thought it was granting *wishes?*"

The coin wasn't heating up, but his face was getting warm from embarrassment. "I found a note . . ." Even though he'd figured out that Nate had left it in his locker, he didn't know why Nate would want him to learn how to use the coin. And he obviously couldn't trust anything Nate told him. "Forget it," Ephraim said.

"You really have no idea what you have there," Zoe said.

"Now I know the coin—or whatever it really is—was bumping me into parallel universes." Only because Jena had figured it out, of course, but he wasn't about to admit that to Zoe. "But at first I thought it was magic. That's how it was advertised."

Zoe laughed. "I'm sorry. I shouldn't be laughing. There's a popular saying, that 'any sufficiently advanced technology is indistinguishable from magic.' At least, to simple minds." She cast him a sly glance.

"If you know so much about it, why don't you enlighten me?" he asked.

"I only know stuff I picked up here and there, when the guys let something slip. I didn't even realize you could activate the coin without the controller," Zoe said. "But I suppose my Ephraim must have figured that out."

"There's a controller too? What does that do?"

She rolled her eyes. "What do you think the 'controller' does?"

Ephraim bit his lip in annoyance.

"Sorry," she said. "It's a small device." She held her hands up and connected her index fingers and thumbs in a rectangle. "It could be mistaken for a cell phone, but it stores numbers for different universes, wherever the coin has been. Like quantum GPS coordinates,

I suppose. And it controls where the coin takes you. It must charge it, too. It's been a while since the coin was plugged in, and you've been using it a lot, I assume."

Ephraim groaned. Every wish he made must have taken him to a random parallel universe, since the coin hadn't received specific coordinates. He'd been using it blindly and draining its battery, if it had one.

"How am I supposed to get home?" he asked.

"I'm sure the controller still has the coordinates for your universe. And I bet it can recharge the coin, too."

It seemed Ephraim needed the controller to leave this universe, but he doubted Nate would jump at the chance to help him unless Ephraim helped *him* first.

"So how did your Ephraim work the coin?" he asked.

"I saw them leave once. They didn't know I was watching. Ephraim slid the coin into the controller, then Nate did something to it. Then Ephraim took the coin back and they disappeared. I didn't quite buy that they were visiting other realities until I saw it for myself."

"But the coin shifted me to other universes without the controller, and Nate followed me to them without the coin. How?"

"No idea. They always worked as a team." Zoe arched her back and stretched, causing Ephraim to lose his train of thought. She sat up and crossed her legs Indian style, curling her toes toward herself. "But I know who would know more about all this," she said.

"I don't think Nate's going to volunteer any info."

"Not him. He and Ephraim got the device from someone else: some man approached them in the park. And yes, I thought that was skeevy too."

"Some guy just handed them the power to travel to parallel universes?"

"They thought he was homeless and crazy, of course, but they humored him. And it turned out he was telling the truth. Or maybe we're the crazy ones." She shrugged. "I don't know if he's still around, though. They avoided the park after that and never mentioned him again."

"How do I find him?"

"I'd start at Greystone Park."

Ephraim stood and paced, passing the blank coin from hand to hand while he worked it all out.

"The coin has only worked for me so far. I know, because my friend Nathan tried it, and so did Jena. If it's keyed to my touch, that means Nate can't use it either, which he knows. So he needs me or one of my duplicates if he wants to visit any more universes, now that we're both here and I can't leave without him." He stopped and looked at Zoe expectantly.

"The same goes for you," Zoe said. "I know what you're thinking, but even if you had the controller, Nate's the only one who can operate it. And getting it from him won't be easy. He carries it all the time."

If Ephraim could steal the controller, maybe he could at least recharge the coin, then take a chance and try "wishing" himself home blindly. He knew that would work. Or Ephraim could try to convince Nate to help him. Both options seemed equally risky.

Ephraim examined a framed photograph on Zoe's desk. In it, Nate and Zoe lounged beside Ephraim on the grassy soccer field behind the high school. They were laughing, their arms draped over his shoulders. It could only have been taken a few years ago, maybe freshman year, but they looked happier than the people they'd grown into. He wondered where those careless kids had gone. Had it been the war? Or had everything changed between them once the coin appeared?

Maybe we're still that happy in another universe, he thought hopefully.

Ephraim turned around. "Did Nate and your Ephraim have a fight?"

Zoe lay back in her bed and stared at the ceiling. "When Ephraim decided to stop using the coin, Nate got furious. He said it wasn't just Ephraim's decision, because it would cut him off from all those universes too. They were in it together, right? Nate actually threatened his family, which obviously didn't go over well."

"Would Nate have really hurt Ephraim's mom?" Ephraim asked.

Zoe was quiet for a moment. "Oh, I'd say so," she said softly.

Of course he would. Nate had killed his own duplicate and executed Jena right in front of him.

"That seems to be Nate's standard response," Ephraim said. "But Ephraim kept working with him after that?"

"He only pretended to. He planned to ditch Nate in another universe, as soon as he had the chance."

"How did Ephraim expect to get back here without the controller?" Ephraim asked.

"He was going to wait until Nate set the coordinates for the return trip, then take the coin before Nate could touch him."

"Wow," Ephraim said. "That's cold."

"I guess it wouldn't have worked anyway, if Nate's figured out how to track the coin with the controller. He would have come after Ephraim eventually," Zoe said.

That was true. So Ephraim would have to take the controller from Nate eventually, or he'd just keep following him—and that would put Ephraim's own family and friends in danger.

"There's something else," Ephraim said. "I've been swapping places with my duplicates in their universes, every time I use the coin." That's why he hadn't figured out what was causing all the changes around him—he was the only thing being changed.

She drew her arms around herself. "That's disturbing."

"But why didn't that happen for your Ephraim? He didn't replace me when he came to my universe," he said. "And Nate co-existed with the native Nathans of all those universes while he was following me."

"You only had the coin. Maybe the controller keeps you from swapping with your other selves."

Ephraim sat back down and rested his elbows on his knees. That could be it. When Nate had grabbed him at the fountain, the presence of the controller—what he'd thought was Nate's cell phone—allowed Ephraim to shift to this universe, where he didn't have a double to switch with.

"What was it like? Did you change bodies or was it just your mind that shifted?" Zoe asked.

Ephraim examined his hands in alarm. He hadn't considered that possibility. Was he still in his own body? He hadn't noticed any differences, but he hadn't been looking for any in himself.

He remembered what had happened back at the diner with Mary Morales. "My clothes always went with me. So I think anything in contact with my skin shifts over too."

"I suppose it doesn't really matter," Zoe said. "You look about the same as my Ephraim, anyway. If that's any consolation."

"Easy for you to say. I've been attached to this body for sixteen years." Ephraim froze as he thought of something else.

"Hey, are you all right?" she asked.

The real consequences of what he'd been doing were finally sinking in. "Basically, all this time I've been knocking other versions of me out of their lives," Ephraim said.

She waved a hand dismissively. "They probably never even noticed," Zoe replied. "You didn't realize what was going on and you were the one doing it. Most adjacent parallel universes, and parallel people, only vary slightly from each other."

"Some of the universes were really different, though. They'd have to be stupid not to notice that something was up."

Zoe smiled wryly. He'd set her up perfectly for another joke at his expense. But instead she said, "I wouldn't worry about them. You have enough to handle on your own, in this universe."

But he did worry. Every time he had wished for something good for himself, he had taken it away from another Ephraim. He had made a lot of people suffer—put other versions of himself through hell. What about the Ephraim who came home to find his mother hospitalized for attempted suicide, when she had been a perfect parent the day before? These weren't strangers—he knew exactly what that would feel like.

"How's my mother in this universe?" he asked suddenly.

Zoe's face paled.

He straightened and looked her in the eyes. "What is it?"

"God, I've wondered what I was going to say to him when he came back." Her voice quavered. "Ephraim, she's dead. She was murdered."

"This happened after your Ephraim left?"

"They found her a few days later. She was killed the day he disappeared."

"I have to go to back my apartment—Ephraim's apartment. You know what I mean."

"Why?"

"I need to know what happened."

"I just told you! You don't want to see what it's like there. Besides, that's one of the first places Nate will look for you."

"I can't really avoid him anyway. He followed me across all those universes. He has me right where he wants me now, on his home territory."

"I'll come with you then," she said.

Ephraim stared at her. The last time he'd accepted Jena's help, she had ended up dead. "No. I'll be fine on my own."

Zoe looked ready to argue, but then she shrugged. "Fine. Just remember the curfew. The cops are looking for you."

"They think he killed his own mother?" Ephraim asked.

"It was suspicious when they couldn't find him, or Nate. But they're also worried that something bad might have happened to you too."

"I'll be careful. Will I see you tomorrow?"

"I'll meet you here after school. You should probably skip it, stay out of sight. Too many questions after you've been gone for so long."

"School? But it's summer vacation."

She snorted. "We haven't had one of those since kindergarten."

Ephraim shuddered. "This is a horrible, horrible place. Thanks, Zoe. For everything. I know this all sucks for you, too."

"I didn't do it for you."

"Can I ask one more favor? Do you have any shoes that'll fit me?" The soles of his feet were sore and black with dirt.

She leaned over the side of the bed and lifted the blanket. She fished around under the bed upside down. A moment later she pulled out first one pink flip flop, then another.

"Thanks." He slipped into them.

Ephraim wanted to hug her good-bye, but he figured she wouldn't want that from a stranger, even—especially—if he resembled her Ephraim.

Then again, he might have been mistaken. As he closed the door of her bedroom, Zoe suddenly looked very lonely.

CHAPTER 21

Ephraim checked the mailboxes outside his building and was relieved to see that he lived in the same apartment. Even better, his key opened the lobby door.

His apartment door was crisscrossed with yellow police tape. He stripped it away from the locks and shakily inserted his key.

He pushed the door open and stale air washed over him along with a musty, rank smell. He gagged and pulled his sweaty T-shirt up to cover his nose and mouth. His own body odor wasn't much of an improvement.

Ephraim flipped on lights as he moved through the quiet apartment. The distinct stench of rot got worse as he went down the hall. He reached the kitchen and turned on the light.

There were no pills this time, no bottle of alcohol. No body. Just blood—everywhere. Brown, dried patches stained the table and the worn linoleum floor. It speckled the oven and stove like tomato sauce.

Ephraim's legs gave out, and he dropped to his knees on the threshold. Whatever had happened in there couldn't have been suicide. It looked like a massacre.

He bolted for his room and slammed the door against the smell. He collapsed onto the bed, pressed his face into a pillow with his eyes screwed shut.

That woman hadn't been his mother. She was no more related to him than the other Ephraim was. The thought didn't comfort him at all; he couldn't help but think of her as the person he'd known all his life. But who had killed her? And why?

Nate.

Ephraim rolled over and sat up. He wiped his eyes dry then fumbled to turn on the floor lamp by his bed.

Just like everything else in this universe, his bedroom was both familiar and unfamiliar all at once. He knew some things there very well: the well-worn books his dad had given him as birthday presents, on the shelf over the desk where they always were; the old stuffed bear Ephraim had insisted on carrying everywhere until he was five; the wooden triceratops skeleton his mother had helped him assemble after his class trip to the American Museum of Natural History.

His furniture was the same, but there were two large widescreen monitors on his desk instead of the thirteen-inch screen he was used to. The computer was gone, likely confiscated by the police, but Ephraim bet it was better than his own refurbished Gateway. Someone had knocked a cardboard box of American Indian arrowheads and rocks onto the carpet, which must be what his double collected instead of coins.

This Ephraim clearly had plenty of money, judging from the LCD TV in the corner, piles of comic books on the floor, and the overstuffed closet filled with clothes, some still with the tags on. Growing up, Ephraim had wanted these things too. He almost felt envious of his double, but then he remembered that the other Ephraim had lost everything that was really valuable—including his life.

He had to get out of here. Not just the apartment, but this universe.

Ephraim turned off the light and stepped back into the hall. He nearly retched again when the smell assaulted him. Now that he knew what it was, it seemed worse than before.

It *was* worse than before. It was stronger on the far end of the hall. There wasn't anything in the bathroom, which only left his mother's bedroom. It would be stupid to go in there. He should just leave now.

Ephraim held his breath and nudged the door open with his toe. It creaked softly and swung away from him, allowing the bathroom light to cast a golden triangle on the bedspread. He pushed the door open the rest of the way. In the dim light Ephraim made out a dark spray of red on the wall and headboard. The cream-colored pillowcase was stiff and soaked a rusty brown.

Someone else had been killed here. Had there been a Jim in his mother's life here, too?

Ephraim spotted a picture frame on the night table. He went inside and turned on the bedside lamp, trying to avoid looking at the bloody bed. He stared hard at the blood-spattered picture.

Ephraim recognized the man in the photograph, even though he hadn't seen him in over seven years. David Scott had his arm around his wife's shoulders, with the other Ephraim standing front center. The picture looked recent—the boy between them looked about fourteen.

If Ephraim's father had stayed with his family in this universe, then the other victim had been . . .

"Dad?" Ephraim said.

CHAPTER 22

Ephraim sat on a bench at Greystone Park. It was eerily quiet there this time of night, without even the gentle splash of water from the old fountain. He couldn't stay in the apartment where his parents had died, but he wasn't ready to go back to face Zoe again either.

Since he'd learned the coin wasn't really magic, that there would be no miracle solution, Ephraim felt even more powerless and alone.

A twig snapped nearby. *So much for being alone.*

With an electric cough, a lamp post near him sputtered to life. Ephraim jumped when he saw a dark shape squatting beneath it. "Who's there?" Ephraim cried. Had Nate been waiting for him here?

The hunched shape unfolded and lengthened. As the shadow shuffled closer, Ephraim saw it was a man, maybe in his forties. He wore a black trenchcoat, had lanky blond hair, and a few days' worth of stubble. He also looked oddly familiar.

"What are you doing here, kid?" the man said. "Why'd you come back?"

Come back?

The man cocked his head and peered at Ephraim's face, shifting so he didn't block the light from the lamp. "My mistake. I had you confused with someone else."

"I get that a lot lately," Ephraim said.

The man sat beside Ephraim on the bench. Ephraim shrank away, but the man didn't stink like the homeless people who usually hung around the park; his clothes even had the fresh smell of detergent to them.

"It's rude to stare," the man said.

Ephraim yawned. "Sorry." He rubbed his eyes. "Do I know you?"

The man reached into the pocket of his coat and pulled out a greasy bag from Twin Donut. He opened it and offered it to Ephraim. "Want?" he asked.

Ephraim hesitated.

"Oh, come on. They're fresh. I bought them this afternoon."

Ephraim hadn't eaten since that morning. He reached hesitantly into the bag and pulled out a gooey Boston Crème donut. The first bite he took of sugar and dough made him feel instantly hungrier. He scarfed it down in three more bites, barely tasting the warm cream inside. He licked the sticky chocolate from his fingers and reached for another one. Before he could ask, the man gave him the bag.

"Keep it," The man patted his stomach. "I lost my appetite when you busted into this universe a few hours ago."

"Thanks," Ephraim said around a jelly donut. "Wait, what?" Ephraim swallowed an unchewed bite painfully and stared at him. "You noticed that?"

"I'm particularly attuned to quantum shifts," the man said. "Or at least my stomach is."

Suddenly Ephraim realized who this was: the man Zoe had mentioned, the one who had given the coin and the controller to this universe's Ephraim and Nate.

Ephraim pulled the coin from his pocket.

The man exhaled. "So you have it now," he said.

"You know what this is?" Ephraim closed his hand around the coin and sat up straighter. "Can you tell me more about it? How does it work?"

"Slow down, Ephraim. We'll get there." He scratched his chin, the stubble sounding like sandpaper against his fingers. "Sorry, that is your name, isn't it?"

"Ephraim Scott."

The man nodded. "So something happened to the other one if you ended up with the coin."

"That about sums it up."

"Lucky you." The man reached over into the bag and absently snagged a donut for himself.

"I thought you said you didn't have an appetite," Ephraim said.

"Don't need one to eat. Chewing helps me think," the man said. He chomped into the donut and chewed thoughtfully.

"Did the coin bring you here too?" Ephraim asked.

The man swallowed. "Or vice versa, depending on how you look at it. I was part of a two-person team exploring parallel universes. Then I lost my partner. Since he was the only one who could use the coin, I was stuck here. I waited a long time to find someone who could help me leave."

"You mean this world's Ephraim and Nate?"

The man narrowed his eyes. "Yeah. I trusted two kids with the most advanced technology this world has ever seen. *That* turned out to be a mistake. Those punks promised to return me to my universe, but then they abandoned me." He brushed powdered sugar from his black pants.

"But why did you pick them? How did you know they'd be able to use the coin and controller? Unless . . ." Ephraim leaned closer and scrutinized the older man. His question came out small and weak. "Who are you?"

The man winked. "Well, just so things don't get too much more confusing, you can call me Nathaniel. I never liked that name, but I grew into it."

Ephraim stared at him, hardly able to believe it. But now that he'd heard it, he knew the man was telling the truth. That was why he'd seemed so familiar. He was looking at a Nathan with another thirty years or so added on.

"You're another Nathan?" he asked.

"Yeah, I'm an analog of your friend. We do have a habit of popping up, don't we?"

"'Analog'?"

"It's our term for doubles in parallel universes. Genetically we're about as identical as clones, but because of the inherent variations in our environments, we're unique individuals."

"Like twins who've been separated at birth?"

"That's a good . . . analogy." Nathaniel laughed.

Ephraim frowned. "You're Nathan's double? But you're so . . . old."

"Thanks, kid. The timeline can differ between some parallel universes—but you need the extra range of the controller to visit those. I suppose technically I'm from one of your possible futures." Nathaniel chewed another bite of donut. A dab of red jelly stuck to the corner of his mouth.

"Why didn't Nate recognize you?" Ephraim asked.

Nathaniel stuck his tongue out to catch the jelly from his lip. The gesture reminded Ephraim a lot of the friend he'd grown up with.

"Even if he somehow suspected it, his mind would have discounted it and come up with some reasonable explanation," Nathaniel said. "I think he probably felt a connection, though, which is why he even bothered humoring my claims about a machine that would let him and his friend travel to parallel universes."

Ephraim weighed the coin in his hand. "So this really is part of some . . . machine?" He was kind of disappointed that there wasn't anything magical about it, in the fairies and wizards sense, no matter what Jena had said about advanced technology being basically the same thing. No, *Zoe* had just told him that, he reminded himself.

Nathaniel plucked the coin from Ephraim's palm and examined it all over, like he was checking for damage. "Hmm. It needs a charge, but otherwise it's in good shape."

Nathaniel held it up between his thumb and forefinger. "This is part of a portable coheron drive," he said. "What we nicknamed the Charon device, since it—"

"Looks like a coin," Ephraim said. He remembered that in Greek mythology, Charon was the ferryman who helped dead souls cross the river Styx to the afterlife in exchange for a coin.

Nathaniel grinned. "That's right. Scientists are big on wordplay. At least our scientists are. This piece happens to be the most important component of the drive, both the engine and navigational guide all in one, while the controller is more like a recording instrument."

"What's it for?" Ephraim asked.

"It could be applied to any number of things, but we used the device to explore and catalog parallel universes. Some of them don't even fully exist until they we observe them ourselves—what we call 'coherence.'"

Ephraim waved his right hand over his head, showing that the last bit of information had gone right over it.

Nathaniel clicked his tongue. "Don't they teach kids basic quantum mechanics these days?"

"I'm a high school student," Ephraim said. "I suppose in the future kids learn that stuff in first grade."

"Of course not. That's when they get into classical physics," Nathaniel replied.

"Right," Ephraim said. He couldn't tell if Nathaniel was kidding or not. "But what's coherence?"

Nathaniel passed the coin back to him. "There's only a handful of people who really understand all this stuff back in my universe, or claim they do. Honestly, I just know which buttons to press. But the way it was taught to me is that whenever something's about to happen, there's a probability wave associated with that moment, which includes every potential outcome. When the event occurs, those possibilities become realities—splitting into one or more parallel universes."

"We figured some of that out already. Well, Jena did, and I mostly got what she said."

"Jena?" Nathaniel looked at Ephraim sharply. "She's here, too?"

"Yes. Sort of. There's a Jena in your world too?"

Nathaniel hesitated, then nodded.

"Is she . . . okay? You acted, I don't know. Like you didn't expect

her to be here or something." Or didn't want her to be there?
Ephraim's Jena—one of them—had just been killed. Had something
similar happened in Nathaniel's universe?

"No no. She's fine. Last I saw her anyway," Nathaniel said.

"Were she and your Ephraim together?" Ephraim asked.

"We're getting way off topic here. You want to know more
about the coin, or what?"

"Yeah, okay. Sorry." Ephraim flipped the coin a couple of times.
Then he thought better of it when he considered he was handling a
precision machine. How many times had he dropped it already? "So
how does it work? I mean, really work?" he asked.

"The disc functions as a gyro—a gyrocompass for the device.
Like the navigational tool used on ships to keep them oriented in
relation to north and south. Only this disc orients to the quantum
coordinates programmed by the controller."

"And without the controller?"

Nathaniel sucked in a sharp breath through his teeth. "It's more
. . . complicated. Risky. You can still use the coin, obviously, but the
coordinates become completely random depending on the position
of the coin."

"So heads up would take you in a different direction than tails up."

"Exactly. Though my partner seemed to be able to subtly influence the outcome and decrease some of that randomness, within the
parameters of the coin's orientation. Like he had a kind of intuition
for it, or vice versa."

Then maybe the coin—or gyro thing—had used Ephraim's
wishes as a guide to the universes visited, just because his mind was
clearly focused on what he wanted. But most of it was still up to
chance. No wonder things never turned out exactly the way he had
expected; it made no difference whether it landed on heads or tails.

"You've run into the other tricky bit already, I imagine. Alone,
the coin conserves energy by swapping you with your analog instead
of just transporting you to the universe directly," Nathaniel said.

"Like a powersave mode. I've never done it before, but my Ephraim did. It was always inconvenient at best. You use it too often, and the coin loses its charge completely."

"The analogs I replaced . . . are they okay?" Ephraim said.

"They were probably confused by the reality shift, if the universe they ended up in is really different from the one they came from. But the process doesn't harm them at all. Physically." He scratched his chin.

"That's a huge relief. And once the coin is drained, it can be recharged?"

"Yes, but only by plugging it into the controller. And this is especially important: you have to say the oath," Nathaniel said.

"What oath?" Ephraim asked.

"You know: 'In brightest day, in blackest night . . .'"

That sounded very familiar.

He had it. The Green Lantern recited that whenever he recharged his ring in its power battery. "*Really?*" Ephraim asked.

"Nah. But we did it anyway." Nathaniel grinned.

"Oh." Apparently older Nathaniel was still a huge comic book geek. Ephraim slid the coin back into his pocket. "I don't think Nate's going to let me charge the coin unless it benefits him somehow."

"No." Nathaniel grimaced. "And he'll do whatever it takes to get it away from you, and into the hands of someone who he can manipulate." Ephraim wondered how this guy knew so much about Nate. Was it just a matter of knowing himself? What had Nathaniel been like at Nate's age?

"Why doesn't the coin work for you or him?" Ephraim asked.

Nathan rubbed his elbow distractedly. "It's a security feature. Having a two-person team ensures that one person can't abuse the technology, and each component is configured for the biometrics of a specific operator. That way, if anyone else comes across the device, they won't be able to use it. But it isn't perfect—the device can't distinguish between subtle variations in users, such as the slight genetic drift you might find in different analogs of the same person. All Ephraims are the same, as far as the coin is concerned."

"What do you think Nate will do next?" Ephraim asked.

"He's stuck here, so he can't find another Ephraim to take your place. So he'll try to convince you to work with him, and wait for his opportunity to ditch you. Or maybe he'll just kill you. He's a little unstable."

"I noticed."

"He won't be able to stand the thought of you having something he can't. Once that coin is recharged, you can get out of here without him."

Ephraim jumped up. "But if we take the controller away from Nate, *you* could use it! I mean . . . would you help me get home?" Ephraim looked at him hopefully.

Nathaniel laughed. "That's funny. I was going to ask for *your* help. I've been waiting to go home for ten years. If you can get the controller, I'll set the coordinates for wherever you want, as long as you promise to drop me off in my own universe first. Deal?"

"Deal."

Nathaniel stood, and they shook hands. It was strange seeing the man his friend might become one day. He'd gotten at least a foot taller than Ephraim.

What had the older Ephraim been like?

Nathaniel tucked his hands into his deep coat pockets. "Good luck, kid."

"Do I find you . . . here?" Ephraim looked around the park dubiously. Nathaniel was probably homeless. In more than one sense of the word, he realized.

"I live in one of the old cottages behind the mansion."

"You're squatting?" Ephraim asked.

"I got a job as a caretaker of the old Greystone property. They're talking about turning the main building into a museum one day, but they can't do that if it's been vandalized. Besides, it helps me keep an eye on things around here," Nathaniel said, turning to leave. "Try to stay out of trouble."

"Hey, I almost forgot," Ephraim called. "Why does the gyro look like a quarter?"

"Ephraim had been carrying that quarter around since high school, doing magic tricks with it. It only seemed appropriate." Nathaniel walked off down a path to the right of the fountain and soon disappeared among the trees.

Ephraim had learned a lot about the coin, but he had even more questions than before. What kind of freaky future universe had Nathaniel come from? What was the purpose of the Charon device? How had Ephraim's older analog died?

The hardest question to answer was: how could he steal the controller from Nate?

Ephraim didn't know this twisted version of his friend well enough to get close to him—but he knew someone who did. And he was counting on her to be as smart as her counterpart in his home universe.

CHAPTER 23

Summer school was worse than Ephraim had imagined. The building wasn't air-conditioned, so by the time he reached his locker he was already drenched in sweat. He spun the dial, hoping its combination was the same.

Ephraim felt a cool hand on his arm. "What are you doing here?" Zoe's voice hissed behind him.

"I've already missed a lot of school," Ephraim said. "I don't want to fall even farther behind."

"Stop fooling around. This is serious. You know you don't belong here." She pushed her bangs out of her face and glared at him.

Ephraim turned and casually leaned against his locker. He ran his eyes over Zoe. She wore a white short-sleeved blouse and khaki shorts with a pair of green flip-flops. Her hair was tied back into a ponytail, and now that he saw her in the daylight he noticed that she was tanner than Jena. "Are you actually worried about me, or do you not want me around because I remind you of him?"

Zoe narrowed her eyes. "I just don't have any interest in giving Nate what he wants. Are you carrying the coin now?"

Ephraim nodded.

"Idiot. That's your only way home. What if he takes it? You'll be stuck here."

"I'm stuck here anyway until I can recharge it, and I don't have a good place to hide it. Besides, I actually came here because I wanted to see you," he said.

She tilted her head. Ephraim described what he'd found at his apartment.

"I warned you not to go there," she said with a sick expression on her face.

"Tell me what happened, Zoe."

"The papers said it looked like a murder-suicide. They think David Scott did it."

"I bet Nate framed him. Did they find a gun? Did the papers say?"

Zoe shrugged and avoided eye contact with him. "You don't know what Ephraim's father was like. He could have done it, I think. The cops wanted to talk to Ephraim, but I told them he was with me that night."

"I suppose it looked suspicious when he disappeared."

She nodded. "Since Nate was gone, too, I told them they'd left on a trip, that he needed time to deal with their deaths."

Ephraim twisted the combination lock to the right and popped the latch. It opened. A folded piece of paper fluttered to the floor. For a moment he thought he was experiencing déjà vu.

Ephraim crouched and opened the note. "Welcome home" was written at the top, in Nate's handwriting. Below it was a dark and grainy photo of Jena's body floating in the fountain.

"Bastard," he said. He couldn't take his eyes away from the grisly image. Jena.

"What is that?" Zoe reached for the paper, and he jerked it away from her grasp.

"You don't want to see this," Ephraim said. He rose slowly, his eyes fixed on the photo.

Zoe slammed her hand against the locker next to his. "Don't do that to me. Don't try to protect me. Let me help you, okay?" She crossed her arms.

More students were filing sullenly into the hallway. They glanced at him and Zoe curiously as they passed—especially him. The sound of lockers slamming, books shuffling, and voices whispering filled the hall.

Ephraim passed the note to her silently. She didn't say anything while he gathered some textbooks and slipped them into his backpack. He didn't have any idea what he would need.

Zoe crumpled up the note and threw it into his locker. "Fuck," she said.

"Are you okay?"

"That was me," she said. "That was *me*! What a sick, twisted bastard."

Ephraim leaned into the locker and retrieved the note, struck by a sudden thought. He smoothed out the note and examined the handwriting. It looked like Nathan's. *Nate's.*

"I know why he did it," Ephraim said.

"What?" Zoe checked the time on her phone and looked down the hall anxiously.

"I know why Nate left me those instructions the day I found the coin! He wasn't helping me at all. He was trying to help himself."

"That sounds about right."

It was just like what had happened with Nathaniel and his partner. Nate had been stranded in Ephraim's universe, the controller useless without the coin to complete it. "He wasn't sure yet that the coin would work for another Ephraim, so he decided to test it out on me." Maybe Nathaniel had told Nate and the other Ephraim about using the coin apart from the controller, and they'd never mentioned it to Zoe.

She tapped the note. "What are we going to do?"

"I don't know. Maybe I can reason with him."

She snorted.

The bell rang for homeroom, and Zoe slammed his locker door shut. "Shit, we have to get to class. Get moving." She propelled him down the hall. The rest of the students had already disappeared, like roaches scuttling away from a bright light.

"Why are you so freaked? Hold on! I don't even know where my first class is," Ephraim said.

"We share the same schedule until third period. I'll fill you in on the rest. Come on! You don't want to be caught in the halls between classes."

Zoe stopped in front of a classroom door, where Ephraim used to take Algebra. She pulled him inside as the last bell ended.

The classroom was stifling. The windows were closed, and twenty other students sat at their desks staring at the front of the room, sweat pouring down their faces.

"Where's the teacher?" Ephraim said as they took two seats in the back.

"No teacher for free period."

"We just . . . sit here?"

"It's only forty minutes. Be quiet now. If they hear us, we'll get called to the guidance office."

"Would that be so bad?" He bet they had air conditioning in the office, at least.

"Do they have corporal punishment where you come from?" Zoe asked.

"No fair making fun of the ignorant visitor," Ephraim said.

"Not so loud," she whispered. "I wish I were making this up."

As Ephraim waited for Zoe in the cafeteria at lunch period, someone sat down across from him. Ephraim almost didn't recognize him, but it was Michael Gupal: he was thin, at least a hundred pounds lighter than his analog in Ephraim's universe.

"Hey," Ephraim said hesitantly.

"What are you doing here?" Michael said.

"Say what?"

"He's back too, isn't he?"

"Who?"

Michael looked around nervously. "You said you'd take care of Nate."

"I did?"

Michael looked terrified.

"What are you so afraid of?" Ephraim asked.

"You know what he's capable of." Michael said. He hesitated

then drew out a folded sheet of paper. He held onto it a little too long when Ephraim tried to take it.

"I found that in my locker this morning," Michael said. "It's just like the other ones. I never should have believed you."

The page had four pictures on it, reminiscent of comic book panels. The first showed Michael with a horrified look on his face, starkly lit by a camera flash. The next picture was of Michael lying in a coffin, dressed in a smart suit, his eyes closed and his skin pale and waxy. The third was a funeral, a man and a woman in black standing over a hole in the ground at a cemetery. The fourth image was of a tombstone: MICHAEL AMIR GUPAL, Beloved Son.

Ephraim thrust the paper back at Michael. "It's obviously faked. Nate is very good with Photoshop," Ephraim said. But he knew the pictures were real—snapshots from a parallel universe, where Nate likely had done unspeakable things to one of Michael's analogs. "I wouldn't worry about it," he said softly. The sight of Jena in the fountain flashed in his mind again. How many deaths had Ephraim caused?

Michael lowered his voice again. "You promised he was going to disappear."

This wasn't even Ephraim's universe. Was it up to him to keep the other Ephraim's promises? He just wanted to get the controller away from Nate and get his own life back.

Then again, if Nate no longer had the controller, he would lose access to those other universes completely. He wouldn't be able to terrorize and kill freely, without fear of consequences. Ephraim might be able to protect countless other people, while also helping himself and Nathaniel return to their homes.

"I'm working on it," Ephraim said. By getting that controller away from Nate, he'd be helping more people than just himself. "Don't worry about these pictures. Nate won't do anything to you, he can only try to frighten you." Ephraim assumed Nate wouldn't do anything that could be traced back to him while he was stuck in his own universe. Michael was probably safe for the moment.

Michael looked behind Ephraim and scrambled up from his seat. "I hope you're right, Ephraim," he said. He slunk away.

Zoe came around the table with a tray of food and took Michael's seat. "What did *he* want?"

"Nate's been frightening kids at school with pictures from other universes."

Zoe grimaced. "It started out as just a game, but it's gotten more serious. Half the school hates or fears him, the other half loves him."

"Loves him? Why?"

"He's loaded. He pays the geeks to do his homework assignments for him. He buys presents to get girls to go out with him for expensive dinners. I think even the principal is on the take. Nate practically runs the school."

"Where does he get all that money?"

Zoe shrugged. "Other universes, I guess."

"How long has this been going on?" he asked.

"A couple of years, since they got the coin and the controller."

"You mean the other Ephraim was part of it?" Ephraim rubbed the back of his neck. "How could he?"

"Ephraim always went along with whatever Nate wanted." Zoe poked at the food on her plate. "I didn't like it either. He finally decided to put a stop to it, and look what happened to him."

"Why don't we just report Nate? In my universe, they take threats from students seriously."

"This isn't your universe. Like I said, Nate has a way of getting what he wants."

"Believe me, I'm aware of that." School was a scary place. The classes were much more advanced than they'd been in the eleventh grade. Most of them seemed to be on a college level, but he supposed that made sense if school ran all year round. Physics class alone demanded advanced calculus that was far beyond his experience. He was surprised that there weren't more students as messed up as Nate.

As they ate, Ephraim related his meeting with Nathaniel the

night before. He was astonished that she actually seemed angry about it.

"That asshole started all this," she said. "He's been here all along, hiding out, while Nate got more and more powerful. My Ephraim would still be alive—" She stabbed her plastic fork into her plate, and they mutually annihilated each other in an explosion of white plastic tines and Styrofoam chips. "Why didn't he do anything?" she howled.

Ephraim ignored the faces staring at them. He lowered his voice to calm her. "What should he have done? Beat up a kid half his age? Even if he'd tried, you've seen how deranged Nate is. And he's got a gun. He may be a teenager, but that doesn't make him any less dangerous."

"I don't know. He should have done something," she said.

"He's willing to help now."

"Only because he wants to go home. Just like you."

"Zoe, that isn't fair," he said.

They each pretended to eat for a little while, though Ephraim was just pushing food around, trying to think of something to say that wouldn't set her off again. The answer fell into his lap, literally, when someone behind him dropped a folded square of notebook paper there and hurried away. Ephraim couldn't tell who it had been.

"One of Nate's followers," Zoe said.

"One of his victims, you mean?" Ephraim said. "Another note." He unfolded it and read it: *Stop by after school. You know where I live.—N²*

"Cute." He crumpled it up and shoved it into his Jell-O container. "He wants to see me," Ephraim said.

"You aren't going," Zoe said.

"I have to talk to him sometime."

"Then you aren't going alone."

"This is a good opportunity. I need him to trust me, Zoe. It's the only way I'll get close enough to steal the controller if he refuses to cooperate. We're in a stalemate right now; he needs me as much as I need him."

"If you're sure." She bit her lip. "Just promise to be careful."

Ephraim wasn't sure at all, but he knew he had to do this. If he didn't show up, or if he brought someone with him, Nate would know he was afraid, and that would make him more vulnerable. Besides, he wasn't going to put Zoe in danger. Nate had already killed her once.

"Don't worry about me," Ephraim said, hoping it was more than optimism.

CHAPTER 24

Shelley answered the door at Nate's house. She seemed as surprised to see Ephraim as he was to see her. She looked a lot different from her analog in the last universe he'd been in: her brown hair was cut short in the back, but her bangs were long and parted on either side of her face. Her eyes were raccooned with mascara, which seemed to be one of the trends around here. He wondered if she and Mary no longer dressed alike in this universe; the Mary he knew would never wear the tight babydoll T-shirt and jean shorts Shelley had on, which were right out of Nathan's wildest dreams.

"You shouldn't be here," Shelley said.

"It's nice to see you too," Ephraim said. "I came to talk to Nate. He invited me."

She held the door open for him. "Upstairs." As Ephraim passed her, she whispered in his ear. "Be careful. Don't trust anything he says." He smelled cigarette smoke on her breath and hair.

Ephraim walked slowly up the stairs to Nate's room. The wooden banister was shaky under his hand. In his universe, it was loose from him and Nathan sliding down it when they were younger. Maybe they'd done the same thing here. When had this version of his friend turned into a monster?

Ephraim tapped on Nate's door.

"Yeah," Nate said.

Ephraim opened the door and saw Nate seated at his desk, thumbing casually through a stack of comic books. For some reason he had on a blue hoodie, with the air conditioning cranked way up.

"Shelley let me in," Ephraim said.

Nate looked up. "Shelley? Oh." He smiled. "I'm glad you decided to come. I wanted to show you something."

Ephraim sat down on the bed and looked around the room warily. Like Ephraim's room, there was a lot of expensive stuff here. Nate had a 40-inch widescreen HD television, and it looked like five video game systems were hooked up to it—including systems he'd never seen, like the Nintendo Revolution and the Sega Slipstream. Stacks of books were piled up on his desk and the floor, and the shelves overflowed with DVDs and comics. A digital SLR camera lay on the floor surrounded by lenses and cables.

Nate dropped a pile of comics next to Ephraim on the bed. "Start with these."

Ephraim picked up a few from the top of the stack. It was a DC/Marvel comic called *Justice X*, a five-part miniseries. He'd never heard of it, but the dates on the covers were from last year.

"Whoa," Ephraim said.

"We snagged that comic from a parallel universe. I also have the PS3 game, which is pretty solid. Good multiplayer." Nate rummaged under the bed. He slid out another bin of comics. "I also have an alternate version of *Paradise X* and *Tales of Earth X* that you wouldn't have seen back in your universe."

"No way." Ephraim grabbed the comics from Nate and flipped through them.

Nate sat down on the floor facing him. Something thumped on the hard wood beside him. The right hand pocket of his hoodie hung low—there was something heavy in it. Ephraim would bet anything Nate had a gun in there. Maybe even the one he'd used to murder Jena.

Ephraim put the comics down on the bed. "These are cool, but this isn't what I'm here for."

"I wanted to show you one of the benefits of being able to visit parallel universes. You haven't even begun to explore all the possibilities. Not your fault, of course; you didn't know what the coin is capable of, with the right partner."

"Why didn't you just approach me instead of lurking and

leaving that note about using the coin to make wishes?" Ephraim asked.

Nate laughed. "I thought that was pretty funny, by the way. A magic coin! Ephraim could be so gullible sometimes."

"Yes, it was very inspired," Ephraim said in a deadpan voice.

Nate beamed, misinterpreting Ephraim's sarcasm as a compliment. He was easy to read, because Ephraim knew his best friend so well, but he hoped Nate had never developed that kind of relationship with his own Ephraim. He might not even be psychologically capable of understanding what another person was thinking or feeling, judging by his behavior. That could be a valuable advantage, likely the only one Ephraim had over Nate.

"I figured you wouldn't believe me until you'd seen it for yourself," Nate said. "I knew once you'd used it, you couldn't give up that power."

"And you probably knew I'd need you and the controller to get back to my own universe," Ephraim said.

"Honestly, I wasn't sure it would work at all. We'd only talked about trying it, but Eph was too afraid to split up." Nate's eyes flashed. "I guess he got over that. He would have taken the coin and left me in your universe, if he hadn't died trying to give me the slip," Nate said.

"So you used me as a guinea pig?" Ephraim scowled. "How did you follow me with the controller?"

"It took me a while to figure out how to switch the device to scan mode, but fortunately I'm good with electronics."

"My Nathan doesn't ever read manuals," Ephraim said.

Nate nodded. "I never needed them either. Tracking the coin was easier than setting up a wireless network, which I was already doing at six. You know, there are some universes that don't even have the Internet. Primitive." Nate cocked his head back and looked at Ephraim through slitted eyelids. "So I gather Zoe's been talking about me and my toy. I'm flattered. It sure didn't take long for her to accept a new Ephraim in her life. And her bed?"

Ephraim's face flushed.

"No, you're not that kind of guy, are you?" Nate said. "We can work on that."

Ephraim cleared his throat. He would have to be careful not to reveal too much, so Nate wouldn't discover he'd been talking to his older analog from a parallel universe. "Zoe says you can't use the coin. The controller's useless on its own. You need me."

"Or another Ephraim." Nate shut his mouth and suddenly looked uncomfortable, like he hadn't meant to say that. His reaction was staged though. He'd meant to say it, to make it clear that Ephraim could be replaced. Fortunately Nate didn't know how easily *he* could be replaced.

Nate put his hands in his sweatshirt pockets, which was only threatening because Ephraim knew he was hiding a gun in his pocket. "And you need the controller if you ever want to get back home," he said. "How about we work together?"

"You killed Nathan and Jena, and who knows who else," Ephraim said. "You manipulated me. You've done nothing but threaten me. That doesn't exactly promote a strong sense of cooperation."

"Sorry about your girlfriend, but there are plenty more where she came from. You'll see," Nate said.

"You want me to join you, or help you find my replacement. Then what? You'll kill me too?"

"As soon as we find another Ephraim who's willing to use the coin, we can take you home. Or to any other universe you want. I have a few choice ones I'd recommend."

"What makes you think another Ephraim will be any more willing to help you? Your Ephraim tried to give up the coin."

"He wasn't going to give it up. He was just trying to keep it for himself—to keep it away from me. He enjoyed using it as much as I did. He's not the Boy Scout you think he was. If he hadn't died first, he would have killed you and taken your place. I mean, he left Zoe behind, right after he—" Nate shrugged.

"After he what?"

"After he killed his parents."

Ephraim stared at Nate. Could it be true? He didn't want to think so.

"You're lying. *You* killed his parents," Ephraim said. "Otherwise how do you know about their deaths? You got back to this universe the same time I did."

"We have the Internet here, Eph. I spent the night catching up on everything I missed while I was gone. If I were you, I'd hire a lawyer before talking to the police about the murder."

Ephraim hadn't even considered that he might be implicated in their deaths. He'd been walking around at school all day; it was only a matter of time before the cops brought him in for questioning after his long absence.

"Crap," Ephraim said. How could he prove he didn't do it? He doubted anyone would believe he was from another universe. He'd probably end up in an asylum, if not jail.

"It would be easier to hide you in another universe," Nate said.

"No!"

Nate looked surprised.

"I . . . I like it here," Ephraim said.

Ephraim had to stay in this universe, because Nathaniel was his best chance of getting and using the controller.

"You've gotten attached to Zoe, I see," Nate said. "She's worth sticking around for. I bet she's the only reason Ephraim stayed here for so long."

Well, there was Zoe too. But Ephraim had Jena waiting for him at home. Only she wasn't really waiting for *him*, exactly, if she'd even noticed he was gone.

"What do I do?" Ephraim asked.

"I have an excellent lawyer," Nathan said. "And I have a few friends in high places. 'Friends' might be too strong a word, but what do you call someone you're blackmailing? You'd be amazed how much dirt comes up in the news in parallel universes, or how many corrupt cops are willing to be paid off. I think I can make this problem go away easily, if there's something in it for me."

"You really had nothing to do with the Scotts' murders?" Ephraim asked.

Nate shook his head sorrowfully. "It's true I didn't discourage Ephraim from his mad plan, but I didn't think he would really go through with it. I thought it was all talk. We talked about a lot of things, didn't do half of them. Like testing the limits of the coin. I'm not denying that I've had to kill people. But I didn't kill them. I liked his mom."

Nate stared at Ephraim. "Ephraim's dad was unstable. He would come around, beat the shit out of Ephraim and Madeline, take their savings, then disappear again. Ephraim must have finally had enough. He thought he'd be leaving this universe for good, so it was his last chance to even the score." Nate shrugged. "I'm surprised he shot his mother too, but that could have been an accident. Then again, he despised her for not standing up to David."

"Why should I trust you?" Ephraim asked.

"You probably shouldn't. I'm not asking you to. I'm saying I didn't do it. And I'm offering to help you avoid getting charged for it, okay?"

Ephraim nodded. As much as he hated it, he did need Nate's help with the situation, if he planned to stay in this universe for a while. Showing his gratitude for the extended offer of friendship might also make Nate more willing to trust Ephraim.

"Thanks," Ephraim said.

"Now that that's settled, let me show you something," Nate said.

Nate went to his desk and turned on the computer. He had a brand-new Mac Pro with two monitors. Ephraim moved over to the desk and stood over Nate as he clicked through images.

These were pictures of people who had been tortured, people

Ephraim recognized. He spotted the one of Michael Gupal's head-stone. These images weren't faked in Photoshop. They were real: pictures from other universes where Nate had done all of these things to actual people—analogs of people Ephraim knew.

Ephraim turned his head away from the screen. The smile on Nate's face sickened him more than the images. He took a breath.

"Did the other Ephraim approve of this?" he asked.

"Like I said, he hated feeling helpless when his father beat him. He needed to take all that anger out on someone."

"What about you?"

"It's fun. I spent my entire life being bullied by these people. They had it coming," Nate said.

Ephraim turned back to the screen, fighting his impulse to walk out. When he saw a thumbnail of the Nathan who had been killed, sprawled under the bleachers, he clicked past it quickly.

"Don't stop—that one's my favorite," Nate said. "It's really noirish, don't you think? I wanted to stay for the funeral; it's always nice to hear people say nice things about you, even when they're lying."

"Why are you showing these to me?" Ephraim asked.

"Just to prove that your Ephraim was complicit in everything I did with the coin. If anything, he was more responsible, since he was the one who made it all possible. He wasn't as nice a guy as you; if you aren't careful, people will take advantage of you."

Ephraim leaned against the desk. "I don't think I'm the Ephraim you want. I can't do that—this sort of thing." His voice cracked.

Nate considered him. "Let's go for a spin." Nate picked up his cell phone. "Do you have the coin on you?"

Ephraim hesitated. He didn't want to go anywhere with Nate, but this could be his only chance. "Yeah."

Nate flicked his hand, and the cover of the cell phone flipped open.

"Is that the controller?" Ephraim asked.

"I forgot. You haven't seen this before." Nate held it up like he was modeling an appliance on a game show.

The half above the hinge featured a glowing screen, while the bottom half had a groove with a number pad beneath it.

"That's it?" Ephraim said.

The controller resembled a cell phone the way the coin resembled a quarter. Ephraim found it hard to believe the inventor would have built such a unique, precision device using spare parts. Then again, camouflaging it as an ordinary object likely would prevent the wrong people from looking at it too closely, just like the coin might find its way into a pay phone, or at worst, someone's coin collection. Even though the Charon device only worked for specific users—Ephraim and Nate—it might be possible for someone to reverse engineer them.

Nate pressed a button, and the screen came to life, displaying strings of numbers. "These are all the coordinates of the realities we've visited so far." He eyed Ephraim. Nate typed in some numbers on the keypad, too fast for Ephraim to catch them. It looked like there were ten digits, and the first was an 8.

Nate extended the controller to him with the bottom half flat. "Please insert twenty-five cents."

Ephraim pulled the coin out of his pocket. It was still just a blank metal disc. He ran his thumb over it, as though he could wear away the surface and reveal the quarter beneath it. He hoped the controller would recharge it. Ephraim fit the coin into the circular space in the controller.

Numbers began scrolling up the screen. The disc shimmered, and George Washington's face reappeared on the coin.

"The controller seems to be downloading coordinates from the coin. These are all the universes you've been to. You've been busy," Nate said.

"Can I see?" Ephraim said casually.

Nate searched his face. "Of course," he said finally.

The controller was made of a smooth light-blue metal, cool to the touch. It felt solid but as light as aluminum. The screen was dead to his touch, and no amount of pressing would bring it to life.

Ephraim had the controller now and the coin. Should he run for it? He glanced at the open bedroom door.

Before he could make up his mind, Nate reached over and pressed his finger to the display. "Let me show you how it works," he said. The moment his skin made contact, it came to life. He scrolled through the lines of numbers then tapped one of them to highlight it. "This button at the bottom sets the coin to whichever coordinate is highlighted."

Nate pressed it, and Ephraim nearly dropped the machine when the coin suddenly floated up from its groove and hovered in mid-air.

"Wow. How does it do that? Magnets?" Ephraim asked.

"You haven't seen anything yet." As Nate scrolled through the list, the coin reoriented itself in the air, turning and rotating with each line he highlighted in the center of the display.

"It *is* like a gyro," Ephraim said.

"A what?" Nate said sharply.

"Uh. I mean, it looks like a gyroscope. One of those navigation things."

This was his chance. But just as Ephraim was about to grab the coin, Nate snatched the controller from Ephraim. He cleared the display and tilted it so Ephraim could see the screen was blank. "Now I'll program it for a random universe," Nate said. "Unless you'd like to 'wish' us to one." He chuckled.

Nate held down the button at the bottom of the keypad. The coin spun and rotated in place, still hovering just above its dock on the controller. It picked up so much speed it turned into a semi-transparent globe in front of them. A warm breeze blew against Ephraim's face, and he smelled burning ozone as the air around the rotating coin heated up. Numbers raced over the screen, too fast for Ephraim to read.

"Round and round it goes. Where it stops, no one knows," Nate said.

When Nate depressed the button, the coin stopped suddenly, frozen in place in mid-air and oriented almost directly vertical.

"Now what?" Ephraim asked.

"Hold onto me, then grab the coin," Nate said.

"Why is that necessary? If we aren't in physical contact when I touch the coin, won't you just follow me like you were doing before?"

Nate rolled his eyes. "It isn't automatic. Even if I have the coordinates you shifted to, the controller still has to track the coin and home in on its signal. That takes time, depending on how far you've gone. And I'd have to deal with the Ephraim who switches places with you. This is much less trouble." Nate smirked. "You're not hoping to get rid of me already?"

"No, I was just curious. Trying to figure out how this all works." Ephraim tried to sound as casual as possible. "So why did I switch with other Ephraims whenever I visited another universe?"

"It must be because the coin wasn't docked in the controller. I've been wondering about it myself. I bet it's a sort of stealth mode, for spying on other universes. If you replace your double, you can move right into his life without even wasting a bullet. Think about it: my Ephraim might have replaced *you* if he'd figured it out sooner."

Ephraim shuddered. He would have just woken up in this wartorn version of the world with a psycho best friend and no idea how he'd gotten there. "You don't seem that broken up about losing your best friend," he commented.

"He *did* betray me in the end. Hard to forgive that. And like I said, there's more where he came from." Nate clapped Ephraim on the shoulder. "I think I like you more, anyway. I've been watching you. You're a loyal friend. But keep in mind, if you ever do think of leaving me behind somewhere, it won't be easy to fool me the same way twice."

While Nate's hand was on his shoulder, Ephraim reached for the coin. He hesitated for a moment, then plucked it out of the air.

Ephraim felt the familiar lurch as they shifted together.

They were still in Nate's room, but it was more like the one

Ephraim remembered. The expensive equipment was gone. His friend's old 20-inch TV was hooked up to a Playstation 2.

Nate carefully closed the controller and tucked it away. Ephraim pocketed the coin. It still felt warm and it vibrated gently. He wondered how much of a charge it had built up. It hadn't been in the controller for long.

Nate smiled as if he knew what Ephraim was thinking. "You could leave the coin in the controller to charge," he said.

He did know what Ephraim was thinking. He was good.

"No, that's okay. It's probably safer for me to hold onto it, in case we have to use it in a hurry."

Nate nodded and looked around the room. "This could have been tricky, if there were another version of me home today. Not that we couldn't handle him between the two of us. We usually leave from the library, which is more isolated."

"Trickier still, if there'd been no house here at all," Ephraim said. Nate paled.

Unless the coin swapped them with their doubles, the Charon device seemed to fix travelers to the same spatial location as they moved from one universe to another. He hoped that with all its safeguards, the coin wouldn't be able to transport him into the middle of another object, or a world with a toxic atmosphere.

Ephraim wandered to the window and looked out at a perfectly ordinary street, a view he was quite familiar with. "Where are we, anyway?" he asked.

Nate grinned. "I don't know! That's what's so great about this—you always end up someplace new. Stick with me, partner."

CHAPTER 25

Nate took Ephraim to the Spanish grocery store a few blocks away from his double's house. He pulled up his hood over his eyes just outside the store.

"What are you doing?" Ephraim asked.

"Watch and learn," Nate said.

Ephraim followed him inside to the register in the front, which was lined with scratch-off lottery tickets and candy. Nate opened his wallet and handed the cashier a ten dollar bill.

"Can you break this?" he asked. Ephraim didn't recognize the picture on the front of the bill, and the paper was tinted orange. It looked like Monopoly money.

Nate studied the cashier carefully, a look of anticipation on his face. He seemed relieved when the man put the bill in the register without even giving the money a second glance. A smile played across his lips as the cashier handed over a five dollar bill and five singles.

Nate examined each bill closely, holding them up to the light. The five dollar bill was blue, but the singles looked a normal green and had the familiar portrait of Washington.

"You think I give you fake money?" the cashier said angrily.

"You can't be too careful these days. These look okay," Nate said. He tucked the money away and reached into the right-hand pocket of his hoodie.

"Nate—" Ephraim said.

"No names!" he snapped at Ephraim. He pulled out his gun and turned back to the cashier. "You. Empty the register," Nathan said calmly, pointing the gun at the cashier.

"Are you nuts?" Ephraim said.

"Chill. This guy's an easy mark in every universe. He's practically our personal ATM."

The cashier glanced between the two of them. "No trouble. Please," he said.

"I know, I know. You have a wife and three kids," Nate said.

"How could you know this?" The man was even more frightened.

"There won't be any trouble, pops. As long as you hand over all your money," Nate said.

Ephraim looked behind the cashier and noticed a security camera behind his head. "He's recording us!" he said.

Ephraim used to worry endlessly about getting detention at school. He'd always tried to follow the rules. Now he was breaking the law. He was *robbing a store*. He shoved one shaking hand into the pocket with the coin.

"Calm down," Nate said. "We'll be long gone before the cops get here."

"But—"

"And where we're going, they can't follow us. Get it?"

The cashier started stacking bills on the counter. Nate nodded to Ephraim. "Take it," Nate said.

Ephraim grabbed two handfuls of money. The panicked cashier held open a paper bag for him, and Ephraim dumped the cash in.

"Uh, thanks. Sorry," Ephraim said.

"Okay, let's go," Nate said.

They exited the store slowly then dodged into the alley behind the store. Nate put the gun back in his pocket.

"They won't catch us, but what about this reality's Ephraim and Nathan?" Ephraim said.

"What about them?"

"They're *us*. They might get caught."

"We don't owe those guys anything."

"How can you screw your other self over that way?"

Nate scowled. "You worry about other people too much."

Sirens sounded in the distance. Ephraim was used to hearing sirens, but this was the first time they were coming for him. He peeked nervously around the side of the store.

"Time for another perfect getaway," Nate said. He pulled out the controller and gestured for the coin. Ephraim slotted it in the circular dock. Nate grabbed Ephraim's arm above the elbow and set the coordinates with his free hand. Ephraim paid close attention, making sure he could operate the controller when the time came. Nate nodded, Ephraim grabbed the coin, and they shifted.

"Now what?" he said. It looked like they hadn't gone anywhere at all.

"We're one universe over from the last one." He folded the controller and slipped it into his jeans. "Back to the *bodega*."

"What?"

Ephraim followed Nate around to the entrance of the store, and they ran through the same process. The cashier responded exactly the way he had before, but this time he offered Ephraim a plastic bag to carry the money in.

"I have my own, thanks," Ephraim said. He held open the paper sack from the previous store.

Ephraim wondered what would happen if one of the cashiers didn't give up so easily and tried to resist them. Nate would probably just kill him and take what he wanted.

After four more identical trips, eerie in how similarly they played out in each universe, Nate finally seemed satisfied, and Ephraim had a dull ache in his stomach; he'd never made so many trips so close together before. Behind the store, Nate scrolled through the list and highlighted a set of coordinates.

"Let's go home," Nate said. By now Ephraim was familiar with the routine. He grabbed the coin while Nate held onto him, and a moment later they were back in Nate's universe—or at least Ephraim assumed that they were. It looked no different from any of the other places they'd been, except it was raining now.

"How'd we do?" Nate said when they returned to his bedroom.

Ephraim unloaded the soggy paper bags of money, and they counted up the bills. Now Ephraim knew where his analog had gotten all that money.

"3,275 dollars. Not bad for this time of day," Nate said. He split up the money and handed half of it to Ephraim. "Just in time, too. I was running low on cash and I want to take Mary Shelley out tonight."

"Both of them?"

Nate just smiled. "With this technology, we can do anything we want, Ephraim."

"Even if we can get away with it, it's still wrong," he said.

"You sound a lot like the other Ephraim did at first. You going to try to double-cross me too?"

"I just . . . I'm still getting used to all this."

"Go spend some of that money and you'll feel better. Tools are made to be used." Nate said. He pulled the gun from his pocket and stashed it in his top desk drawer. He kept the controller tucked safely in his other pocket.

Ephraim nodded and turned away, wondering if that was how Nate viewed him—as a tool.

He was going to stop Nate, one way or another. All he needed was a plan.

"There's plenty more where I came from?" Zoe said. She pounded her fist on the kitchen table. "He really said that?"

Ephraim flipped the cheese omelet with the spatula one last time and lowered the flame on the stove.

"I can't believe you're actually working for him," Zoe said.

"*With* him," Ephraim corrected. He turned from the stove to see her glaring. He was making Zoe dinner in exchange for the use of her couch. Mr. Kim hadn't been happy about the arrangement or Ephraim's apparent return to Zoe's life after a long absence. Zoe had pointedly reminded him that Ephraim had nowhere to go, and he had finally assented.

When Ephraim arrived at the house, Mr. Kim had awkwardly offered his condolences, then immediately gone out. Zoe thought her father would probably stay at his girlfriend's, as he did on weekends.

"I'm just pretending to cooperate with Nate," Ephraim said. "We both know we're using each other. It's just a matter of who gets to take advantage first." Ephraim turned off the burner and sliced the omelet in half. He slid each portion onto a plate.

Zoe took a bite of her omelet. "Mmm. This sure beats take-out. I'm tired of Chinese and Mexican."

Ephraim glanced at her. "Yeah."

She was right, though. The eggs weren't half bad. They ate in a companionable silence for a while. Ephraim kept trying to think of a plan, but his mind kept circling back to his conversation with Nate.

He sighed. "Zoe. Nate said that Ephraim killed his own parents before he left."

Zoe clenched her fork. "You believe him?"

"I didn't know your Ephraim. You did. You tell me. Could he have done it?"

Zoe shoved her omelet around on her plate.

"He could have. He'd talked about it before, a couple of times. When he was angry. His father was a real asshole. He deserved what happened to him." Her shoulders slumped. "But I don't think he would have killed Maddy."

"So, did he or didn't he?"

"Do you think you could kill someone?" Zoe asked.

"We're different people," Ephraim said.

"I know," Zoe said. "You seem a little . . ."

"Nicer? Cuter?"

"I was going to say a little more naive."

"Oh."

"But it works for you. Ephraim was always so . . . grown up. He carried the world on his shoulders. It's like he was impatient to become an adult."

"Maybe he didn't have a choice." Ephraim's mom had always needed him to be the responsible one. It seemed that hadn't been any different for his analog—worse, if his father was around to make things difficult.

"Maybe. I can't help but compare the two of you. It's surreal, sitting here like we always did, but you being so different. He didn't have your sense of humor, either." She forked another bite of omelet into her mouth. "He also couldn't cook."

"This is barely considered cooking."

Ephraim also had to keep reminding himself that this girl wasn't the one he had been hopelessly infatuated with since the second grade. Aside from her appearance, he knew she wasn't the same person. She was a lot more confident for one, and had a quicker temper, too. Physically, she seemed more comfortable with her body and was more athletic, but was still as intelligent as Jena.

"What's she like?" Zoe asked.

Ephraim looked at her suspiciously.

"I know that look on your face," Zoe said. "You're thinking about someone. It isn't hard to guess who."

He cleared his throat. "Jena's great. I mean, just like you. You have similarities, of course. She's really popular at school. She's the smartest student in the whole country, I think."

Zoe laughed. "Not all that much like me, then. I don't have many friends. And I hate school."

"But you're so good at science and computer stuff."

"Doesn't mean I have to like it."

"If I had to go to school six days a week all year round, I'd hate it too. About the only thing I liked about it was seeing Jena every day. Your Ephraim probably felt the same way about you. I wonder why he didn't take you with him?"

"What?" Zoe's fork clattered to the table.

"Um. I mean, if the other Ephraim wasn't planning to come back here, why didn't he take you with him?" From her stunned look, he knew he'd really stuck his foot in it.

"Why do you think he wasn't coming back?"

He stared at his plate, the bits of yellow egg scattered across the cheese-streaked grape leaf pattern at the center of it.

"Nate said . . ."

"Oh! Nate said. I thought you didn't trust him?"

"I don't!"

"Then why would you believe anything he said?"

"I—"

"I'm sure he had a good reason for it." Zoe slid her chair back and tossed her fork down on the plate. "He would have taken me if he could have, but that Charon machine only works for you and Nate."

"But I—" Ephraim cut off his words. She obviously wouldn't want to hear that he'd shifted with other people before. The question was, had the other Ephraim known he could or not?

"Thanks for dinner. I'm going to bed early." Zoe said. She stormed out of the kitchen. The door swung back and forth behind her. Ephraim poked at the lukewarm remains of his omelet and pushed the plate away from him.

He wouldn't be able to sleep if he left things with Zoe that way. At the rate that the people closest to him were disappearing, he didn't know if he'd have another chance to smooth things over, and he couldn't afford to lose another friendship, if he could even call it that.

He climbed the steps to the second floor and approached her room. He couldn't see a light under her door. He knocked softly, then more loudly.

He was about to tiptoe back downstairs when the door opened. Zoe had changed into a long T-shirt with a purple unicorn prancing on a rainbow.

"What now?"

Okay, so she was still a little upset.

"I just wanted to say that I'm sorry," Ephraim said.

"For what?" Zoe asked.

"I was really insensitive. I shouldn't have said . . . what I said."

She stared at him for a second then stepped onto the landing in socked feet.

"It's not your fault I reacted that way . . ." She leaned against the wall and hugged her arms around herself. "I've been thinking the same thing to myself since he left. He didn't even say good-bye."

Ephraim drew closer to her. "Look, I know I'm not him, but I'm going to finish whatever he was trying to do. You're right—he did know what he was doing. He probably just didn't want you to get hurt. I can relate to that."

Zoe sniffed a little. She rubbed at her eyes with the back of her hand.

Ephraim forged ahead, the words rushing out of his mouth. "His mistake was he trusted the wrong person, then tried to handle the problem himself. I'm going to need your help. If I say or do something completely idiotic, tell me—and make me listen. Even though we just met, I think you know me better than I know myself."

"Don't worry. I'll definitely let you know when you do something stupid."

They looked at each other awkwardly.

"You must be really tired," Ephraim said.

"No, not really. Did you want to do something?"

"Well . . . I saw your dad has *The Twilight Zone* on DVD, and I thought it would be fun to watch some. Together."

Zoe tilted her head to one side. Then she smiled. "You're on."

She chose the episodes. Ephraim had seen most of them in reruns when he was a kid, but it was different watching them as an adult, especially with Zoe. She knew all sorts of trivia about the show and filled him in as they viewed some of her favorites. She ended the mini-marathon with a special episode, just for him she said, one called "Penny for Your Thoughts," about a magic quarter that allows a man to read people's minds.

When the show ended, she switched off the television and turned to Ephraim. "Two bits for your thoughts," she said. "Doesn't have the same ring, does it?"

Ephraim kissed her. He couldn't stop himself. She started to pull away, but then she leaned into him and kissed back.

A moment later, they separated. She frowned.

"Was that stupid?" he asked.

"Now *that's* a stupid question." She dropped the remote on the coffee table and stood up. "Time for bed. For real this time. And that isn't an invitation."

"I didn't think it was," Ephraim said.

"Good. This doesn't change anything, all right? We shouldn't have done that, but I wanted to see what it was like." She shook her head. "It was different."

Different-good?

"Good night, Zoe," Ephraim said.

"Did she like you too?" Zoe asked softly.

"Who?"

She smiled. "Best answer. Good night, Eph."

She went up the stairs. Ephraim sat alone on the couch, replaying what had just happened. He'd never dared to try that with Jena. Even though he'd wanted to, those sorts of scenes happened only in his fantasies. But it had been so easy with Zoe, so natural, and she had seemed to want it, too. Like a wish come true.

He was really starting to like Zoe, he thought guiltily. He had criticized Nathan for his casual interest in both of the twins, so how could Ephraim like both Zoe and Jena? On top of that, he was actually jealous of the Ephraim she'd loved so much, the guy who had left her behind for another universe. He couldn't replace his analog in Zoe's life, and even if he could, it wouldn't be right.

He had to stop Nate and get out of this world before he did something really stupid. Like fall in love with Zoe.

CHAPTER 26

Nate and Ephraim went on several trips to parallel universes over the next few days. Despite Ephraim's private apprehension, Nate didn't seem intent on robbing or murdering all the time. Instead, they went to comic book shops and video game stores to pick up things you couldn't get in Nate's universe, the way they used to hang out at the mall. It was ludicrous to imagine this kind of power being used just to buy more stuff, but at least no one was getting hurt. And they were actually getting comfortable with each other.

He feared that wouldn't last. Ephraim figured he was under probation while Nate tried to figure out if his friendship was sincere. Eventually, Ephraim would have to prove himself by helping Nate hurt someone. He had to figure out how to get the controller before that happened.

But Ephraim had to admit, using the coin could be fun. It was easy to convince Nate that he was enjoying himself, because he *was*. Though he'd begun to recognize the attraction of it—there were countless universes out there to explore—he was actually disappointed that so many of them were similar to his own, aside from a few subtle and not-so-subtle differences.

There were worlds where everyone drove hybrid electric cars; Ephraim didn't spot a single SUV on the road, and all the parking meters were equipped with sleek charging stations for car batteries.

They visited a version of Summerside where everyone bizarrely had a Boston accent. Ephraim and Nate drew stares whenever they spoke—apparently they sounded like they didn't come from anywhere in particular.

One universe was completely devoid of franchise fast food, the first McDonald's restaurant having apparently failed, barely a footnote in history. The absence was striking on Central Avenue, where mom-and-pop businesses that had shut down long ago still thrived, and the Starbucks coffee shops and chain stores that had slowly crept in to replace them had disappeared entirely.

Ephraim began to pick up on little details he'd noticed in his first experiments with the coin, things he'd discounted at first but which he now saw as slight variations that implied more significant differences. But he was still getting bored of all the *sameness*. There were no parallel universes where people had superpowers, or the laws of physics were wildly different, or there were two suns. Perhaps there were earths with dinosaurs out there, Nate suggested, but it seemed that the most inventive realities remained in the realm of comic books and movies. Or maybe the device couldn't or wouldn't allow them to visit those worlds.

"How can you be bored? We're traveling to parallel universes! No one else can do that," Nate said. "Every trip we take is amazing."

"I just want to see something . . . new. That's all," Ephraim said.

Nate nodded. "That's the spirit. Let's see what this thing's got."

They set the controller on random and each time the coin stopped spinning, Nate checked the coordinates. He shook his head, then set it spinning again three times before he was satisfied.

"I feel good about these numbers. Let's try it," Nate said. He put a hand on Ephraim's shoulder, and Ephraim took the coin.

The first thing Ephraim noticed was a change in light from the warmth of noon to a cooler pre-dawn brightness, though it was still hotter than it should be in July. The sky was gray but not overcast. He couldn't see any clouds, but heavy pollution in the air muted the sun somehow, and the back of his throat tickled. Nate sneezed a couple of times beside him.

The next thing he noticed was how much *nothing* there was. The park across the street was gone, and the ground was barren as far as he could see, dry and pitted with a scraggly dead tree jutting out of the ground here and there. They were surrounded by miles of black chain link fence topped by coils of barbed wire.

"This world doesn't look very friendly," Ephraim said. "Where are we?"

Nate grabbed his arm and spun him around to face the library. The building had been replaced by a squat concrete structure, a large bunker or some kind of military facility. They trudged toward the large steel doors slowly, passing a couple of muddy green Jeeps parked in front. Nate stopped and picked up a flyer from a pile on the dashboard of one of the vehicles. His face paled.

"What is it?" Ephraim asked.

Nate handed him the flyer and pulled out the controller.

"Get the coin ready, Ephraim. We're leaving," Nate said.

Ephraim read the flyer. It showed a picture of Uncle Sam in a top hat and red, white, and blue. He was pointing, like in the old war posters Ephraim had seen in Social Studies class. But the bold red letters along the bottom read, "I Own You." The words at the bottom announced that all men and women age 16 and older were being drafted for the US Army to fight in the war against the Soviets, as of June 1.

"Ephraim, the coin," Nate said. "Now." He was punching some numbers into the controller.

Ephraim dropped the flyer to retrieve the coin from his pocket. The paper was swept up by a sudden gust of warm, gritty wind and shot away from him. It caught briefly on the barbed wire along the fence, then ripped free and fluttered across the parched land.

Nate grabbed the coin from his hand.

"Hey!" Ephraim said.

The coin was orienting itself above the controller now.

"We don't have time for this. Ephraim, this is a recruitment center. And they want us." Nate pointed at Ephraim like Uncle Sam in the poster. No, he was pointing behind Ephraim.

Ephraim turned and saw a Jeep rumbling toward them.

Someone shouted at them. A camouflaged soldier climbed out with an assault rifle at his elbow and sauntered toward them, his combat boots kicking up plumes of dirt.

"How'd you get in here?" the soldier called. "What's your unit? Why aren't you in uniform?"

"Shit. Take the coin," Nate hissed.

The soldier was leveling his weapon at them now. He said something that sounded like a question in Russian. His expression was all business, just like the gun, but Ephraim abruptly recognized him. It was Michael Gupal, who was only a year older than him and Nate.

Nate grabbed onto Ephraim's arm with a vice-like grip, and Ephraim reached for the coin. He nearly dropped it, but as soon as his hand made contact, they were away. He imagined the shocked look on Michael's face as they disappeared.

The universe they were in was the complete opposite of the one they'd left behind. The land around them was covered in lush wilderness. Not only were the buildings gone, but dense trees and a small lake occupied the site of Greystone Park, a stark contrast to the artificially created woodland Ephraim was used to.

"Thank God," Nate said. "That was too close. Good thing I had these coordinates memorized." He spat into the long grass. Ephraim could taste the last universe in the grit in his mouth too, but it felt wrong to taint the unspoiled land they were standing on.

"This area has never been settled," Nate said in a low tone. Ephraim was surprised at the wistfulness he heard in his voice. He expected Nate to say that it was the perfect place to bury a body, not treat the land with the surprising reverence he obviously had for it.

Nate turned around slowly, his arms spread wide. He tilted his head back and drew in a deep breath.

Ephraim had never smelled fresher air. He was aware of the sounds of life all around them. Birds chattered in the trees, and he heard rustling in the foliage. It was warm but pleasant for a day in July, unlike the record heat wave hitting Nate's universe and the almost unbearable temperatures in the militaristic universe they'd stumbled into.

"Eph and I came here a lot," Nate said. "We hiked all through this forest. It goes on forever. We've never seen anyone else here, but we found signs of American Indians here and there. There's a burial mound three miles north. Eph was collecting arrowheads and old stuff like that. We think they all must have died or moved on." He sighed. "This is one of my favorite places, in any universe."

"Thanks for sharing it," Ephraim said. He agreed that the place had appeal, but he was unnerved at the idea that in this universe, he'd never even existed. Everything he knew, everyone he loved, was missing—and the world seemed better for it.

Ephraim ignored his scenic surroundings and focused on Nate. The other boy rested with his back against a tree, one hand tucked into the pocket of his sweatshirt where he carried the controller. No chance of getting it away from Nate while he dozed off, but Ephraim might be able to take the gun from the other pocket or prevent Nate from reaching it first.

Through all their travels, Ephraim had never allowed himself to relax, always waiting for a moment to steal the controller without getting injured or killed in the process. But he almost felt that they had a real friendship now. That scared him as much as he hoped that Nate believed it, too.

He couldn't let Nate's resemblance to his best friend prevent him from acting. There was a large rock nearby. If Ephraim could grab that—

Nate opened his eyes and yawned. He checked his cell phone for the time and got to his feet. He dusted off his pants and approached Ephraim.

"I'd love to stay longer, but we have one more stop to make," Nate said. "It's just about lunchtime."

"I think I've had enough excitement for one day." One lifetime, even. "Where are we going now?" Ephraim asked.

He hid his disappointment at another missed opportunity. He pulled out the coin and slid it into the controller; they had done this together so many times, they each knew their roles automatically. Nate seemed to pay careful attention to the coordinates this time, as though he were looking for a specific one that he didn't use often.

Nate looked up and walked five paces to the large rock Ephraim had spotted. He gestured Ephraim over and directed him to stand in a certain place beside him on the other side of the rock. He grabbed onto Ephraim's arm with one hand and held the controller out with the other. Ephraim took the coin, and in an instant they were standing inside the bus shelter across from the Summerside Public Library, shaded from the hot noon sun. The library was open, which told him they weren't back in Nate's universe or one of its close approximations.

"Where are we?" Ephraim asked. He turned around and saw Greystone Park behind them, looking the same as usual.

"Does anything look familiar?" Nate said.

Ephraim laughed. "Everything does," he said. "I'm kind of getting used to that."

Nate grinned. "You're home, Eph."

Ephraim looked around, but there was no easy way to tell this universe apart from many of the others he'd been to.

"I'm home?" Ephraim said. He felt a sudden thrill of happiness, before it was tempered by suspicion. "Why?"

"I thought you wanted to come back here," Nate said.

"I did. I do. But I'm confused. Do you want to get rid of me?" He eyed the pocket where Nate always kept his gun.

"It's time to make a decision, Eph," Nate said. "We can continue to be a team. I'd like to. Or if you think you still want out of our arrangement, you can stay here, where you belong."

"That's it? No strings?"

"Just one," Nate said. He pointed at the library.

Ephraim saw another Ephraim walk out and sit next to the big stone lion to the right of the stairs. This was the first time he'd actually seen one of his analogs, aside from the picture of the dead Ephraim. Somehow that made this all more real, even though he'd already been to so many different universes.

"How is that possible? If this is my universe, then I'm the Ephraim that belongs here. Who the hell is that?"

"When you made that first wish, he's the Ephraim you exchanged with. I saw it happen. He took your place."

The library doors slid open. Jena appeared. Ephraim's jaw clenched. He hadn't considered the fact that she was still alive in this universe, but it made sense—he'd only seen one of her analogs die, after all, several universes away. This was a different Jena entirely—not as different as Zoe, but not the same girl Nathan had killed, either. This Jena still didn't know anything about the coin or how Ephraim had tried to use it to make her interested in him.

"Looks like he got your girl, Eph." Nate sat on the bus bench and stretched out his legs. He laid the controller beside him then folded his hands in his lap.

"How do I know this is really my home reality?" Ephraim said.

"You can look around some more if you want. Go home and talk to your mom. She's probably out of the hospital by now, steadily drinking herself back into a stupor. I wonder how this Ephraim handled that whole mess in your place."

Ephraim's confusion turned to anger. The Ephraim across the street had been living his life all this time. There was no telling what he'd done in the last month since Ephraim had accidentally left it. His analog and Jena laughed, and she leaned against his arm.

Ephraim sat down. He suddenly felt conspicuous. What if one of them glanced over and saw him at the bus stop? But it didn't look like those two had eyes for anyone but each other.

"If there are two of me here, how can I stay here?" Ephraim said. "How can I get my old life back?"

Nathan looked at him. "We'd have to get rid of him," he said.

"How do you mean?" Ephraim said.

"That's the deal, Eph. The way I see it, you have two options. You can try to talk to him, convince him to take the coin and leave this universe with me. Then you can step in and enjoy the fruits of his labor with Jena. It looks like he's already gotten farther than you ever did. But hopefully not too far yet, eh? Maybe you can learn something."

So here was Nate's test of loyalty, sooner than he'd thought it would come. Ephraim was tempted—he could just pass the responsibility to someone else. It would be easy to tell himself that it wasn't his problem, but he didn't believe that anymore. There was no distinction between *him* and *them*. All the Ephraims in all the universes, good and bad, were him. But he was the only one with the coin.

"And the other option?" Ephraim asked. He already knew what it would be.

"We could just kill him and you could reclaim your rightful place here. With her." He cracked his knuckles. "It might be kind of fun; I've never killed an Ephraim before." He cocked his head. "Directly. It's nothing personal. My grudge isn't with you, you know."

Ephraim leaned forward and stared at the other Ephraim. "The coin swapped us before. Couldn't we do that again?"

"That's not how this works," Nate said. "I need a partner. I'd rather it be you, honestly. I don't want to have to go through this all over again." He licked his lips. "You know, if you really prefer this universe, I could also replace this universe's Nathan so we could both live here. This place has a lot going for it compared to mine. I guess the grass is always greener on the other side of the wormhole."

Ephraim remembered the first time he'd met the Nathan of his home universe, when he boldly challenged the bullies harassing him—drawing their attention and taking a bad beating in his place. They'd been inseparable since. Ephraim couldn't let Nate hurt his best friend. Some habits were hard to break. There'd be nothing to stop him if Ephraim decided to stay here after all; that would just give Nate a fresh universe to play with.

Ephraim picked up the controller. Nate didn't seem to care. He flipped it open, but there wasn't the tiniest flicker of activity from it. What he'd been told about the biometric security feature was true—it was useless to him without Nate.

What if Ephraim just destroyed the controller? Keep Nate here so he couldn't get back to his own universe to take revenge on Zoe. Of course, there would be the little problem of a second Ephraim—he wouldn't be able to go back to his life while another version of himself was around. There'd also be two Nathans in this universe, one of them armed and deranged.

"What do you think, Eph?" Nate asked. "No pressure." Despite his light tone, Ephraim was aware that Nate's hands were now in his pockets, and that one of those pockets held his gun.

He had no choice but to keep playing along, and stick close to Nate until he could make his move, whatever it might be. There had to be a way to get to him, something he was overlooking.

Ephraim closed the controller. Remembering Nathaniel, he was suddenly struck by an idea. What Nate really wanted was total control over the coin. He needed an Ephraim around to activate it for him, but what if he thought he didn't need a partner after all? His desire to be in charge could be the best way to get to him.

"What if there's another option?" Ephraim asked.

"Like what?" Nate asked suspiciously.

"Hear me out. I was wondering if there might be a universe out there where you can use the coin instead of me?" Ephraim said. "Say there's another universe with a coin and a controller, but our roles are reversed?" Just imagining it filled Ephraim with dread. He hoped there was no such place, but he needed Nate to believe there could be.

"I don't know. You think that's possible?" Nate looked intrigued, though. Ephraim could practically see the wheels turning. Nate pulled his hands from his pockets.

"In an infinity of universes, isn't anything possible?" Ephraim asked.

"I should have thought of that before," Nate said. "If we could find a universe like that, sure. We could part ways, if that's what you want."

Ephraim realized he'd made a mistake. Nate seemed so taken with the concept, he might want to look for that universe right away. Ephraim assumed such a universe didn't exist. The coin seemed unique so far, but if he was wrong and Nate got one of his own, there'd be no way of stopping him from spreading his hate and anger throughout the multiverse.

Ephraim needed more time to work on his plan, and he would definitely need some help to pull it off. In the meantime, he had to convince Nate that he didn't want to give up the coin and access to all those universes after all. That shouldn't be too hard for Nate to buy, considering how attached he'd become to his travels.

Ephraim pursed his lips. "Did you mean what you said before? That you like partnering with me?"

Nate look surprised, but he covered for it quickly. "Well, yeah. I feel like we're starting to get each other. It's kind of like having my best friend back." He lowered his eyes. That might have been the first completely honest thing Ephraim had heard Nate say.

For all his bravado, maybe Nate just missed Ephraim, the way Ephraim had when he thought he'd lost Nathan. Being betrayed by your partner had to hurt, and with all of Nate's anger and frustration, it was easy to see how that might turn to hate. Nate had spent his whole life being mocked and kicked around, it made sense for him to snatch at power wherever he could. Nate wasn't a good guy by any stretch of the imagination, but Ephraim thought he was beginning to understand him.

"Me too," Ephraim said. "These last few days have been good. It's not just the coin." He swallowed. "It's hanging out with you. I don't like a lot of what you've done, but we can work on that." He smiled.

Nate's eyes widened. "Really?" he said.

Ephraim handed him the controller. "I've made up my mind. I want to continue working with you, and working on our friendship. I don't think I belong here anymore. I can't give up all those other universes." Ephraim pulled out the coin. "I can't give this up again. I tried to once. . . . You were right—it's the only thing I have going for me."

Ephraim thought regurgitating Nate's words back to him— telling him what he wanted to hear—might make his lies sound more like the truth.

"Are you sure?" Nate asked. He frowned, betraying skepticism, and maybe disappointment. He flipped the controller open with a flick of his wrist, training his eyes on Ephraim the whole time.

"I'm sure," Ephraim said.

"What about Jena?" Nate said.

Ephraim looked past Nate to the Jena on the library stairs. She seemed happy, there with her Ephraim. "There are more of her out there," Ephraim said. "Besides, I sort of have a thing for Zoe." As soon as he said it, he was disturbed to realize it was actually true. Nate bought it.

Nate started typing with his thumbs on the keypad, like he was texting someone. "Then I'm deleting the coordinates of this universe from the controller," he said. "If you want to do this, there's no going back, Eph. The odds of us finding exactly this one again randomly . . . well. I've never been very good with math, but it's a long shot. Are you really okay with that?"

Was Nate bluffing him? He hoped so. If he was wrong, Ephraim might never see this universe again. Could he make that sacrifice?

It was worth it if he could shut Nate down, once and for all. And what better way to prove that he was being genuine?

"Go ahead," Ephraim said.

The controller beeped three times, and he saw the ten-digit string of numbers disappear from the screen. He suddenly felt faint.

It was too late to change his mind now. He just had to hope his plan would work, that all of this wouldn't be for nothing.

"Good man," Nate said. "Let's go home."

Ephraim slotted the coin into the controller and took one final look at his home universe before it disappeared forever.

CHAPTER 27

"You did the right thing. You know that," Zoe said.

"That doesn't make me feel any better." Ephraim said as he leaned back against the dusty bookshelf. They were sitting in the first-floor stacks of the shuttered Summerside Public Library. The building was closed and many of the books were gone, but Zoe still had the keys, and it seemed like a perfect place to meet. It was the last place Nate would look for them.

Zoe sat across from him, an electric lantern between them. Sitting here with her in the dark made him think about those stories of couples fooling around in the library stacks.

"So when will you tell me what your big plan is?" Zoe asked. "You seem pretty excited about it."

"I want to wait for the others to get here, so I don't have to repeat it all." He grinned. "Besides, it's more fun to keep you in the dark."

"Ha ha." She flicked the switch on the lantern, and they were plunged into darkness. "See how you like it."

"Hey!" He waited for his eyes to adjust, but the windowless room stayed black.

"Come on, Zoe. Turn the light back on."

"I didn't know you were afraid of the dark," she said.

"Yes, you did. Your Ephraim was probably afraid too. Unfair advantage."

"Did you also have a little nightlight to help you sleep?" Zoe said. Her voice sounded closer.

"Not since I was six," he lied.

"Ephraim always wanted to keep the lights on, when we . . ." Her voice was definitely closer.

"What are you up to?" Ephraim asked.

Zoe giggled, and he felt warm breath on his cheek.

He heard a shuffling noise a few aisles down.

"What was that?" he said. He turned his head but still couldn't see.

"Never mind," she whispered by his ear. "It's probably just a rat."

"A rat!" he said.

Suddenly a bright light shined on both of them.

"Guys! Get a room," a girl's voice said.

Ephraim squinted in the glare of the flashlight and shielded his eyes with a hand.

Zoe pecked him on the cheek.

"Got ya. That's what you get for teasing me," she said.

"It's hardly the same thing," he said.

Zoe turned on the lantern on the floor. At first he thought it was Mary, but she would never wear a skirt that short and snug.

"What're *you* doing here?" Ephraim said. Just like that, their whole plan was ruined before it had even started. If Shelley was here, Nate knew they were up to something. He might even be skulking in the stacks.

"What's your problem?" Shelley said. "Zoe said you wanted my help."

"I'm just a little paranoid because your boyfriend wants to kill me."

"He's not my boyfriend anymore. He just doesn't know it yet." Shelley sighed. "Look, I don't know what's going on. But if you don't want my help, I'll just go."

Ephraim whispered to Zoe. "I asked you to call Mary," he said.

Zoe pushed her hair back, leaving a smudge of dust across her forehead.

"I did."

"Believe it or not, I can tell the difference between them," he said.

"Them? Ephraim, this is Mary Shelley Morales," Zoe said.

Ephraim frowned. "Mary Shelley's one person? Her?"

"Yes. *Her*," Mary Shelley said. "It turns out sound travels pretty well in a library. Maybe that's why librarians are always shushing people."

"You don't have a twin sister?" he asked her.

"Nope. It's just me and myself," Mary Shelley replied.

"In my universe, you're identical twins. Named Mary and Shelley." Ephraim stared at the girl standing between them.

Mary Shelley pointed her flashlight down at her feet. "I always wanted a sister," she said. "But it would be weird to have one who looks just like me."

Nathaniel spoke from behind her. "Wait. It gets weirder."

Mary Shelley jumped and screamed. Zoe spun, swinging her lantern around like a weapon. Nathaniel stepped back. He held a glow stick in one fist, like a tiny Jedi lightsaber, its green light feeble in the light from the lantern.

"Who the hell are you?" Mary Shelley demanded.

Nathaniel grinned. His face had a greenish tint from the glow stick. He did look a little frightening. "It's good to see you too, M.S.," Nathaniel said.

She squinted at him. "Do I know you?"

Ephraim stood up and brushed dirt off the back of his shorts. "It's all right. He's a friend. His name is Nathaniel."

"Nathaniel?" Mary Shelley asked. "I bet that isn't just an odd coincidence."

"He's one of Nate's analogs, an older version of him from a parallel universe," Ephraim said. He was surprised at how normal those words sounded to him now.

Mary Shelley shined her light in his face. "There's a resemblance, I'll admit," she said.

Ephraim nodded to Nathaniel. "Thanks for coming. You know Mary Shelley, I guess," Ephraim said.

"Just one of her in my universe too," Nathaniel said wistfully. "I haven't seen her since high school."

"And this is Zoe Kim," Ephraim said. He indicated her with his flashlight.

"Zoe." Nathaniel stared at her intently. "Nice to meet you."

Zoe put a hand on Ephraim's arm. "Now that we're all here, time you told us your plan, isn't it?"

Ephraim sat and gestured that they should gather around him on the floor. Mary Shelley had some difficulty with that, given her miniskirt. He looked away politely as she arranged her legs the best she could. Zoe grinned at his discomfort.

"I think we all agree that Nate needs to be stopped," Ephraim said. Each of them nodded in agreement. "I think he'll pretty much do whatever it takes to control the coin. He's already done terrible things and I don't see him changing anytime soon."

"He's gotten worse," Mary Shelley said. "A lot worse."

"My Ephraim had been worried about him for a while," Zoe said. "That's one of the reasons he finally decided to escape. It stopped being a game with Nate."

Ephraim drew a circle in the dust next to his knee. "But without an Ephraim analog to use the coin, Nate is essentially powerless."

Mary Shelley flicked her flashlight beam on and off nervously. "Nate was ripping pissed that he couldn't use the coin." She pursed her lips. "If he could have, I think he would have taken it from Ephraim a long time ago."

"I was never that rotten," Nathaniel said. "But I will admit that sometimes I felt more like a sidekick than a real partner. I can see how that might get to him."

"The Nathan analog I shared the coin with felt the same way," Ephraim said. "So I think we can use Nate's feelings, greed, and ambition against him. What if he didn't need me anymore? What if he had a coin that he could use?"

"I'm sure he'd be thrilled," Zoe said. "But how do we get him one?"

"And why would we give him that kind of power? We're supposed to be taking his power away," Mary Shelley said. She pulled a

cigarette out of a purse and put it between her lips. Ephraim made
eye contact with her and slowly shook his head. If Nate smelled cigarette smoke in the library, it might make him suspicious, and they
desperately needed the element of total surprise. Annoyed, she
tucked the cigarette behind her ear and went back to flicking her
flashlight.

"There aren't any other coins," Nathaniel said.

"Are you sure?" Zoe said.

"Absolutely. But we did have a backup controller, safely in my
universe."

"I'm actually glad to hear that," Ephraim said. "But I think
Nate will grasp at any chance at all to get a coin of his own, one that
he can use without a partner. He wants to believe it's possible, and
we'll make him think it is," Ephraim said.

"I have a radical suggestion," Mary Shelley said. "Let's just kill
him. Take the controller from Nate and give it to Nathaniel." Mary
Shelley pointed the flashlight at the older man. He blinked as the
light centered on his face.

"That does sound tempting," Zoe said.

"No," Ephraim said.

"Think about what he did to all the other Nathans." Zoe's voice
got harder. "To Jena. What'll he do when you take away the only
thing he cares about? Whether you stay or not, this is our home.
Nate can still do damage here. We need to get rid of him."

The anger in her face scared Ephraim more than the thought of
what she had in mind.

They were all silent for a moment. Ephraim glanced at
Nathaniel before he spoke.

"I agree that he probably deserves to suffer for what he's done.
But that still doesn't make it right," Ephraim said.

Mary Shelley laughed acidly. "This is why Nate's going to win,"
she said. "He doesn't care about what's 'right.' And I don't either. I
want him to pay for hurting me. For making me hate myself."

Ephraim looked at her. He hadn't known that Nate had crossed that line with her.

"I'm sorry he hurt you," Ephraim said. "And I won't pardon him for it, because abuse is unforgivable. But look. Killing Nate won't change what he's done. We can't bring those people he murdered back to life." Their analogs existed in other universes, they were right here in front of him, but that didn't mean the individuals were replaceable. Each was unique in his or her own way.

He had to believe that. He had to embrace the idea that his life mattered, that he had something to contribute that no one else could—and this was probably his moment to do it.

"So, my plan," Ephraim said. "We have two challenges: get the controller from Nate, and neutralize him as a threat—preferably without killing him. Okay?"

"I don't particularly care about keeping him alive. Since he's an evil asshole and all," Mary Shelley said.

"Well, *I* care. Now, we shouldn't try to overpower him while he's armed. I don't want to take a chance of someone else getting shot. So we have to trick him into giving up his gun, or catch him off guard. For that, I'll need your help. *Everyone's* help."

Silence again. Zoe took his hand and squeezed it. Mary Shelley sighed.

"Whatever you need," Nathaniel said.

Ephraim rubbed his hands together. "Great. Now first . . . does anyone have some spare change?"

After they'd gone over the plan a few times and everyone understood the parts they would play, Ephraim called Nate from a pay phone. Ephraim was nervous; he'd never been a good liar. But Nate agreed to meet him.

Ephraim waited near the library steps, lounging at the base of a lion statue. Finally, a shiny red Chevy roared up and parked by the curb. Nate climbed out and slammed the door.

Nate sauntered over to Ephraim, his hands in the pockets of his hoodie. Ephraim didn't know how he could stand wearing that thing in the summer, but he knew Nate wore it to conceal his gun.

"Hey," Nate said.

"Hey." Ephraim knocked on one of the lion's stone paws for luck and hopped down. "Thanks for coming."

"No problem. What's up?" Nate asked.

"Did you bring the controller?"

Nate patted his left pocket.

"Good," Ephraim said. "Remember our conversation the other day, about finding a version of you who can use the coin?"

Nate nodded.

"I want to try it," Ephraim said.

"Yeah?" Nate's asked. His voice was even, but Ephraim recognized his friend's restrained excitement and apprehension. "Why? You said you liked working with me."

"I do. But   think of what we could do with two coins," Ephraim said.

"Oh, I have been," Nate said. Ephraim thought it was more likely he'd been thinking about what he could do if he didn't need a partner to use the Charon device.

"We'd be real partners then. Equals," Ephraim said. "And let's be honest. I'm sort of holding you back."

"That's true."

"I might want to quit one day too, settle down with Zoe, and I can't do that with this in my life. But I don't want to screw you over either."

Nate narrowed his eyes. "So why'd you want to meet here?"

"I needed a safe place to hide the coin. I can't leave it at Zoe's place. The other Ephraim abandoned her, and I'm worried she'll try to get rid of the coin to keep me in this universe." He smiled. "Or just to spite you."

"You should work on your taste in women," Nate said. "No offense."

"Well, I finally figured out that there's only one analog of Mary Shelley in this universe, and you've got dibs on her," Ephraim said.

Nate glanced at him sharply. "Where did you hear that word?"

Ephraim swallowed. "What word? Dibs?"

"Analog. I've only heard one other person use it in reference to parallel universe doubles."

"Oh." Ephraim scratched distractedly behind his right ear. "Zoe, I think. She has a big SAT vocabulary."

"What's an SAT?"

"A form of torture in my universe. Now I remember. That's what she calls Ephraim. My analog. She must have picked up the term from him."

"Sure." Nate dropped it, but he was still suspicious. "Anyway, if you're really worried about the coin's safety, I could hold onto the coin for you," Nate said.

"I considered that. But it seemed better to keep it where no one would think to look for it. Thus, the library."

"Certainly no one would think to look here, especially since it's been closed for ages, and Ephraim never liked it much," Nate said. "How did you get in?"

Ephraim dangled his key ring. "I work here, remember? And the locks are the same as in my universe."

He unlocked the door, and Nate followed him inside slowly, looking around the murky lobby with his hand on the gun in his pocket.

"I stashed it back here," Ephraim said, leading the way to the stacks behind the checkout counter. Nate trailed behind him in silence. They reached the even darker room, and Ephraim picked up Mary Shelley's flashlight, where he'd hidden it just inside the door.

He hoped everyone was already in place. As he wandered between two shelves, he sneezed loudly, the arranged signal to let them know they were there and the plan was on. He rubbed his arm against his nose.

"The only drawback is I'm allergic to all this dust," he said to Nate.

Ephraim heard the safety hammer on Nate's gun click softly as he released it. He couldn't risk attacking Nate here, though it would have been much less trouble than what they had in store for him.

"Almost there," Ephraim said lightly, hands clenched.

He stopped in front of a dust-covered bookshelf that was still loaded with abandoned books. Zoe had come up with the plan to lure Nate into the library, and she picked the book he had hidden the coin inside.

Ephraim slid it off the shelf and shone his flashlight on the spine.

"*Labyrinths*," Nate said.

"Page 29." Ephraim shook the book, and the coin dropped into his palm. He reshelved the book dutifully.

He tucked the flashlight between his elbow and side, pointing away from where the others were hidden, just behind the shelf in the next aisle over. He glanced at Nate. "So I'm going to make a wish, and you'll follow with the controller."

"But you'll switch places with another Ephraim," Nate said.

"I'm sure you can handle him," Ephraim said. "Besides, it might make it easier to get the coin from your analog."

Nate grinned. "I get it now. I'll get a coin and you'll get your own controller. Smart, Ephraim. And here I thought maybe you really wanted to help me."

"There's nothing wrong with us both coming out ahead," Ephraim said. "You ready?"

Nate flipped open the controller. "I'll be right behind you."

It was hard not to interpret that as a threat.

Ephraim didn't know how much time he would have once he and the others reached the other universe, but it probably wouldn't take Nate long to lock onto the coin. He hoped they would have enough time to get into position.

Someone's sneaker squeaked against a floor tile behind him.

"What was that?" Nate peered into the darkness, moving his head up and down to look through the bare shelves. If he spotted the others now it would be all over. "Shine the light behind you," Nate said.

"It was probably just a rat," Ephraim said.

"A rat!" Nate put his hand back in the pocket with the gun. That was his solution to everything.

"Shh, I'm trying to concentrate," Ephraim said. He tilted the coin heads up in his hand and closed his eyes, keeping his mind as blank as possible while he spoke. "I wish that I were in a universe where Nate can use the coin instead of me."

The coin wasn't getting hot. Did that mean it couldn't grant his wish? He hoped so. Nathaniel had seemed pretty sure that this was the only coin.

In his mind, Ephraim focused as clearly as he could on a universe without any analogs of Nathan, Zoe, Mary Shelley, or him. It wouldn't do for any of them to switch places with their counterparts there. The metal warmed up gradually in his hand. He kept thinking about the universe he wanted to visit until the coin was finally painfully hot. He flipped the quarter into the air.

And deliberately missed it on its way down. It hit the tiles and rolled away from him, but also away from where Zoe, Mary Shelley, and Nathaniel were hidden. Damn. That's what he got for relying on chance.

"Whoops!" he said. "Where'd it go?"

"Dumbass. I think it went over there," Nate said.

Ephraim scurried after the rolling coin, then pretended to stumble. He dropped the flashlight and the light went out.

"Shit," Nate said in an exasperated voice.

Ephraim kept moving toward where he'd seen the coin disappear and hunched down.

"Eph?" Nate called.

"I can't find it!" he said. Ephraim felt the darkness closing in around him. He struggled to breathe, and his palms became cold and wet. Maybe this was a bad plan, like Mary Shelley had said it was. Of course Nate would realize what was going on. And he'd never give them another opportunity to stop him.

"Hold on," Nate said. His face lit up with the glow from the controller. "Where are you?"

"I think I see it," Ephraim said, knocking books off the shelves to cover the soft footfalls of the others heading toward him. Some metal bookends clattered, and he heard Mary Shelley's muffled curse. Ephraim sneezed loudly.

Nate came closer, holding the controller out in front of him to light his way. Then Ephraim felt hands on his shoulder and back. He couldn't tell how many, but he hoped that all three of them were in contact with him or each other. He groped for the coin in the dirt. Come on, he thought. He needed to find it *now*.

The glow from the controller's screen grew closer. Someone slapped the coin into Ephraim's hand, and a moment later he was . . . still in the stacks, but the glow of the emergency lights showed that the library was back in operation.

Zoe was still holding his hand. She gave it an encouraging squeeze before letting go, and he closed his fingers around the coin.

"Everyone here?" he asked. He turned around and the motion sensors triggered the fluorescents overhead, flooding the aisle with light. He, Zoe, Mary Shelley, and Nathaniel squinted and blinked at each other, smiling broadly. Then Zoe and Mary Shelley darted away with barf bags pressed to their faces. Ephraim and Nathaniel exchanged uncomfortable looks and pretended they couldn't hear the girls retching behind the shelves.

A moment later Mary Shelley and Zoe emerged with pained expressions.

"This is a stupid, stupid plan," Mary Shelley said.

"That was so close," Zoe said.

"It's still close—we don't have a lot of time. He's gonna be coming through any second, as soon as the controller locks onto the coin's coordinates. You guys get out of here and head for the fountain. We won't be far behind."

The door to the stacks had just creaked closed when Nate popped in next to Ephraim, accompanied by a burst of static electricity and a soft popping sound. Ephraim nearly jumped out of his skin.

"Holy crap!" Ephraim said. "Is that what it looks like when we do that?"

"Amateur," Nate said. He closed the controller and tucked it away in his hoodie. "I expected another Ephraim to take your place, but no one appeared. I guess you don't exist here. Weird, huh?"

Ephraim shrugged. But that reminded him to check the coin, as Nate would expect him to. Since Zoe had handed the coin to him in the dark, he had no idea if it had landed on heads or tails. As it happened, it was neither.

The coin was blank again.

CHAPTER 28

Ephraim trailed slowly behind Nate as they crossed the street to Greystone Park, trying to give the others more time to get ready for them. Nate was impatient; it was getting dark and the park would close in a little while. Dusk settled around them while they neared the fountain, the sun tinting everything an ominous red as it sank behind the treeline.

"Why do you want to walk through the park?" Nate asked him.

"You got the coin and controller there, so I thought it was a good place to start looking for your analog," Ephraim said.

"I think my house would be better. I mean, that's where I'd look for me."

"Well, it's on the way, so we might as well check it first." Ephraim pretended to sound frustrated.

"Fine. But come *on*," Nate said.

Ephraim fiddled with the coin in his pocket. "Coming." He had checked it again and again, but there was no getting around it. The coin was out of power. That last wish—the effort of shifting four people without exchanging them with analogs—had completely drained it.

If they failed to get the controller from Nate, they would all be stranded here. Wherever "here" was.

"Should we swing by the fountain?" Nate asked. Ephraim hadn't even noticed them enter the park.

"Yeah," Ephraim said. That played into his plan perfectly. He headed for a side path that led into a short maze of hedges, and Nate followed.

Ephraim stopped short just before the hedges opened onto the plaza and pointed.

Nathaniel stood next to the fountain with Mary Shelley. She was holding her cell phone out, waving it around like a Geiger counter. Ephraim groaned to himself—they hadn't explained to her how the controller worked, so she was making it up as she went along. Nathaniel was much more collected. He put a hand on her shoulder and said very clearly, "Set the coordinates for the next universe." He reached into his pocket and pulled out a quarter. It glinted in the waning sunlight.

"Is that supposed to be me?" Nate asked. "He's so old."

"Shelley's with him. It must be you." Ephraim said. He winced when he heard his flat delivery, but Nate didn't notice. He was too caught up in the scene playing out for his benefit.

Nate shaded his eyes with his hand. "It *is* me," he said in amazement.

In the plaza, Nathaniel flipped the coin a couple of times. Then he mimed fitting it in the cell phone in Mary Shelley's hand.

"So how do you want to—" Ephraim began.

Before Ephraim could stop him, Nate stepped out between two hedges, drawing his gun. "Hold it right there, pops," Nate said.

Mary Shelley released a very effective B-movie scream, which may not have been part of her act—there *was* a gun pointed in her direction. Nathaniel purposely fumbled the coin and it fell onto the cobblestones between him and Nate.

"Ephraim," Nate called. "Fetch that coin for me will you? And get the controller from that hot chick. Robbing the cradle, eh, old man? What universe did you find her in?"

Ephraim winked at Mary Shelley when he took the cell phone from her. He scooped up the quarter and returned to Nate.

Nate couldn't hold the gun and take both the quarter and cell phone from Ephraim.

"Give me the gun. I'll cover them," Ephraim said.

Nate just smiled as he reached for the quarter. Ephraim handed it to him, trying to keep his hand from shaking from excitement and nervousness. It wouldn't be long now.

Nate held his gun on Nathaniel while he checked out the quarter. Satisfied for the moment, he slipped it into his pocket.

"Now let me see that controller," Nate said.

Nate might not have noticed that the quarter was a perfectly ordinary coin, but he wouldn't be fooled by Mary Shelley's cell phone. Ephraim didn't know what else to do, so he dropped the phone at Nate's feet.

"What the hell is wrong with you? You're such a fucking klutz today, Eph."

Nate knelt to pick up the phone.

Ephraim saw his moment. He yelled, "Get down!" then kicked the gun out of Nate's hand. It clattered against stone somewhere to their side, but it didn't go off.

A moment later, he realized he should have kicked Nate in the face instead, when Nate tackled Ephraim's legs and brought him down hard.

"What the fuck?" Nate said. Ephraim's foot connected with his jaw, and he ducked away.

"The jig is up, Nate," Zoe said. She darted from behind a hedge and snatched the gun. In one smooth movement, she tossed it underhand into the fountain. "I always wanted to say that," she said, smiling.

Nate scrambled away from Ephraim and turned to face the four of them. He wiped a smear of blood from his chin.

"Give me some credit, guys," Nate said. He reached behind him and pulled a second, smaller pistol from the waistband of his jeans. "In some universes, they practically give these away to anyone who wants them."

"Shit," Ephraim said.

Nate cocked back the safety and aimed the gun at Zoe. "If anyone moves, Zoe dies. Or Jena, or whoever you are." He gestured at Nathaniel and Mary Shelley. "All of you stand over there. You too, Ephraim."

"You can't shoot all of us," Mary Shelley said.

"Actually, I can," Nate said. "Six bullets and only four of you."

"Too bad someone threw the other gun in the effing fountain," Mary Shelley said.

Ephraim held his hands out. "Nate. This was all a setup. That coin in your pocket's only worth twenty-five cents. You won't be going to any more universes if you kill me, or anyone else."

Nate pulled out the quarter. His lips moved, and he flipped the coin, catching it in one hand. When nothing happened he cursed and threw it into the fountain. "I'll just take your coin from your dead body, the same way you did. And I'll find another Ephraim here."

"This universe doesn't have an Ephraim," Ephraim said. "I wished for a universe where analogs of you and I don't exist."

"You can't do that. The coin doesn't work that way."

"It drained all the power from the coin to do it, but it brought us here," Ephraim said.

"Eph." Zoe groaned.

Ephraim winced. He'd just given away the fact that they couldn't leave without the controller either.

Nate waved the gun at Nathaniel. "I recognize you now. You're the geezer who gave us the coin and controller. You're another me?"

Nathaniel grimaced. "Unfortunately."

"What happened to you?"

"I grew up. You should try it."

"If you came from my universe, this must be Zoe and Mary Shelley." Nate smiled thinly. "They were in the library with us. You're trickier than I thought, Ephraim. A lot trickier than the Ephraim I knew. I shouldn't have underestimated you."

"Come on, Nate," Ephraim said. "It's over. We're all prepared to stay in this universe if it means stopping you from hurting anyone else." This wasn't going exactly as planned, but he could still salvage the situation if he got the controller from Nate.

Ephraim stepped forward and jumped when the gun swiveled in his direction, then back toward the girls. Nate's aim was getting wilder, but this close, chances were he would hit *someone*. "Nate. Just give me the controller and the gun and we'll take you wherever you want to go. I promise."

The gun fired, the shot echoing through the park.

"No!" Ephraim turned to Zoe—he couldn't stand to lose her again. But she was fine.

Nathaniel fell next to her, clutching his left side. Bright red blossomed on his flannel shirt.

He stared at Nate in disbelief. "You little shit."

"Nathaniel!" Ephraim rushed to his side.

"He stepped in front of me," Zoe said.

"I'll . . . be all right." Nathaniel grunted. His breath wheezed and his hand was slick with blood. "Damn. This is a new shirt."

"Why did you do that?" Mary Shelley screamed at Nate. "You didn't have to do that!"

"My finger slipped," Nate said casually. He pulled back the safety. "I'm so nervous I can barely hold this gun steady." He pointed it straight at Zoe.

Zoe took a panicked step back.

Ephraim launched himself at Nate, careful to get between him and Zoe. He wasn't going to let any more people die in his place. He didn't care about the controller or his home universe or any of that anymore. He had only two things on his mind: stopping Nate and protecting his friends.

Nate swung the gun toward Ephraim but hesitated before pulling the trigger, just long enough for Ephraim to shove him onto the hard cobblestones around the fountain. Ephraim heard the gun drop next to them and another shot go off. He hoped it hadn't hit anyone else.

Nate pushed Ephraim into the cement of the fountain and ground his back against the rim of the basin. Nate let him go, then jabbed him in the chest with his elbow.

Ephraim groaned. "Is this really what you want? To be like all those kids who beat you up through elementary school? Just another bully?"

Nate punched him in the left cheek, and Ephraim felt the impact vibrate through his skull as his head whipped right.

Nate punched him again on his left ear. Ephraim flopped over.

"I helped you though," Ephraim choked. "I used to protect you. I bet your Ephraim did too."

"You always thought you were better than me," Nate said. "You were worse than they were, because you pretended to be my friend. And then you betrayed me."

Ephraim opened his eyes.

"I *am* better than you." Ephraim spat. Bright-red saliva splashed on Nate's shirt.

Ephraim's vision blurred—he saw two Nates looming over him, indistinct and overlapping. Through the ringing pain he heard distant voices, distorted like he was underwater.

"Wait," Zoe said. "You might hit Ephraim!"

"Let go!" Mary Shelley said.

"Have you ever fired a gun before?"

"Get out of my way."

Ephraim clasped an arm to his stomach. Scissors of pain cut through him, and he started to feel nauseous. It was as if this was happening to someone else. He liked it that way. It was happening to another Ephraim. He let himself drift toward unconsciousness. This wasn't his problem anymore . . .

Another gunshot snapped him out of it. His vision focused, and he forgot the pain for the moment. Nate had frozen with a hand in one of Ephraim's pockets. They both exchanged a frightened glance and scrambled away from each other, then looked over at Mary Shelley and Zoe.

Mary Shelley crouched beside Nathaniel's body, looking more shocked than any of them. "Did I hurt anyone?" she asked. She clenched the smoking gun double-handed, knuckles white. Her chin bled from a cut just below her lip.

"Just yourself," Zoe said angrily. "That kickback is a bitch, isn't it? Give me that before you actually shoot someone."

Mary Shelley passed her the gun with a wince, massaging her jaw. Zoe pointed the gun evenly at Nate. "I'm a better shot than she is. You okay, Ephraim?"

"Nothing a week in bed won't fix." He stood up shakily, aching with every movement. He grinned at her. "Especially with someone cute nursing me back to health."

"Don't get fresh. I'm holding a gun, you know," Zoe said.

He put his hands up in mock surrender.

"Now give Ephraim the controller," Zoe said to Nate. "Slowly."

Nate didn't move. Ephraim reached into the left pocket of Nate's hoodie to retrieve the device. Nate just glared at him sullenly. He patted Nate down, just in case he was hiding another weapon, and pulled his digital camera out of a back pocket. He joined Zoe and Mary Shelley and knelt to check on Nathaniel. His eyes were closed, and his breathing sounded shallow.

"Nathaniel?" Mary Shelley asked.

Nathaniel's eyelids fluttered, and he spoke through gritted teeth. "It hurts like hell, but I think he missed anything important. I'll probably need some stitches."

"If he damaged any organs, at least we have a perfect donor," Mary Shelley said. She glared over at Nate, who was sulking by the fountain.

"Cool it," Ephraim said.

Nathaniel's eyes flew open. "Ephraim. You got the controller."

"Yeah." Ephraim flipped it open, but it didn't switch on. He tried to put it in Nathaniel's left hand, but the man's grip was too feeble to hold it. His right hand was pressed to his side. Blood dripped between the fingers. Ephraim's stomach lurched, and he looked away. He didn't want to watch another friend die like this.

"I don't know if I'm going to be able to fulfill my part of the bargain," Nathaniel said.

"We'll get you home," Ephraim said. "Don't you worry."

Zoe grimaced. "We'll force Nate to help us," she said.

Nate sat on the edge of the fountain, arms folded and looking at all of them calmly. "I'm not doing shit for you," he said.

"I'm not giving him the controller again," Ephraim said. "Not after all this."

"Then I guess we don't need him for anything," Mary Shelley said. "Shoot him, Zoe."

Nate glanced at Mary Shelley, and his expression changed. Softened. "I care about you, M.S.," he said softly.

"You were obsessed with me. I was just another thing you wanted. But I was never enough."

Nathaniel groaned. "The biometrics . . ." He pushed himself up with his jaw clenched, and Mary Shelley bent down to lift his shoulders. Nathaniel coughed and pointed at Zoe. "Give the controller to Jena." He licked his lips. "Sorry. *Zoe*."

Ephraim stared at him. "What?"

"Go on."

Ephraim shrugged and passed the controller to Zoe. She exchanged it for the gun, which felt like a cold, ugly weight in his palm. It wasn't like the plastic guns he'd played video games with. This gun had actually killed people. He pointed it unsteadily at Nate; the controller in Zoe's hands held most of his attention.

Zoe flipped open the controller, and the screen flashed to life.

"It's working," she said in amazement.

"Why?" Ephraim asked.

"Our Jena was part of the team, too," Nathaniel said. "She's the one who came up with the nickname Charon for the device."

That sounded like Jena, all right.

"You've been holding out on us, old man," Ephraim said. "Why didn't you share that before?"

Nathaniel raised his eyebrows apologetically. "I worried that . . . if I told you, you wouldn't need me."

Zoe put a hand on Ephraim's shoulder. "So she and your Ephraim," Zoe said. "They explored universes together?"

Nathaniel regarded both of them. "Actually, they never did."

"So others can use the coin and the controller," Ephraim said. "How many?"

"I only know of four people—not counting their analogs, of course. But the device can be programmed for any pair of users back at the lab."

Nate was leaning forward, literally on the edge of his seat, obviously eavesdropping on their conversation.

"Now's clearly not the time to get into this," Nathaniel said.

"You're right. But I hope you can give me some answers later," Ephraim said.

Nathaniel groaned. "So do I."

"What are we going to do?" Zoe said.

Ephraim still had the gun on Nate, but they couldn't keep him hostage forever. "I don't know. We can't kill Nate and we can't let him loose. He's messed up and he won't ever change," Ephraim said.

"You might be wrong." Nathaniel said. "I was like him once, maybe even angrier. I'm not proud of it, but I became a better person, largely thanks to the Ephraim I knew."

Nate laughed again. "You'll never get home without my help, Ephraim. I memorized your home coordinates before I deleted them. I'm the only one who can get you home."

"Assuming I believe you, I'd already resigned myself to giving up my universe. The place isn't the thing, it's about the people. Universes might be interchangeable, but people aren't. If I never get back home, I could make a good life for myself anywhere," Ephraim said. He and Zoe made brief eye contact.

"Eph." Nathaniel rolled his head to the side to look up at him. "Even if the controller doesn't remember your universe, you do. The coin can take you wherever you want to go, especially if it's been there before. You just have to think about it clearly. Follow your instincts."

"First we have to get you fixed up," Ephraim said.

"Never mind that. Mary Shelley can help me to a hospital." She was already calling for an ambulance on her cell phone. "You take care of Nate," he said.

"You trust us to come back for you?" Ephraim asked.

"I trust you with my life," Nathaniel said.

"We'll get you home," Ephraim said. "I wish I knew what to do with Nate, though." He laughed, realizing what he'd just said.

"Too bad we can't wish him to the cornfield," Zoe said.

Nathaniel raised an eyebrow.

"Like in that episode of *The Twilight Zone*," she explained. "This creepy little kid had the power to control reality with his mind. He sent people to 'the cornfield' when he didn't like them. Of course, that was probably just a euphemism for killing them . . ."

Ephraim snapped his fingers. "Zoe, the cornfield is a great idea. That's exactly what we'll do."

CHAPTER 29

"Where the hell are we?" Nate asked. He yanked the arm Ephraim was gripping tightly. Ephraim let him go, and Nate scrambled away from him and Zoe.

"A place you haven't explored yet," Ephraim said. "I know how much you like new places."

"Hell is right," Zoe said. "This isn't a cornfield. It's more like a minefield."

The fountain was gone. The landscape was barren—all the trees had been cut down, and the park was surrounded by miles of high, black chain link fencing. A building was visible in the distance—not the library but some kind of military structure. Green Jeeps rumbled around it, and Ephraim saw two distant helmeted soldiers looking toward them. He and Zoe should probably get out of there soon.

"Is this what you had in mind, Ephraim?" Zoe tucked the controller into the waistband of her denim shorts with her left hand while her right held the gun steady on Nate. He'd have to ask her one day why she was so comfortable with guns. Part of him didn't want to know.

"It's exactly what I had in mind," Ephraim said. The coin was cooling in his hand. He ran his thumb over the reeded edge.

It had taken him a few minutes to locate the right coordinates among those stored in the controller, but he'd remembered visiting this militaristic universe with Nate after a string of heists in sequential universes, before the trip to the virgin woodland Nate liked. Ephraim had wavered between the two options, but in the end, he'd allowed his feelings to influence his decision. He couldn't justify giving Nate his own personal paradise, no matter how difficult it might be for him to survive there without the use of technology.

"This place is practically post-apocalyptic," Nate said. "You can't leave me here." He peeled off his hoodie and tossed it on the ground. The temperature was almost unbearably hot here.

"That's the idea. You won't be able to do any more damage in this universe," Ephraim said.

"You aren't really going to ditch me here," Nate said. "That isn't like you, Ephraim. Your analog maybe, but you're different. You're better. Isn't he, Zoe?"

"Don't talk to me," Zoe said. She pulled back the safety on the gun. "Please, give me an excuse to use this."

"Zoe," Ephraim said.

"Oh. Good cop, bad cop. I get it. You're trying to scare me, Ephraim. Fine, I'm scared. Now get us out of here," Nate said.

Zoe used the toe of her flip-flop to nudge a torn scrap of paper on the ground, half-covered in red dirt. "Look at this," she said.

It was one of those draft flyers for the US Army, announcing the mandatory recruitment of all able-bodied citizens 16 or older to join the fight against the USSR.

Ephraim picked it up and handed it to Nate. "Here you go, soldier. Now you can kill as much as you want to."

Nate's face went white when he saw it. "No, Ephraim. You can't do this."

"You like guns so much, you should love it here," he said.

"No. Please." Nate crumpled the flyer. "Listen, just send me back to the universe with the wilderness. The coordinates are in the controller. I know them by heart. I'll stay there, I promise. I won't hurt anyone because there's no one to hurt. I don't deserve this."

"Don't listen to him, Ephraim," Zoe cautioned.

Ephraim clenched his jaw. "You're right, Nate. You don't deserve this. You deserve worse. Maybe I shouldn't stop Zoe from shooting you for everything you've done. But we aren't killers."

"It's the same thing as killing me if you leave me here," Nate said.

"At least you'll have a fighting chance, and maybe you'll even manage to accomplish some good for once in your life."

"Look." Nate licked his lips, his eyes crazed. "I was lying before, about your analog killing his parents. I was with Ephraim when he found them that night, already dead. David Scott killed Madeline, just like the police said. That's why Ephraim took off. He was upset."

Ephraim stared at Nate. "Of course he didn't kill them. I didn't need proof of his innocence—I know myself and what I'm capable of."

"Don't be so sure," Nate said. But his words lacked conviction. He was desperate. "I didn't kill him," he said softly. "I know you both think I pushed him into traffic, but Ephraim was so distracted, it really was an accident. He told me I was on my own from now on, and not to follow him, and he walked right in front of that bus."

"Shut up," Zoe said. Her hand was trembling.

There was suddenly a lot of activity near the compound. A dust cloud moved toward them—three of the Jeeps were fast approaching their end of the field.

"Time to go," Ephraim said.

Zoe put the gun's safety back on before tucking it into her jeans, then tied Nate's hoodie around her waist to conceal it. She pulled out the controller and flipped it open. Ephraim slid the coin into its groove, and she selected the coordinates for the previous universe. "The scary thing is, if I'm reading these numbers right, the subgroup for this universe isn't too far off from my own," she whispered.

"We just have to hope this never becomes our reality," Ephraim said.

"Eph?" Nate whined. He kneeled in the dirt, watching the army Jeeps approach. He didn't look so tough anymore.

Ephraim held up the digital camera he'd confiscated from Nate and flashed a picture of him. "I always want to remember you that way," Ephraim said.

Nate stared up at him, rage building behind his expressionless face.

Zoe linked her arm securely through Ephraim's and pushed a button on the controller. The coin slowly lifted and hovered.

"Have a good life, Nate," Zoe said. Then Ephraim took the floating coin.

Nate's wail was cut short when Ephraim and Zoe shifted. But the chilling echo of his despair followed them into the next universe.

They checked on Nathaniel and Mary Shelley at Summerside General. Nathaniel's chest was bandaged and color had returned to his face. He was cleared to leave, though the doctor recommended staying overnight.

"How's Nate?" Nathaniel said.

"How can you still be concerned for him after everything he's done?" Ephraim asked.

"Because he's still me, as much as I hate to admit it." Nathaniel climbed out of the bed, his face pinched with pain. Mary Shelley helped him stand. "Let's get out of here. This isn't a bad universe though; the health care system is a lot better. They didn't even care that I don't have medical insurance."

"That could come in handy," Ephraim said. "I can just pop over when I need an operation."

Nathaniel eyed him. "So you plan to keep using the coin?"

"I have a few things to make up for, as much as I can. Then . . ." He shrugged. "Maybe I'll try to get home. After that, I don't know. It's tempting . . . but that's probably a good reason to get rid of it for good."

They went back to the library, where they all linked hands outside. Zoe set the coordinates for her home universe, and a moment later they were standing outside the familiar ruined building.

Mary Shelley cleared her throat. "Well, I'm not much for goodbyes. My house is only a few blocks from here, and I'm already late for dinner. So . . ."

Ephraim hugged her. "Thanks for your help," he said.

"Sure. You stay out of trouble." She kissed him on the cheek.

She waved to Nathaniel and Zoe, who didn't seem to notice because they had their heads bent over the controller, then walked off down the street.

"We found Nathaniel's home coordinates," Zoe said. "Right at the top of the list."

Nathaniel insisted they depart from the center of Greystone Park, so for the last time, the three of them went across the street and gathered in front of the dry and cracked fountain.

"Are you ready to go home?" Ephraim said to Nathaniel. He was curious to see what the future would be like—*might* be like.

Nathaniel nodded.

Ephraim slotted the coin into the controller. He was envious; it wouldn't be this easy for Ephraim to get home; but of course, he hadn't been waiting years to have the chance.

"I think you should do the honors," Nathaniel told Zoe.

She took the controller from him and set the coin spinning. When it froze in place, Ephraim held out his arm, and Zoe and Nathaniel gripped it firmly. He deftly plucked the coin from midair.

They appeared inside a large courtyard surrounded on all sides by smooth steel walls rising ten stories high, which roughly outlined the perimeter of the courtyard surrounding the Memorial Fountain. The only exit seemed to be through four wide doors set into each wall, which looked like the massive doors on a bank vault.

"Holy shit," Zoe said. "Where are we?"

An alarm went off, reverberating through the enclosed court-yard. Nathaniel hurried over to one of the doors and placed his palm against a panel beside it. The alarm stopped, and the door whooshed open. He glanced inside longingly before turning back to them.

"Sorry about that. Uh, welcome to the Everett Institute for Research in Relative States, Wave Mechanics Probability, and Many-Worlds Travel," Nathaniel said.

"That's a mouthful," Ephraim said. He tried to make a sensible acronym out of it and failed.

"That's why we usually just refer to it as the Crossroads," Nathaniel said. "But I call it home, sweet home."

"You live here?" Ephraim asked. There was a ten-foot-high statue of Atlas in the center of the courtyard, roughly where the fountain should be. The Titan's arms held a vertical ring in which a six-inch-thick brass disc was suspended horizontally. Two other brass rings framed it at different angles.

"I had to move out of my mom's house eventually," Nathaniel said. "And working here has its privileges. Hopefully they haven't replaced me yet, since I've been gone so long." He smiled proudly at the machine Ephraim was staring at. "That's our Coheron Drive. Isn't she beautiful? I helped build her."

Ephraim glanced at the coin in his hand. Zoe patted his shoulder comfortingly. "Don't worry. Size doesn't matter in quantum mechanics," she said. "It's how you use it."

Nathaniel tilted his head back and drew in a deep breath. Ephraim looked up and saw a square patch of sky above the atrium, which was covered by a skylight.

"Thank you, both of you. Don't take this the wrong way, but I hope we never meet again." Nathaniel extended a hand to Ephraim.

"Oh, I'm sure I'll see you around—one of you, anyway," Ephraim said. They shook hands warmly.

Zoe hugged Nathaniel.

He winced.

"Sorry. Good luck," she said.

"Keep an eye on him, okay? Remember what I told you," Nathaniel said.

"Sure thing," Zoe said.

Nathaniel stepped inside the open doorway, waved at them, and pressed another button that shut the door behind him. Ephraim itched to check out the inside of this impressive building and explore a universe twenty-five years into his future, but he had other things to take care of right now.

"So where next, boss?" Zoe asked.

Ephraim took one last look at the supersized version of his coin, wondering how it worked. "Can you set the controller for the reality I was in before yours?" He handed her the coin, and she worked the controller silently, the tip of her tongue peeking from the corner of her mouth.

"That's the one where I died, isn't it?" she whispered.

"Not you," he said firmly.

She held out the controller to him, the coin hovering over it and dimly reflecting the glow of the lamp above them.

"When I arrived in your universe, there was no analog of me to swap with. So right now there shouldn't be an Ephraim in the universe I left." No Ephraim, and no Jena. It might put a drain on the coin, but he didn't have to worry about that with the controller in easy reach. He took Zoe's hand, waited for her nod, and took the coin.

They shifted.

Ephraim heard the fountain burbling behind him again, but he didn't turn to look at it. He was sure the water had been thoroughly cleaned by now, but he wasn't anxious to revive his memories of Jena's death.

Zoe slipped her hand from his and drew her arms around her stomach. "I'm getting used to the shifts. But just the same, I'm glad I didn't eat anything before we left."

The plaza was brighter than it should be just after sundown; at this time in the evening, the fountain lights and water were usually turned off.

Zoe turned and gasped. "You have to see this," she said. She pulled at his elbow.

Reluctantly, he looked at the fountain. It was surrounded by vases of flowers and piles of books. As they approached it to get a better look, they found notes and memories of Jena scrawled in chalk on the concrete around the fountain. Pictures of Jena and her friends were propped up against its base, and dozens of burning candles floated in the water.

"Wow," Zoe said. Her eyes filled with tears.

"Yeah," Ephraim said.

"I feel like Tom Sawyer and Huck Finn visiting their own funeral," Zoe said. She sat down on the edge of the fountain and stared at the lights on the water. They reflected off the silver coins beneath them, shimmering like stars. The fountain was full of more coins than he'd ever seen—all wishes for Jena, he imagined. He dipped a cupped hand into the water and poured it out. It was cold. The motion set some of the candles gently floating away from him.

Ephraim looked around nervously, peering into the deepening shadows around the fountain. "We should probably get going," he said. "We don't want anyone to see you here."

"'The report of my death was an exaggeration,'" Zoe said. She wiped her eyes and sniffled. "You're right. What now?"

"Hopefully, the controller has coordinates for all the universes I've visited since I found this damn coin." Except the coordinates he really cared about, which he'd seen Nate delete. "I didn't know what I was doing before, but every time I made a wish, I bumped an analog of mine out of his life and into someone else's. I want to return all of them to where they belong. If we work backwards, that ought to put everything straight."

Zoe's mouth opened, but she didn't say anything, just braced the controller between her hands in her lap.

"I must have gone to nearly a dozen universes. All I need is for you to set the coordinates, then I'll grab the coin and shift ahead on my own, so I swap with my analog," he said. "Are you sure you're up to this?"

Zoe nodded. The coin spun in the air and then froze in position.

"Okay then. You know how to follow with the controller," he went on. Nathaniel had given her a tutorial on the controller's advanced features, and she was a quick study. She knew as much about it as he did now. "It's late, so the other Ephraims should all be

home. But give me a minute to get somewhere private." He looked
around. "You may want to hide too, unless you want to deal with the
confused analog who takes my place."

"I'll be all right," Zoe said.

"When you catch up to me, we'll just set the next coordinates.
Wash, rinse, repeat. We'll go through all of them, starting from this
universe and working our way to back to my first wish."

"Got it," Zoe said. She took a deep breath. "Do you really have to
do this? I'm sure those people don't even realize what's happened to
them. It might disrupt their lives even more if we shift them again."

"They belong in their own universes," he said.

"But didn't you say that Nathan came with you a couple of
times? And . . . Jena?"

"I know I can't set everything right for everyone." He couldn't
bring all those dead people back to life, for instance. "But I'd like to
fix as much as possible."

"Fair enough." She stood. "It's going to be a long night. Are you
ready?"

Ephraim reached for the coin.

The first trip went well. Ephraim found himself in his own bed. It
was extremely comforting after everything he had been through. He
sat up and looked around the dark room, for once not wanting to catalog the differences. If he pretended, this could be home. Maybe this
was a foolish mission. Hadn't he said it himself? The universe didn't
matter, the people did. He could just stay here.

"No," he said. That would be selfish. He wasn't doing this for
himself, he was doing it for all the other Ephraims . . . the ones he
had pushed out of their lives.

He waited for an hour, but Zoe didn't appear. He paced around
the living room wondering what had gone wrong, or if she'd changed
her mind. He kept flipping the coin in the dark, wondering whether
he should go looking for her. Finally someone buzzed the apartment.

"Zoe?" he whispered into the intercom.

"Who do you think?" She sounded annoyed. He buzzed her in.

She pounded on the door when she got upstairs, and he let her in.

"Easy," he said. "Don't wake my mother."

"I hate you," she said. She was panting heavily. "I managed to track your coin. But when I got to this universe, I was still in the fucking park and you weren't there. I ran the whole way here, in the *dark*." She stared at him. He smoothed his messy hair self-consciously. "Gee, I hope I didn't wake you," she said.

"Crap. Sorry!" Ephraim said. "I completely forgot the controller wouldn't move you to my location. I thought it was strange when you didn't show up."

"Know what else was weird? Seeing another Ephraim take your place. Your analog was very disoriented. And naked. He also thought I was part of his screwy dream—until I kicked him to prove he was awake and that I wasn't interested." She grinned.

Ephraim winced. "Was that necessary?"

"I'm not completely evil. I gave him Nate's hoodie so he could get home without getting arrested for indecent exposure."

"Such a Samaritan." He looked at her sidelong. "So . . . did you, uh, see anything?"

She smirked. "Nothing I haven't seen before, lover."

He led Zoe to his bathroom. "It should be safe for you to wait in here. If you pop into a universe and you don't know where I am, just wait here for me. I'll come to you next time."

"Hopefully this will be easier from here on out," Zoe said.

Ephraim slotted the coin in the controller, and she set the next coordinate. "Next stop: more of the same," she said.

The coin flashed as it spun, then stopped, torqued at a weird angle. He sighed and reached for it.

A few universes later Ephraim was sitting on his couch. The television was on, some movie he didn't recognize, but it was old, the black-and-white images flickering in the dark room. Jim snored beside him, his head lolling forward on his chest, his left hand still in a half-full popcorn bowl.

Ephraim got up quietly and snuck a handful of popcorn. Jim's breathing sputtered in his sleep. Ephraim edged out of the living room and into the bathroom next to his room, where he waited for Zoe to appear.

Zoe popped in and promptly banged a knee against the toilet tank.

"Ow," she said.

"Shhhh!" Ephraim whispered. "We have to be very very quiet."

"Are we hunting wabbits?" Zoe said with an arched eyebrow as he slotted the coin into the controller.

"It's duck season," he said.

"Rabbit season." She laughed.

"Duck season."

"Rabbit season." Zoe set the next coordinate.

"Rabbit season!" Ephraim said, and grabbed the coin.

Ephraim was in bed again, but the sound of soft breathing in the dark room told him he wasn't alone this time. He held his own breath as he slowly rolled his head to the left.

Mary was sleeping there, curled onto her side, her brown hair falling over her cheek. Ephraim froze.

He waited for what seemed like a long time, then slowly eased himself out of the bed. He was clothed, of course, but he saw a pair of boxer shorts he recognized on the floor, near a pile of his and Mary's clothing. He shook his head and tiptoed into the bathroom. Just as he closed the door, Zoe popped in behind him.

"Duck season!" she said, her voice reverberating in the tiny room. "Fire!"

"Ahh!" Ephraim whirled around. "You scared me."

Zoe blinked at him in the fluorescent light from the mirror over the sink.

Mary's voice came from the bedroom. "Ephraim?"

Zoe's mouth fell open. "What was that? Do you have a girl over? Who is it? Is it me?"

Zoe leaned over and started to turn the doorknob.

"What are you doing?" he hissed.

"I'm just going to take a peek."

"Ephraim? Are you all right?" Mary called.

"That sounds like Mary," Zoe said. "Or is it Shelley in this world? Or both? It's both of them, isn't it? You dog."

"We don't have time for this." Ephraim dropped the coin into the controller, and Zoe straightened.

"You're no fun. You must come from Boring World." She cocked an eyebrow. "Sure you don't want me to give you two a few minutes here?"

Ephraim waved his hand. "Let's just get on with it, all right?"

"Okay. Sorry."

As Ephraim took the coin, he thought that the analog he had replaced likely wouldn't thank him for snatching him away from *this* borrowed reality.

Ephraim found himself in another bathroom, but it definitely wasn't at his house and he didn't recognize it. He was crouched over the toilet; judging from the smell of the mess in the bowl, his other self couldn't hold his liquor. He gagged and backed away.

"Nice going, party animal," he said.

The pounding bass in the walls told him a party was going on outside. But who was he with?

He exited the bathroom and scanned the crowd. He spotted Mary and Shelley dancing together in a corner of the club. He slipped out quietly and discovered he was at least still in Summerside. He thought it might have been Mary and Shelley's house.

He jogged back to his apartment, appreciating what Zoe had gone through to get there from the park. He snuck in, worried he'd find his mother waiting for him, and slipped into his bedroom. Zoe was sitting in front of the television playing video games. She glanced up when he came in, dripping with sweat.

"Well, this sure isn't Boring World," Zoe said. "Where were you?"

"My other self was at a party somewhere."

"I figured when I saw how drunk he was when he swapped with you. He's sleeping it off on the bathroom floor in the last universe." Zoe walked up behind him and put an arm around Ephraim's waist. Her hand held the controller. Ephraim dropped the coin into it, and she tucked herself in closer, turning her head to yawn into his shoulder. He wondered why she was suddenly being so friendly, but he wasn't about to complain. He put an arm around her, wanting to stay that way with her for a while.

"He'll have a hard time explaining that, along with a nasty hangover," Ephraim said. "Hey. We're almost done, Zoe. I should get going."

She nodded and disentangled herself from him. When she was clear, he grabbed the coin.

In the next universe he was sitting at a computer with porn on the screen. He quickly turned off the monitor, just as he felt a tingling sensation along the tops of his bare arms. Zoe popped in, the air crackling and rushing around her as she displaced it. Her eyes swept the room with a smile on her face.

She brushed her hair casually away from her eyes, like she hadn't just stepped through from another universe.

"Oops. I forgot to go into the bathroom first," she said. "I hope I didn't interrupt anything." She giggled.

Ephraim glanced at the dark screen. "You caught him in the act, didn't you?"

"*Awkward.* I mean, it's one thing if your mother walks in on you, and another when you're pulled into a parallel universe and appear right in front of a girl who looks like your crush."

Ephraim sighed.

"He screamed and bolted for the bathroom," Zoe said. "Which is why I couldn't go in there. You sure you're helping these guys? That one is probably going to need therapy after this."

"How many are left?" Ephraim asked. He yawned. The first gray light of dawn was creeping through the window. It was morning already. He felt like he had been shifting through universes for his whole life. He tried to ignore the dull ache in his stomach.

"We're nearly there. Just a couple more coordinates," Zoe said. She lowered the controller. "Something smells good."

Then he smelled it too: cooking bacon.

He pictured his mother in the next room, cooking breakfast for him. He wanted to stay here more than anything, but she was someone else's mom. He had stolen that other Ephraim's happiness, and if he was going to get his old life back, he had to take it *all* back.

He thought about his first few wishes. "Three more trips to go," he said.

"We only have two more coordinates."

He grimaced. "I know."

They shifted twice more without incident. Ephraim had simply appeared in bed each time. These analogs sure knew how to have fun.

"That's it," Zoe said.

"I'm sure there's a pattern to these coordinates," he said. "The first few numbers look the same." Those must indicate a particular subset of the multiverse, with the rest of the digits zeroing in on the specific variations.

"Okay," Zoe said. She punched in the first few digits. "Are we close enough to your home that you can just make it there on your own?"

"I think it's just one shift over, but I made a pretty big wish that first time." He wondered what he would find when he got back there. Nate had said his mother was drinking again. He hoped it wasn't true, but if it was . . . he would have to find some way to help his mother. There were no magic solutions to that problem, no matter how much he might want one.

Ephraim closed his eyes. "I'm going to try."

Zoe set the coin spinning, and he put his hand over hers, on the controller. Though the coin slowed, it didn't stop moving. Eventually it settled in a sluggish, wobbly sort of state, turning over and over. Heads. Tails. Heads. Tails.

Ephraim remembered that on his first wish the coin had come up heads. Of course now he knew that the coin's orientation only affected the spatial direction of his shift; if he'd been directing the coin with his thoughts, maybe he'd chosen "bad" universes because subconsciously he thought tails was a worse outcome than heads. It was all in his mind. Heads and tails were a matter of perspective.

He tried to keep as much of his home universe in his thoughts as he could, most especially his mother, Nathan, and Jena as he remembered them. He readied himself to snatch the coin. When it was horizontal with tails facing up, it abruptly stopped. Zoe looked at him doubtfully.

Tails. That had to be right, if he was truly traveling back the way he came. It didn't mean anything more than that.

He closed his eyes, and, because it couldn't hurt, he muttered, "There's no place like home." Then he took his hand away from around Zoe's and the controller, gently slid it under the coin, and closed his fingers over it.

The shift felt different from all the other times. He felt the usual twinge and lurch in his stomach, like it was compressing then expanding, but then he felt an additional little tug to one side as he came through into another universe that looked just like the last. He fell to his knees, dropping the coin on the soft carpet.

He gulped in air. He smelled stale cigarette smoke.

He wanted to check before Zoe arrived. He bolted up from the floor and ran to the kitchen. He opened the cabinet above the refrigerator and saw his mother's liquor stash, tall clear bottles lined up like enemy soldiers. He never thought he'd be happy to see those little bastards again.

He crept into the living room and was faced with another familiar sight. His mother was passed out on the sofa, an empty bottle turned on its side and an ash snake of a forgotten cigarette perched precariously on the clay ashtray he'd made her in the third grade. He'd meant it to be a candy bowl.

Ephraim went back to the bedroom and waited for Zoe.

"Did it work?" Zoe said behind him.

Ephraim jumped at her sudden appearance. "I'm going to have to get you a little bell if you keep doing that," he said. Then he hugged her. Zoe tensed up at first, but gradually he felt her relax in his arms.

"I think I made it." He put his hand on the doorknob. "If this isn't home, then it's really close enough."

"Splendid," Zoe said. "So what now?"

"I want to show you something. Oh! Guess we'll need this." He retrieved the coin from the floor where it had dropped, and pocketed it.

"Don't forget these," Zoe said. She held out his wallet and keys.

"But I have my—" He checked his other pockets and came up with a duplicate wallet and keys.

"Where did you find those?" he said quietly.

"Just over there on your desk." Zoe pointed.

He grinned. His mother must have returned those to his analog when she got home from the hospital. Zoe was holding the proof that he'd really made it home.

She came to the same realization.

"Oh," she said. She opened the wallet.

"Are you going to be okay?"

She sniffed and slipped the wallet into her pocket. "Yeah. You said you had something to show me?"

Ephraim scratched at his neck where a branch was tickling him. He and Zoe were hiding behind a tree and watching Jena's house across the street. It was already morning, the world covered in a gray light from an overcast sky. It looked like it was going to rain.

"Why are we spying on my house?" she said.

"Wait for it," Ephraim said. He was conscious of her breathing right next to his face, the closeness of her arm to his.

The front door opened. "There," he said.

Linda Kim turned to close the door, then stooped to retrieve the newspaper. She tucked it under her arm and walked to the driveway, jingling a key ring.

"Momma?" Zoe said. She half-rose. Ephraim put an arm on her shoulder.

Mrs. Kim paused and peered across the street at their hiding place. She walked to the edge of the lawn and looked directly at them for a moment.

"She can't possibly see us," Ephraim whispered. Zoe didn't say anything.

Mrs. Kim finally turned and got into her car. She backed the vehicle out of the driveway and drove right past them.

Zoe clung to the trunk of the tree. "I've only seen her in pictures," she said.

"I thought—"

"I appreciate what you tried to do for me, Ephraim. Thank you."

"You're upset," he said, disappointed.

"I'm happy I got to see her, but . . ." She took a wavery breath and looked at the front of the house. "This is all just too much. It's been one thing after another. I'm tired."

Ephraim wasn't sure if he had done the right thing, bringing her there.

"I'm ready to go home now," Zoe said.

So soon? Ephraim thought.

Zoe flipped open the controller. "Actually . . . how do we get me home?" she asked, staring at the little display. "This thing won't take me back on my own, and the coin won't work for me."

Ephraim nodded. "Now that we have the coordinates of this reality . . ." He paused so he and Zoe could confirm that was just the case. "I'll just take you back to your own reality with the coin and the controller, then pop back here on my own with just the coin. Unless . . ."

Zoe tossed her head back, and her hair flipped over her shoulder. "What?"

"Unless you think you'd want to stay?" Ephraim tried to keep the neediness out of his voice, but when he failed, he thought it best to go the whole way. "I really like you, Zoe. You're the one thing I'll miss from all of this."

"Oh." Zoe smiled a bit sadly. "That's tempting, but you said it: we all belong in our own universes. There's no room for me here." She glanced up at the house. Ephraim turned, and saw Jena staring at them from her open window.

He still couldn't get that image of Jena's floating body out of his head, but here, in this reality, right now, she was very much alive.

Ephraim turned back to Zoe.

"I have to go," she said.

"Okay. If that's what you want, let's take you home," he said.

Zoe scrolled back to her universe's coordinates, at the other end of the list. They were so many worlds apart. Ephraim popped the coin into place. It had barely stopped spinning when he took Zoe's hand in his left. He led her behind a tree blocking them from Jena's view. Then he closed his right hand over the coin.

Zoe looked as relieved to be home as he must have. She looked around as though checking off things against her memory of them.

"Such a gentleman. You walked me back to my home dimension." She squeezed his hand.

"My pleasure, madam. It has been an honor traveling with you."

They unclasped hands at the same time.

"So," Zoe said. "I guess this is good-bye. You'll be seeing another me in a minute, but I'll never see you again, will I?"

Ephraim raised his hand and brushed some hair away from her cheek. "She isn't you," Ephraim said.

Zoe closed her eyes and took a deep breath. When she opened them she smiled. "Well, then, you'd better leave. Before something else happens."

Ephraim didn't think he'd be upset with what she was suggesting, but he knew the longer he stayed, the harder it would be to leave—not this place, but her.

He nodded until he trusted himself to speak. Even so his voice sounded thick.

"So, just set the coordinates for my home reality. There's no one back there to swap with me, so you don't have to worry about dealing with another one of me." He licked his lips. "But just to be safe, I want you to destroy that controller when I'm clear. It's the only way to make sure it can't be used again, by anyone."

"Nathaniel said you might want me to do that. I think he was a little disappointed, thinking we might follow in his footsteps."

"We have to follow our own paths," Ephraim said.

He flipped the coin once, and it flashed in the early morning sunlight. He caught it.

"I wish—" he began.

"No more wishes."

Zoe guided his hand to the controller, and he slipped the coin into its slot. Zoe turned it on, and when the coin stopped spinning, he looked straight into her eyes. A dozen things to say ran through his head, but in the end all he could say was, "Good-bye, Zoe."

"Be seeing you," she said.

He took the coin.

Ephraim heard a short shriek. He looked up and saw the girl he'd just left behind in another universe. For a moment he thought maybe he hadn't gone anywhere after all. Maybe the coin had stopped working, or he hadn't wanted to leave badly enough . . .

But it only took a moment to confirm this wasn't Zoe. She pushed up her glasses, eyes wide behind the lavender frames.

"Jena," he said.

"Ephraim?" she asked. She sounded scared. "How did you do that?"

"Sorry if I startled you. It's . . . complicated," he said. There was no way he could convince her it was just a magic trick, when he'd appeared a few feet right in front of her. He didn't want to lie to her, anyway. That had gotten him into trouble with her elsewhere, and she'd proven herself more than capable of handling the truth.

"I thought I saw someone with you a second ago. A girl," Jena said. She looked around. "Where'd she go?"

"I can explain, but it'll take a while. And you might not believe me," he said. Especially since he couldn't prove any of it this time with a demonstration. Then again, he still had Nate's camera, which was full of pictures of other universes. "Do you think we could talk?" he asked.

"I was just about to leave for work."

"I'll walk you to the library and tell you everything," he said.

"Okay. I expect this will be interesting."

"Maybe you can also fill me in on a few things I've missed."

She looked puzzled. "You say that like you've been gone for a while."

"I have been."

"But I saw you last night," she said. "What's that in your hand?"

"A souvenir," he said. "A coin."

Ephraim opened his hand. The coin was only a polished silver disc now, cold and ordinary. Pushing him through to his own universe without swapping him into an analog had drained its charge completely. And by now, Zoe would have destroyed the controller— cutting his only link back to her. Now they'd never see each other again.

He looked at Jena and wondered if they could ever have the kind of relationship that Zoe had shared with her Ephraim.

He couldn't be satisfied with things simply returning to normal, not after seeing all those possibilities. If he made the right choices, he knew he could get his mother the help she needed and improve his friendship with Nathan. He could tell Jena how he'd always felt about her, confident that there was a good chance she felt the same way.

He flipped the coin and caught it.

"Heads or tails?" Jena asked.

Ephraim rubbed his thumb over the smooth disc. He glanced down and smiled when he saw the blank face of it.

"Heads."